THE AUTOBIOGRAPHY OF
BENJAMIN SISKO

THE UNIQUE CAREER OF DEEP SPACE 9'S LEGENDARY CAPTAIN, AND BAJOR'S EMISSARY

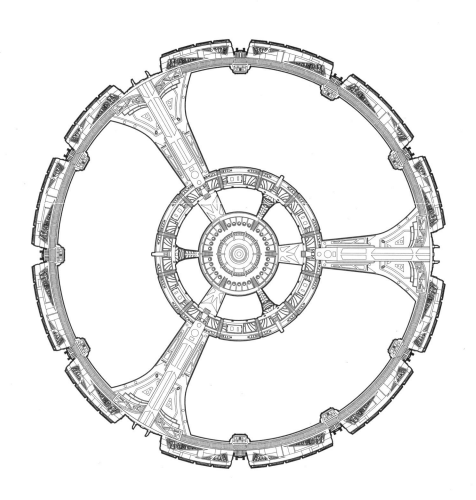

THE AUTOBIOGRAPHY OF
BENJAMIN SISKO

THE UNIQUE CAREER OF DEEP SPACE 9'S LEGENDARY CAPTAIN, AND BAJOR'S EMISSARY

BY
JAKE SISKO

EDITED BY DEREK TYLER ATTICO

TITAN BOOKS

The Autobiography of Benjamin Sisko
Hardback edition ISBN: 9781803366234
E-book edition ISBN: 9781803366241

Published by Titan Books
A division of Titan Publishing Group Ltd
144 Southwark Street, London SE1 0UP
www.titanbooks.com

First edition: November 2023
10 9 8 7 6 5 4 3 2 1

Illustrations: Russell Walks
Editor: George Sandison
Interior design: Adrian McLaughlin

A CIP catalogue record for this title is available from the British Library.

Printed and bound by the CPI Group (UK) Ltd, Croydon, CR0 4YY

Did you enjoy this book? We love to hear from our readers. Please e-mail us at:
readerfeedback@titanemail.com or write to Reader Feedback at the above address.

To receive advance information, news, competitions, and exclusive offers online, please
sign up for the Titan newsletter on our website: www.titanbooks.com.

CONTENTS

INTRODUCTION BY JAKE SISKO 9

CHAPTER ONE 15

CHAPTER TWO 17

CHAPTER THREE 29

CHAPTER FOUR 43

CHAPTER FIVE 53

CHAPTER SIX 65

CHAPTER SEVEN 77

CHAPTER EIGHT 85

CHAPTER NINE 99

CHAPTER TEN 107

CHAPTER ELEVEN 119

CHAPTER TWELVE 127

CHAPTER THIRTEEN 143

CHAPTER FOURTEEN 149

CHAPTER FIFTEEN 155

CHAPTER SIXTEEN 171

CHAPTER SEVENTEEN 181

CHAPTER EIGHTEEN 191

CHAPTER NINETEEN 205

CHAPTER TWENTY 209

CHAPTER TWENTY-ONE 215

CHAPTER TWENTY-TWO 225

CHAPTER TWENTY-THREE 231

CHAPTER TWENTY-FOUR 237

CHAPTER TWENTY-FIVE 241

CHAPTER TWENTY-SIX 245
CHAPTER TWENTY-SEVEN 249
CHAPTER TWENTY-EIGHT 257

CONCLUSION 259
ACKNOWLEDGMENTS 261
ABOUT THE AUTHOR 263

*Dedicated to everyone who is reclaiming their story
and speaking their truth.*

INTRODUCTION

BY JAKE SISKO

THERE WERE NO SHIPS ON THE UPPER OR LOWER PYLONS. No protests or pilgrimages on the promenade. No station repairs that needed immediate attention. No scheduled vessels coming through the wormhole.

Deep Space 9 was quiet.

The silence unnerved Lieutenant Nog as he sat at the situation table in the center of ops. On the night shift, the silence would have made sense. At night, with most of the promenade shops closed and station personnel in their quarters or asleep, there was simply nothing to hear.

But now, at 0630 hours, on the day shift of the first anniversary of the end of the war, and Captain Sisko's disappearance, this wasn't what Nog expected. The Ferengi had been thinking about the seventh Rule of Acquisition all morning: "Keep your ears open." However, the ambient noise in the operations center was barely above twenty decibels.

There was more sound coming from the computers at the different stations in ops than the people manning them. No one was talking, and if they were, it was only to ask and answer the occasional question. The lieutenant looked around at the people in Bajoran and Starfleet uniforms; even the Starfleet operating system in the computers was an indication of what had been saved by winning the Dominion War. At the same time, the station's Cardassian architecture would always be a reminder of just how close they'd come to losing everything. Nog realized maybe the silence on the station wasn't silence at all, but a way for everyone to reflect on what had happened.

And whom they'd lost.

Without warning, the dormant sensor array at the situation table was activated. Years ago, Jadzia Dax had fine-tuned the station's sensors to detect a sudden surge in neutrino emissions. Nog watched the emissions rise steadily on the early detection system, which could mean only one thing.

The wormhole was opening.

Outside the station, light, energy, and gravity coalesced at a single point, and neutrinos surged.

A whirlpool of light and color spiraled open, gaseous clouds miles in diameter blossomed into existence. At the center, not a rip or tear in space, but a doorway. And within the open doorway, a blazing tunnel of energy beckoned.

Nog flashed a quick look at the trans-wormhole subspace communications relay that connected the Alpha Quadrant to the Gamma Quadrant. Seventy thousand light-years separated the two relay stations, but a subspace filament made communication nearly instantaneous. You would know when something had entered the wormhole and was taking the two-minute trip to the other side.

However, no ship had entered the wormhole.

Lieutenant Nog had seen what the Bajorans called the Celestial Temple of the Prophets open many times before. But it was rare for the stable wormhole to do so without something entering or exiting. He tapped the communications console on the monitoring station. "Colonel, the wormhole is opening, but no ships have entered or exited."

Less than ten seconds later, Colonel Kira Nerys stepped out of the station commander's office. Gripping a baseball, she paused atop the short staircase that elevated the office above everything else in the operations center. As all eyes turned to her, she focused on the empty iris of the Cardassian display that sat high above ops for everyone to see. "On screen," Kira commanded as she descended the stairs.

Like an ever-watchful eye, the elliptical viewscreen snapped to life. The wormhole appeared as it had thousands of times before.

But this time, something was different.

The energy at the heart of the doorway that always blazed like an infinite sun began to pulsate.

Nog didn't bother to hide the anxiety he was feeling as he said, "That's… new."

Lieutenant Commander Amir's attention was pulled away from the main viewscreen to the external sensor readout, at the science station he was manning. The half Andorian, half Vulcan's antennae shot up in surprise from his head full of white hair as his blue-green-skinned hands raced over the panel.

"Something's happening in there. I'm reading a massive buildup of tachyon energy," he said. The science officer looked up, his face filled with concern. "The wave pattern is similar to what we see with some directed energy weapons, Colonel."

Colonel Kira knew her science officer wasn't prone to make rash judgments or mistakes. As she stood next to Nog at the situation table, her eyes went back to the viewscreen. Amir was right. Something was going on inside the wormhole. The energy at the heart of what the Prophets had constructed was pulsating, fluctuating, and changing somehow. Kira couldn't allow herself to think about what that meant for the Prophets or anyone else inside the Celestial Temple. Right now her responsibility was for the station, and quite possibly everyone in the Alpha Quadrant.

The Bajoran commander of Deep Space 9 felt her grip tighten on the baseball as she ordered, "Shields!"

Less than a second after the order was given, a tight beam of energy erupted from deep within the wormhole and slammed into the forcefields that activated around Deep Space 9. The entire station shook from the strength of the impact on the shields.

Chief Engineer Tekoa was shaking her head frantically as she spoke, her soft brown eyes unable to mask her confusion. "I—I don't understand it. No structural damage to the station; shield integrity at full strength. With the amount of power that beam is generating, it should have blown a hole in our shields, but it didn't."

The colonel could see it on Tekoa's face. The station's new Bajoran chief engineer didn't know why or how, but somehow they'd gotten lucky. Kira looked over at the science officer. She hoped the young man had some answers. "Amir?"

The Andorian-Vulcan raised an eyebrow.

"Colonel, while the beam has the power of a *Sovereign* class ship phaser bank, it appears to have been attenuated to a non-lethal frequency. But I have no idea why this has been done."

Nog interjected: "I know why." The lieutenant tapped a few buttons at his communications station, and the entire situation table began to display the information from his monitor. A cross-section evaluation of the beam that was still impacting the shields. "The beam's strength is probably just to ensure the fidelity of the communication. There's a compressed message encrypted within the beam." Nog looked up at Kira. "With Captain Sisko's old command codes. He's sending us something."

Kira looked down at the baseball, the object that had become so much more than an essential tool used in a game. It had become a symbol of a presence that was as much a part of the station as the bulkheads and duranium girders that held the station together. A presence that could be felt in the laughter of the promenade on good days and in the fortitude of her new staff on bad days. But it was also a promise that had been made, and perhaps most importantly, for her, it embodied something this commander of Deep Space 9 and former freedom fighter had used all her life to guide her.

Faith.

The colonel looked up at the viewscreen and the continuous energy beam that emanated from within the Celestial Temple and gave the only order she could. "Lower the shields."

✦

A NOTE TO THE READER

What you've just read is an account of the events that transpired as relayed to me by Deep Space 9's senior staff from interviews I conducted with them over a two-day period after what is now known as the *Sisko Event*.

There has been a great deal of speculation about what or who actually came through the wormhole that day. The rumors range from the mildly entertaining to the absurd. Some believe the wormhole has now become a conduit to the far future and that Captain Sisko returned after negotiating for wormhole technology on behalf of the Federation. Others have started a religion known as 'The Sisko', the followers of which think Ben Sisko now exists everywhere in the universe and should be worshipped as a deity. Conspiracy theorists even believe the wormhole is a creation of the Federation and the Dominion, that the war was really a plot set up by both governments to consolidate power in two quadrants. A deal brokered by Ben Sisko.

My stepmother, Kasidy Yates-Sisko, has recently been forced to raise my sister at an undisclosed location, away from prying eyes and the paparazzi. There are new "Sisko sightings" throughout the Federation nearly every day, and the speculations have become endless.

As a writer and journalist, my first duty isn't to the Federation, Starfleet, or even my lifelong friends. My responsibility has been, and will always be, to the truth.

The truth is that everyone wants a piece of Benjamin Sisko.

The Bajoran people want to preserve the sanctity and deeds of the Emissary. The Cult of the Pah Wraiths want to defile everything the Emissary stood for. Starfleet wants their captain back. Me, I just want to see my father. And the truth is, no one will get what they want.

But maybe, for now, that's okay.

It has taken me nearly two years to sort through the gift my father sent me in the beam that struck Deep Space 9 that day. Over fifty hours of video, with some moments that I can only describe as *jarring*. I'm not sure how my father was able to send the signal. Perhaps, now that he's in the wormhole with the aliens the Bajorans believe are prophets, he's learned some tricks from them— honestly, the how doesn't really matter to me. What does is that he was able to send it. In the time it's taken me to go through the video, I've come to see, understand, and relate to my father in a way I never could have before.

What I've transcribed from the video, what you're about to read, isn't what any of us really wants. But, it may be precisely what the Alpha Quadrant needs.

Benjamin Lafayette Sisko, in his own words.

Jake Sisko
Stardate 55902.0

CHAPTER ONE

WHAT YOU LEAVE BEHIND—2375

JAKE. SON.

I was on Bajor, in the fire caves, with Dukat.

Falling.

But now I'm here, in the wormhole, with the Prophets. They saved me. It's only been a few minutes, but the spaces between seconds feel like decades. It's not easy to explain, son. Time. The future, present and past are all unraveling and coalescing around me, through me.

I need to talk to you. I need to do this now before I talk to Kasidy, and while it's all still... linear for me.

The Prophets saved me, and they have work for me to do, things they want to teach me. But before I'll allow any of that to happen, I wanted, *needed* to talk to you. To send this transmission to you.

A few years ago, when you came with me to watch the wormhole inversion, there was an accident I never told you about. I was trapped in subspace, and while I was there, I experienced a different timeline. What was minutes for me there was years, even decades, on the outside, in normal space-time.

I wasn't dead or even lost. I was stuck somewhere outside of time. In that timeline, son, knowing I was out there somewhere, you lived a life of mourning and obsession, with only fleeting moments of happiness. You were so preoccupied with trying to find me, save me, that you let your life and loves slip away.

I know I've only been in here for a few minutes, but I'm thinking now about how me being here, in the wormhole with the Prophets, could feel like that to you. Jake, I think of you in that timeline and how your sadness twisted into obsession, how in the end you had nothing and no one. I don't want to see you go through that now, son. I won't lie to you, I don't know when I'll be back, but it doesn't mean I can't be in your life.

When I was around your age, my father started talking to me differently. We'd have conversations, it was always father and son, but it also became man to man. Honestly, a lot of it was me just listening to your grandfather as he told me about his life and what he learned along the way. At the time, I often didn't see the point he was trying to make to whatever story he was telling me, but as I got older and I began to live my own life, I found myself thinking about the things he told me about his more and more.

There's so much I never talked about with you, about me, about our family. I just thought I would when the time came; that we'd be having these conversations in person. But life isn't always what we expect or what we plan. When I get back, we'll do this the right way, but for now, right now, let your old man tell you about his life and some of the things he's learned along the way.

CHAPTER TWO

FAMILY—2332-2338

MY FIRST MEMORY IS OF HOLDING MY MOTHER'S HAND.

I was a baby, no more than a year old. My small fingers reached out, exploring the boundaries of my new world, and I found her. Those little hands held onto the enormity of her fingers, and even though I couldn't remember her face, or really anything about how she looked. But I could feel her, feel her love for me, feel the safety and comfort she gave me. My whole life, that feeling has never really left me. I always wondered how I could remember something from such a young age. I understand now that I could hold onto that memory because part of my lineage isn't linear.

Now, I realize that memory isn't of Mama, the woman that raised me, the woman I thought was my mother, Elizabeth Sisko. That memory is of my birthmother, my father's *first* wife, the woman that a wormhole alien inhabited to orchestrate my birth.

Sarah.

Now that I'm here in the wormhole, it's easier to understand that the love I felt, and thought was from one woman, was actually from two—one human, and one that existed outside of time. When I made first contact with the entities that live here, in the wormhole, we didn't just communicate— we helped each other. I gave them an understanding beyond themselves, and they helped me to look within myself.

Jake, this may be hard for you to understand, but Sarah, or rather the entity that inhabited her, knew me, saw me save her people time and again, and cared about my well-being long before she went back in time to conceive me.

Because it had happened, she ensured it would happen.

I know Sarah, in her own way, loves me, but she didn't raise me. The truth is Elizabeth Cohen Sisko is the only mother I've ever known.

Thinking about her now, Jake, I realize we never really talked a lot about your grandmother. I know you've seen pictures and even a few holographic recordings of her, but that was well after she was a mom with four kids. I want to talk to you about what she was like before that, back when I was still an only child, like you are now. In those early days, before my brothers and sister showed up, and with my father working, it felt like it was just Mama and me.

She was my first best friend.

Back then, Mama had long, thick, black and brown dreadlocks that framed her round face perfectly. Her small button nose and high cheekbones would lighten up every smile. Every night she'd read to me, her voice soft and gentle, like a melody that soothed you whenever you heard it. Some nights she would read Aesop's fables. On others, it would be African folktales, or mythology from different cultures. Her brown eyes would light up with excitement as she took on the personalities and voices of the characters. I was always so enthralled that I fought to stay awake, but I'd always lose that battle only to dream of faraway lands and mysterious creatures. Mama would leave a nightlight on, and usually that was enough. But sometimes, I'd look at the shadows on my wall and imagine the monster from the story we'd just read together. On really bad nights, I'd wake up screaming, and Mama would come into my room and stay or let me sleep with her and Dad.

After this had been happening off and on for about a week, Mama told me she had found a new book for me. It was a small, thin book titled: *Life Doesn't Frighten Me And Other Poems* by Maya Angelou. I remember that before I knew anything about Maya Angelou, I immediately liked her name because it said she was an angel, and Mama told me angels protected people. The book wasn't much bigger than my hand. We opened it together, and almost immediately, as Mama read and acted out the poem, it put me at ease. The words of this woman—this angel—told me that even though things might look and feel scary sometimes, in the end, there is nothing to be afraid of.

The book quickly became my favorite, and even though I never told Mama, I would often pull it out at night, feeling their power emanating off the page as I read the words aloud in the quiet of my room.

Our days were just as much fun as our nights. Every morning, class would begin. Even before I realized Mama was a teacher, she was homeschooling me. Over breakfast every day, she would ask me about the story she had read to me the night before. She'd want to know what I thought about the monster, or the characters. Sometimes she would ask me what I would've done differently if I were in the story, or if I were telling it. One-word answers were never allowed in our house. "Sentences or not at all," Mama would say.

Whenever I didn't know a word, she wouldn't just teach it to me, she'd explain the etymology in a way that I promise you was fascinating to me at four years old. And whenever I didn't understand something, whether it was a word, something in a story, a math problem, or just why the sky was blue, she never lost her patience, and she explained it to me (sometimes in a hundred different ways) until I got it and could describe back to her what I understood.

That was Mama.

Before Elizabeth Cohen was my mother, she was an orphan, a second-grade teacher, and a photographer. Her parents Sonya and Alonzo were Starfleet officers aboard the *U.S.S. Leondegrance*. They were killed during a First Contact mission gone wrong. Captain Nyota Uhura brought the *Leondegrance* back to Earth, to take "Tin Lizzy" to her godparents in New Orleans. The story goes that Captain Uhura brought little Elizabeth to her godparents in an antigrav stroller that looked like the tins that mints were kept in centuries ago. And the name Tin Lizzy was born.

As a kid, Mama grew up not wanting anything to do with Starfleet, but she was fascinated with people. When Elizabeth was five, she'd beg to go to the park—not to play with other kids, but to people-watch. She was mesmerized by all the different species but didn't really understand that they came from different worlds. Since they were on Earth, they were human. For hours after a visit to the park, Elizabeth would talk about the human with the pointy ears, or the human with the blue skin, or the human that looked like a cat. This would often go on throughout dinner and well into her bedtime. After several of these conversations, her godparents got her a holo-camera, probably more for them than it was for her. She'd capture images from the day's park adventure and then project them into the living room or fall asleep to them in bed nearly every night.

By the time she was a teen, she'd gone retro and turned in her holo-camera for an old-style camera that used film. As a kid, I'd spend hours with Mama in her studio, watching her develop pictures she'd taken. We'd be standing together in the near darkness of the small developing room, and magic would happen right in front of me. I'd hold her hand in the fading sunset emanating from the light panel above us. She'd slip a sheet of paper into a tray filled with liquid, and an image would slowly, patiently appear. It was as if she had the ability to breathe life into those sheets of paper.

Mama was a talented, even gifted photographer. So much so that some of her pictures still hang in the New Orleans Museum of Art. But as gifted as she was, she would be the first to say teaching was her true calling.

I've been in Starfleet for over twenty years. I've seen some very impressive technology and breakthroughs, but the truth is that the future isn't built with technology or even by engineers. The future is built by teachers. Every mind that is educated, every consciousness that is opened to new ideas and different ways of thinking, is a brick paving the way toward tomorrow.

Mama was in her fifth year of teaching at Dorothy Mae Taylor Elementary when she learned of a new weekly cultural program being instituted at the school. Once a week, a local chef would cook non-replicated meals for the student body with pots, pans, and real ingredients. The idea being to give the student body a completely authentic taste of New Orleans cuisine and Cajun cooking.

As the story goes, after about a month of different dishes like red beans and rice, po' boys, jambalaya, and even Hubig's pies, she went to meet the talented but impractical chef that had devoted his life to an extinct, archaic, and unnecessary career.

They were married three months later.

In my life, I've met and been friends with a lot of people that are married. Honestly, son, a lot of the time, people are married for more than what's apparent and less than what everyone else thinks. For some, it's just because the two work well together—convenience. For others, it's out of a physical attraction, and for the select few, it really is because of that thing everyone wants when they wed.

Love.

Even as a kid, I could see that what Mama and Dad had was special. Your grandfather always told me he didn't know what he did that made Elizabeth fall in love with him and want to spend the rest of her life with him, but he was glad she did.

Mama was four years older than Dad, and he always thought that her maturity and insight were part of it. "Your mother saw the world in a way that wasn't like anyone else," he used to say to me. "She didn't let her past or pain become an obstacle in guiding her future."

After he told me about Sarah, he told me he had no intention of getting in another relationship. The pain was just too great. But when he met Elizabeth, she started to court him! She would write letters to him by hand, when no one does that anymore. Your grandpa told me that reading those letters, it was like she had found a way to put all the emotion and sincerity of her soul on the page. Those letters helped him to let go of the pain he was holding onto from Sarah and make room in his heart for Mama.

I wish you could've seen them together, Jake. They had an ease with each other that just made them fit. In many ways, being around them as a kid helped me understand what I wanted for myself in a relationship and helped me recognize a little about what that should look like. But it wasn't just Dad and Mama. Your great-grandparents—my Grandpa James, and Grandma Octavia—had that too. In my earliest memories of them, they were already in their sixties. Grandpa James was bald when I met him, something I'm pretty sure was by choice. He was tall and thin, which is where all the Sisko men got it from, I guess. His grin and the way he laughed were like nothing else I'd ever seen or heard. Both were so filled with joy and always made him appear much younger than he was. Grandma Octavia was shorter than Grandpa, and her long dark hair with streaks of gray just seemed to highlight the electricity in her eyes whenever she got excited about something. She never held back how she felt about anything. The whole family could always expect her to tell the truth and let us know when we weren't.

I know we've never really talked a lot about it, Jake, but you know there was a time Sisko's wasn't just a restaurant in New Orleans. Grandpa James and Grandma Octavia ran the hotel next door while Dad was the head chef. Sisko's was one of the only remaining pre-war hotels not just in New Orleans but on Earth.

Everything I knew about the world and everyone in it existed in and around those two buildings.

We all lived in the brownstone over the restaurant just like your grandfather does now. The hotel was five floors of Louisiana, where time stood still. Nineteenth-century furniture and architecture alongside New Orleans culture that goes a lot farther back than that. Grandpa James would tell me stories of how Siskos have been living in, and serving, the New Orleans community for centuries. All the way back to Antoine Dubois Sisko, a free man, and officer in the Corps D'Afrique. He fought in the Civil War for the Union and aided in the capture of New Orleans from the Confederacy. Isaiah Sisko, a photorealism painter, lost his house in the Tremé during Hurricane Katrina. With no home and no money, he became a street artist and squatter in two abandoned buildings in the French Quarter. After rebuilding his life, Isaiah bought the buildings, and opened an art gallery and halfway house for artists and musicians.

During World War III, when the world was tearing itself apart, the people of New Orleans did what they've done throughout history in every crisis, whether it was a natural or man-made disaster: they banded together.

By then, the Sisko property had been transformed into a hotel and jazz club, and Clora Sisko ran both. Everything went to hell while Clora was pregnant, but she didn't let that stop her from helping people. She used her trumpet as a beacon to lead people out of the darkness and into the safety of the hotel and club.

When the family business was passed to Grandpa James, he was a young man. But, to his father's disappointment, music wasn't in his soul. For my grandfather, it was the other half of New Orleans's beating heart that captivated him. That other foundational element that sustained and carried slaves through those darkest of times, that would remind them of their culture, their identity, and their true homes, far away across the ocean on another continent.

Creole cooking.

Louisiana cuisine came as naturally to Grandpa James as breathing. So when Sisko's was handed to him, he transformed the jazz club into a creole restaurant. Grandma Octavia ran the hotel, and from the stories Grandpa James told me, it changed everything. Before the restaurant, people would come from all over Earth to hear the live music. But a few months after the restaurant opened, they got their first customers from off world. At first, it was humans from Luna, then Mars, and then Starfleet. After that, it was Tellarites, Andorians, and on occasion, a Vulcan or two. They would come in to sample the creole cuisine and sometimes stay a couple of nights to experience an authentic nineteenth-century hotel.

Everything was cooked by hand, just like Dad does now. Real meat, fish and spices, pots, and pans on an electric stove. But back then, it wasn't just in the kitchen like it is now: this was everywhere throughout the Sisko household. No replicators. No computer or communicators. No transporters. All of our doors had knobs on them, and we used cellular phones instead of the global communications network. The hotel had a transporter and communicators, but that was only a convenience for the guests.

In our house, New Orleans, and most of Louisiana, new technology and the change it represented weren't welcomed.

You have to understand, son. Since its birth, New Orleans has always been a story written in the deep rhythms of music and food. A city built out of the many diverse cultures that used music and food as its foundations. From the creation of New Orleans until the twenty-second century, that meant it was a service industry city.

With the advent of replicators and holodecks, the future was telling New Orleans it was no longer relevant or necessary. Craving a bowl of authentic gumbo? Don't worry, this slot in the wall will turn resequenced protein into a meal that will taste just as good as the real thing. No time to see some live jazz? No problem, there's a holodeck program that will make you think you're right back at the moment jazz was born, listening to the real thing. I can't think of a greater sin, Jake, than to eat resequenced-protein-turned-into-gumbo in New Orleans, or watch a holodeck jazz session while in the birthplace of such an original art form. But that was what the future threatened to take from New Orleans—from all of us actually.

Just like the Amish did centuries ago, New Orleanians rejected the notion that new technology meant better. Even though the United Earth government didn't necessarily agree, it respected places like New Orleans that held onto tradition over technology. And as a result, the city is still one of the few places on Earth that hasn't just preserved the history and culture of the past, but thrives because of that commitment to history.

That preservation of history and culture was more than a philosophy for my grandfather—it was a sacrosanct edict. One of the ways it manifested was through the restaurant. For Grandpa James, traditional Creole cuisine was a way to hold onto his past. A past that was rarely written about in history books, but was written within family recipes kept in bibles passed down through the decades. This was a way of paying homage and respect to those first generations of Creole cooks, many of whom were brought to what was once called America as slaves.

In a lot of ways, Jake, your grandfather was even more serious about preserving and respecting the past than my grandfather. Somewhere along the way, cooking became more than something Dad did. It was part of who he was. I never saw my father sterner than when he was in our restaurant's kitchen.

When I was about four or five, he'd sit me out of the way on top of a counter in the back of the kitchen next to the freezer. Whenever I sat back there, I felt like I was in the audience watching a play. Dad would tell me, "Benjamin, I only have three rules when you're in my kitchen. I'm not Dad—call me Chef, always. Raise your hand if you have a question, don't touch anything unless I say it's okay, and don't eat anything unless I say it's okay."

I knew that was four, but one of the first things I learned while in Chef Sisko's kitchen was that "Yes, Chef," was the only acceptable answer. Besides, the last rule was always the hardest. From my vantage point, I could see and smell everything. The aromas of things being chopped or cooking would float their way to me, making my mouth water and my stomach ache with anticipation. I've been to the Gamma Quadrant and back, but some of the best things I've ever tasted in my life were in that man's kitchen.

I'd watch the kitchen crew cooking, cutting, cleaning, and arranging food on dishes like they were works of art. Everyone would work independently, but also in unison, not unlike the bridge of a starship.

My first lessons of discipline, structure, and order came from those days in my father's kitchen. I also learned how to work with people, and, most importantly, how to treat them. From Nathan Greene, his sous chef, all the way down to the waiting staff, I never saw my father raise his voice to anyone. When someone did something he didn't like, he'd look them straight in the eyes and tell them. Usually, it was off to the side, but on occasion it was in front of everyone, and it was always done with respect. After talking to them, he'd move on from whatever it was, expecting them to take him seriously, even if he was friendly afterward. When I first saw that, I realized he was the same way with his kids, and it made me feel good to know we were being treated the same way he treated adults. It made me feel like even when I disagreed with whatever Dad said, I knew he was being fair.

My father worked harder than I've ever seen anyone work. Running a restaurant and kitchen crew. Coming up with new dishes all the time, taking over a cooking station from one of his cooks at a moment's notice, the entire staff preparing everything without twenty-fourth century automation. Sometimes during the week, the only way any of the family would get to see him would be to sit in the back of the kitchen and watch him work. There were days I'd wake up and go to sleep without seeing my father at all, but on those days, there was always a note on my nightstand when I woke up. *Idea for a new pastry is in the fridge. Need your input. Love, Chef.*

We'd get notes like that during the week but we all also knew the rule. Weekends were for the family, with no exceptions. Nathan was in charge of the kitchen on the weekends, and when my grandfather retired from cooking and running the kitchen he became the restaurant's maître d'. Grandma never stopped running the hotel, but on the weekends they both found someone else to take over.

✦

My grandparents would take me fishing every Sunday morning. We'd go out to Lake Pontchartrain, sometimes even catch fish good enough to cook in the kitchen.

One Sunday morning, I was sitting on the edge of the pier with Grandma Octavia while Grandpa stood next to me, leaning on the guardrail, tugging on his fishing pole. My toes teased the water's surface, skimming across the smooth glass-like surface, creating intersecting ripples. I loved fishing, loved going to the lake, but the mysteries under the water captivated and terrified me. I never said any of this to anyone, but my grandparents, as somehow all grandparents do, knew.

I could feel Grandma Octavia looking at me. After a long silence, she finally spoke. "There's nothing in there to be afraid of, Benjamin," she said.

I remember letting out a barely audible "I know," as I stared into the unknown. I felt her hand on my back, and the next thing I knew I was in the lake swallowing water, my legs kicking, my arms reaching, grasping for anything and everything. The look on my grandfather's face must have mirrored my own. He dropped his fishing pole and was about to dive in and get me when Grandma Octavia spoke, without taking her eyes off me: "Stay right where you are, James Sisko. That boy has got to learn sometime."

I kicked so hard I felt like I was running in place, and I saw my grandfather open his mouth to say something, close it, then open it again. Finally, he closed it and squatted at the edge of the pier. I was only a few feet away from the edge but it might have well been a mile. He said, "C'mon Ben, you can do it!"

Even in my panic, I realized it was the first time Grandpa had called me Ben and not Benjamin. But as I slipped under the surface, I didn't know if I'd hear him say it again. I thrashed around in some mad dance of confused limbs. This was exactly what I'd envisioned, what I feared every time I'd looked into the water, and now here I was! I looked up at the surface and the shapes of my grandparents. Now both of them appeared to be moving. But I noticed something else.

I wasn't that far from the surface.

I realized if I didn't just kick but use my hands maybe I could get back to the top before I sank any deeper. So while I was kicking, I started to use my arms to reach up and push down the water that was on top of me. At first, it didn't work, but when I started kicking up and scooping down at the same time, I could feel myself slowly rising. And I broke the surface.

As I kicked and paddled back to the dock, I felt bigger, stronger and a little braver than when I went in. Grandpa was laughing and clapping so hard I thought he was going to fall in with me. Grandma wasn't laughing, but she was smiling, and crying. This was the first time I remember being truly afraid, and even though it wouldn't be the last, I learned fear could be conquered.

✦

When I was four, Mama had Judith Josephine Sisko. Mama loved the famed twentieth-century dancer, singer, and actress Josephine Baker, and that's where Judith's middle name came from. Mama always said that when she was in high school, she found Josephine Baker intriguing because she was a woman that blazed her own trail when it was nearly impossible for a woman to do so. Because Mama was an orphan, she wanted Judith to feel tied to that kind of strength, independence, and self-reliance. Since birth, we all just called her JJ, and the nickname stuck.

I remember that before she had JJ, I'd see her eating desserts from the kitchen all the time. Sweet potato pie, bread pudding, peach cobbler, and sometimes even Hubig's pies dipped in chocolate. I remember one day asking Mama why she got to have all those wonderful desserts when I wasn't allowed to. She said, "Because I'm having a baby, honey." I looked at her belly and told her that I wanted to have a baby too. She laughed and told me that one day I would, but my wife would do all the work.

Jake, we both have something else special in common. We've both been an only child and soon, you're going to have a sibling. Thankfully I know you'll be a better older brother than I was at the start. When JJ was born, I couldn't believe how little she was. I was a giant by comparison. Her tiny hands would reach out, and it was like her whole world depended on grabbing my finger. I remember thinking there was no way I was ever that small.

I felt the shift of attention from me to my sister, and I didn't like it. Whenever Judith cried, grinned, or did anything really, Mama and Dad would be there for her. They put the baby in my room, and there were so many nights Dad would be in there with us, gently rocking Judith in his arms while I went to sleep. I'd wake up in the middle of the night or early in the morning from her crying, and Dad would still be there, usually in his chef's apron from the night before or a clean one to start the day. I'd ask him where Mama was, and he'd say to me, "Your Mama's sleeping. She did all the work. Now it's my turn."

One day I was in a particular mood for a four-year-old, my arms folded as I walked through the house with a frown just as sour. Grandpa James saw me, and when he asked what was wrong, I started complaining about Judith. This probably wasn't the first time he heard my litany because he interrupted me right away. "Boy, you don't understand," he said. "You're the big brother. Now, who do you think Judith is going to look up to when she gets to your age? And you'll be there to tell her how to do everything the right way!" Grandpa James laughed, probably because I was smiling so hard. I've always loved my grandparents, but I remember after that conversation thinking Grandpa James was the smartest person I knew. He was my Dad's dad, so he had to be. A year after that, David and Elias were born, and I could see that what he was saying was true. Judith would start laughing and clapping her hands when I was with her and would cry whenever I left the room. I was hoping the same would happen with my twin brothers. Being a big brother wasn't so bad after all.

CHAPTER THREE

ABSENCE—2339

BY THE TIME I WAS SIX OUR HOUSE WAS FILLED WITH KIDS. Judith was two, and the twins, David and Elias, were one. My sister was learning to walk and my brothers were getting comfortable with their first words, "no" and "ball." Mama left teaching kids in high school to homeschool Judith and me. When the twins came, Dad worked fewer hours in the kitchen to help raise all of us.

One afternoon I was doing homework in my room and heard someone playing the piano in the restaurant lobby. I'd heard the piano before, but this sounded different. I could actually feel the music. It was so good I couldn't concentrate on my schoolwork. I closed my book and ran out of my room. Halfway down the stairs, I looked over the staircase to the piano to see who was playing. I didn't realize my mouth was open until I closed it.

"Grandma?"

Her hands were moving across the piano keys in a blur. She looked up at me laughing. "Come sit next to me, baby!" she said.

I nearly jumped down the rest of the stairs and sat next to Grandma Octavia. She was moving in rhythm to the music as she coaxed me to the piano. Usually, people played something slow and subdued while customers ate. Sometimes during live music sessions, I'd hear something exciting, but it was always part of a group and never by itself. Now I felt like the notes were floating over my head and were going to take me away with them. I couldn't stop clapping my hands and tapping my feet. When she finished, I gave Grandma a big hug. "What kind of music is that?" I asked.

"Jazz, Benjamin." Grandma made fists with her hands quickly several times and then held her hands up in front of her and shook them out as if they were wet to relieve tension. "That was 'C Jam Blues' by the one and only jazz master, Oscar Peterson. It's been a long time since I pulled that one out of me, but when jazz gets in you, it has to get out. Did you feel it, baby? Did you feel the music get inside you?"

I remember shaking my head so hard I felt it might fall off. "Again, again!" I demanded.

Grandma put her hands over the keys, about to play, then slowly pulled them back. She turned to me and had a knowing grin on her face I'd never seen before. "You know, Benjamin, Oscar Peterson was younger than you, five years old, when he started playing piano. He had a lot inside him that he had to get out. Do you want me to teach you how to play so you can get all that jazz out of you too?" Grandma put her hands on both of my shoulders and looked me straight in the eye. "Now, before you say anything, I'm not going to teach you if you're going to quit when it gets hard, and it's gonna get hard, but I promise even then, we'll make it fun. But if you finish what you start, no matter what happens, you'll never waste your time or others', and you'll never be disappointed in yourself. Do we have a deal?"

My grandmother held out her hand to shake it. I could see it on her face. She was deadly serious, and she didn't want to be disappointed, but this was the first time I could remember wanting to do the hard work, so I didn't disappoint myself.

"Deal," I said.

✦

I used to love sleeping with my parents. We'd have this nightly ritual we'd go through. Mama would put me to bed, and read to me. If I didn't go to sleep by the time she was finished, she'd give me a kiss, turn the light out, and leave the door to my room open just enough so a sliver of light from the hall could seep inside. After a few minutes, I'd get up. With my stuffed alligator, Mister Bayou, in tow, I'd go to my parents' room and get in bed with them. They never said anything. We had an understanding. One night after Judith was born, I had been tucked in but couldn't fall asleep. I went to my parent's room and found Judith already sleeping between them, right where I usually slept. Mama saw my disappointment and did her best to make me feel better as she kept her voice low.

"You're such a big boy now, Benjamin, and a big brother. Why don't we let your baby sister sleep here tonight, okay?" she said.

Even though I was only six years old, I knew what Mama was doing. I wanted to cry and say no. But she was right; Judith was just a baby, and after all, I was six! So I nodded and left the room, dragging Mister Bayou behind me.

When I got back out into the hall, I dreaded the thought of going back to my room. And then I noticed a light coming from the third floor. I climbed up the staircase and walked into my grandparents' bedroom. Grandpa was in bed reading, and Grandma was combing her long silver and black hair in front of her mirror. They both stopped what they were doing and looked at each other and then at me.

Grandma Octavia laughed and said, "Well, I guess it's time for bed!"

After that, I had a new ritual that took me up the staircase a couple of times a week. Sleeping with my grandparents was an adventure. On some nights, we'd just go to sleep, but most of the time, they'd be waiting for me, and the fun would begin. We'd listen to music or dance for hours. Sometimes we'd talk about the family, and what they were like when they were my age. Sometimes my grandparents would ask me what I wanted to be when I grew up. I'd just shrug my shoulders and continue playing with Mister Bayou.

Grandpa James was always talking about cooking. So I wasn't surprised one night, when the three of us were in bed talking, and he said, "Benjamin, there's nothing wrong with learning how to cook and running a kitchen. I'm a chef, and so is your daddy. You're gonna be one too."

Grandma Octavia leaned over towards me but was looking at her husband when she spoke. "Or not, baby."

The intensity in Grandpa's face softened into a smile as he looked at his wife. "Or not, Benjamin. You can do anything you put your mind to, and whatever you decide, it's going to be spectacular!"

✦

I was six when I hit Judith and made her cry.

My little sister was always hitting me. With everyone else, she used words. JJ was one of those three-year-olds that spoke clearly and didn't engage in 'baby talk.' Even at two-and-a-half, her brown eyes were so expressive, and after spending a lot of time with Grandma Octavia, JJ's *no* became, *no thank you*.

But when it came to her big brother, her language of choice was her fists. When she was little everyone thought it was cute, even me. But as she got older, I started to feel the force of her blows, on my leg, my back, and even in the face! That was until one time, without thinking, I punched her back. It was in the arm, of course, and not hard, just enough to tell her to stop in her own language. Judith started crying so loud that the whole house came to see what was going on.

Every time my father asked me what happened, I had an excuse for what I'd done. Another excuse to justify my actions. Finally, he just looked at me and said, "Hitting is wrong, Benjamin, and that's your little sister. What message are you sending as a big brother? We raised you better than that!" My father crouched down so we were eye to eye. "Excuses are like lies, Benjamin. You can't hide behind them. When you try, they just point to the truth, son."

My father had talked to me before, but it was rare when he came down to my level. Whenever he did, it was because he wanted, and needed, me to not just listen to what he was saying, but to do my best to understand him. "Yes, sir," I whispered.

Judith came over to me and kissed me on the side of my head where she had just hit me, then she wrapped her little arms around my neck and gave me a hug. "Sowwy," she said.

✦

One evening I went to my grandparents' bedroom, and the door was closed. I tried turning the knob and couldn't believe that the door was locked! As I was twisting the knob back and forth, Grandpa James came to the door. His usual pleasant grin was gone, and as he looked down at me he looked like he was somewhere else, far away. It was almost like he didn't recognize me. "Not tonight, Benjamin. Grandma isn't feeling well."

As he closed the door, I could see my grandmother in bed behind him. Grandma Octavia had an authority and strength in everything she did, even when she sat up in bed, but now, suddenly, she looked frail. She was slouched down and staring off into space. I stayed at the closed door for a minute, not really knowing what to do. Finally, I decided to go downstairs, and as I got back to the second floor, Dad was waiting for me.

"Something's wrong with Grandma," I said.

My dad looked at me, his face looking like Grandpa's had just a few minutes ago. "I know, baby," he said, finally.

Dad picked me up and carried me to my parents' bedroom. Judith was asleep in my old spot, but Mama was awake watching the twins sleep in their crib. My father put me in bed next to Judith, then he got in, and then Mama.

That night we all slept together.

✦

Early the following day, a tall man wearing a brown jacket with black pants came to the house. He had silver hair and black eyes, and carried a small black shoulder bag with a long thin strap. He wore seriousness on his face like it was part of his attire.

My father told me he was Grandma's doctor. I later learned he was her neurologist. While Mama watched my siblings, I followed my father and the doctor up to the third floor. When I followed them into my grandparents' bedroom, Grandma was in almost the same exact position I saw her in the night before. She just sat there, staring off into space. The doctor reached into the black bag and pulled out a small device that started making weird sounds when he flipped it open. He passed it over her slowly, and the thing started beeping intensely when he raised it over her head. After studying it for a moment, he put it away and then pulled out a thick stick-like device. He pressed it to Grandma's neck, and a second later she looked up and smiled the smile I'd seen a thousand times before. You have to understand, Jake. Because of our family's views about technology, I'd never seen a tricorder or hypospray before, much less a Betazoid neurologist.

Later, Dad told me Grandma had a rare form of epilepsy her entire life. As a child, she was often found staring blankly into space and would later claim she'd had visions. Once the seizures were properly diagnosed and medication prescribed, she hadn't had an episode for years—until now. The doctor said that even though she felt better now, Grandma had a tumor in her brain, and she needed an operation to have it removed before it got any worse. Whatever this man had done, I was happy he'd brought my grandmother back from wherever she was, and at the same time I was beginning to understand there was a much larger world than what I was seeing.

Later the same day, Miss Vee stopped by the house. In Louisiana and New Orleans there's always been one medicine rooted in science, and another type of medicine passed down through the generations. Miss Vee was an Obeah doctor, a herbologist, and a soothsayer. My grandparents would argue whenever she would come over, which was too often as far as Grandpa was concerned. He said once that Miss Vee was a witch doctor. I knew from watching *The Wizard of Oz* that there were good witches and bad ones. No one ever said which side Miss Vee was on. I overheard Grandpa tell my parents that he learned Grandma had stopped taking her medication a long time ago. Miss Vee had given her a gris-gris—a talisman to wear that would protect her from the seizures—but it didn't seem to protect her from the brain tumor.

While everyone was talking, I snuck back upstairs. The door was shut, and instead of knocking, I just held my breath and turned the knob. Grandma was sitting at her dresser, combing her hair, looking absolutely beautiful. I couldn't hold back anymore and ran to her, crying as I hugged her.

"Everyone says you're sick. Are you okay?" I said.

I'd forgotten how confident she was always, even in her laugh, as she held my face and gave me a kiss on my forehead. "It's okay, Benjamin, everything is going to work out just fine, you'll see," she said.

Grandma wiped my tears and everything just seemed to melt away. My fear and confusion, the anxiety I was feeling about the possibility of losing her, the shadow and finality of death that I was never really conscious of until that day. All of it evaporated, and was forgotten in her smile.

"I'm hungry," I said, as I wiped away what was left of my tears.

We both laughed. Grandma promptly turned me around and gave me a pat on my backside. As I ran out of the room, I could hear her voice trailing behind me. "Go tell my son his mother said to make my grandson anything he wants in the kitchen, and I'll see you tonight at bedtime, Mister Sisko."

I never saw her again.

✦

Sometimes, Jake, you don't really see something or someone until they're gone. I didn't understand how much my grandmother and mother held our family together until it started to fall apart.

Grandma Octavia was a force of nature in both my life and the Sisko household, just as necessary as oxygen or gravity. When she passed away, something broke in the family. The hotel and restaurant closed, and my father and grandfather stopped smiling, stopped laughing, and stopped talking. The house was so quiet the first few days after she left. It was like she took a part of all of us with her. Judith kept asking where Grandma was and didn't understand when she was told she was in Heaven. My baby brothers Elias and David were too young to understand, or express the sorrow everyone was going through and how it made them feel, so they just cried all the time. I watched as everything and everyone stopped, frozen in the amber of grief.

Except for Mama.

Our homeschooling never stopped, but instead of our regular classes, Mom let Judith and me talk about whatever we wanted. And it wasn't just that we talked. She listened. At the same time, Mama was cleaning up after four kids, including two three-year-olds. Not to mention cooking for all of us, usually with Elias or David on her hip or in a stroller nearby as she did so. Because we were grieving, it didn't mean life stopped. Whenever I think back to that time, it's clear Mama was our teacher, counselor, cook, and organizer.

Slowly, patiently, she started to put all of us back together. But I often think about who was there for her. My father did what he could through his grief, but in many ways, Mama was alone during this time. Jake, when you're married and have children of your own, you're going to understand that no relationship is ever wholly equal. It constantly shifts. Sometimes you give more, and sometimes your partner does. But through it all, never lose sight of what the woman in your life and mother of your children goes through all by herself without ever saying anything, simply for the love, care, and cohesion of her family. My mom went through it, Jennifer did, Kasidy is going through it now, and one day your wife will as well. Always keep that in mind, son, and you'll be a better husband for it.

✦

On the day of the funeral, we weren't whole, but we were no longer entirely broken either. And we weren't alone. I remember looking out of the window of my room and seeing car after car pull up out front. It was always a variation of the same thing. Someone would get out of their vehicle with a home-cooked dish in hand, stay for a while, and talk to my parents or grandfather. They would usually have a story about Grandma I had never heard before, like when she used to sing and play the piano to liven up a party, or when someone said Grandma Octavia knew how to drive an eighteen-wheeler and a stick shift.

As the funeral approached, I wasn't sure what to expect. I overheard some adults saying Grandma was going to be put in her resting place, but Mama had told us Grandma was already in Heaven, so that didn't make sense to me. While I was thinking about all this, I was standing in front of the mirror in my room, getting dressed. Mama had laid out my "good clothes" for the funeral. A crisp white shirt and black suit that I only wore at fancy restaurants, or when friends of my grandparents' came over to visit. I was trying to attach my clip-on tie to my shirt when I noticed my father was in the doorway to my room watching me. He also had on a black suit and shoes, but with a real tie. He just stood there looking at me for a moment before he finally spoke.

"Everything okay, Benjamin?" he said.

I was paying more attention to the clip-on than him when I glanced up at his reflection in the mirror. "Yeah," was really all I had time for at the moment.

Dad chuckled as he came into my room. "I can see that. Hey, I brought you something I think you might like," he said. He crouched in front of me, coming down to my eye level, and pulled something out of his suit's pocket.

A real tie, but sized for a kid. For me.

It was a paisley solid black. My father handed the tie to me and said, "How about we grow up a little today?"

My face said everything. I threw my clip-on tie onto my bed next to us. My father raised my shirt collar up and slipped the tie around my neck. Then he loosened his tie, so it hung as well. Without waiting, I immediately started messing with it, trying to tie the tie. My father didn't say anything, he just watched me work. By the time I was finished, I had a knot more appropriate for a shoelace than a necktie.

Dad sighed as he started to undo the mess I had made. "I know you're excited, Ben, but patience is important. Taking the time to listen and do something the right way will always be more important than fast and first. Do you understand, son?"

I nodded.

"Okay, we'll do it together, slowly. Watch what I do, then follow me," he said.

My dad shortened the tie so that the fat end was longer than the skinny end, then he folded the fat end over the skinny end, making an X of the two strips. "How are you feeling about Grandma's funeral?" He asked, his chin down, staring at his tie.

I followed what he did, without saying anything.

My father ignored my silence and moved on to the next part. He looped the fat end of the tie under, across, behind, and then finally through the top end to make the knot for the tie. He grinned, then repeated the entire process slower the second time and looked up at me when he was done.

I slowly started to repeat what he showed me. Looking down at my work as I put my fat strip under my X, I decided to answer him without looking up. "Well, will Grandma be there? I mean, will we see her?" I asked.

After a few moments of silence, he cleared his throat and then answered. "No, no, Grandma's gone, Ben. Her soul, her spirit, everything that made her who she was, is in Heaven now." Dad evened out the tie knot I made, making sure the seams of the tie weren't facing out. Then he smoothed out everything and finally put my collar back down. "The funeral is a way for everyone that's here to remember her, and to say goodbye to her. To celebrate her life, and keep her in our hearts and thoughts."

"Kind of like the going away party Mama had at the school when she stopped teaching there so she could teach us at home?" I wondered.

"Kind of, but we celebrate everything in the person's life. Not just one event, do you understand?" Dad questioned.

I nodded, and my dad kissed me on the forehead then stood up, smiling. "That is one good-looking tie you're wearing, Mister Sisko. Good job, son!"

I smiled back at my father and realized that, somehow, I felt a little less sad about Grandma leaving.

✦

New Orleans isn't really a city. It's a community.

When it came time for the funeral, I remember hearing the crowd in the restaurant before I saw anyone. I'd watched groups perform live music in the restaurant courtyard countless times. But I had never heard so many different instruments together, or voices in the restaurant.

As I headed downstairs, I stopped mid-way on the staircase. From my vantage point, it was like I'd stepped into another world. All the tables and chairs had been swallowed up in a sea of people. I could see the restaurant and the courtyard were filled with people; some I knew, most I'd never seen before. Everyone was very well dressed, with suits of all cuts and colors for the men and beautiful dresses with audacious hats for the women. Many of them had instruments. I'd never seen so many in one place. Trombones, trumpets, and saxophones. I saw a tuba, some tambourines, guitars, a pair of drums, and even a violin. With the musicians warming up and people talking, none of it sounded like anything, except noise.

In the crowd, I spotted Mama. I thought she was making her way over to me, but she stopped at the piano. She sat down, and started to play slowly, 'Just a Closer Walk to Thee'. A few of the horns in the crowd joined in, and everyone in the restaurant started to organize into two lines starting at the front door. I saw my dad up in the front of the line. He started swaying back and forth in rhythm to the music, and then everyone else started to follow him, marching in place as everyone with an instrument joined in.

Dad opened the restaurant doors, and the street outside was crowded with people. Where cars were usually parked, I saw a horse-drawn hearse, and I knew Grandma's coffin was inside. My father marched outside in rhythm to the old bible hymn, and everyone in the restaurant started to trail slowly behind him. I'd never seen one before, but after hearing enough about them from my grandparents, I realized that this was a second-line funeral progression honoring Grandma. All the women in the crowd pulled out white handkerchiefs in unison and started waving them in step as everyone began to march out of the restaurant.

While about half of the people were still inside, Mama looked up at me on the staircase. Her eyes told me to come down and sit next to her. Once I sat down, she turned to me. "C Jam Blues, just like Grandma taught you. I'm going to lead you in."

I let my hands hover over the keys and closed my eyes. Mama was picking up the pace, infusing jazz into the bible hymn. And in that moment I could feel everything Grandma had taught me. The jazz inside me was clamoring to get out.

I opened my eyes and started to play.

✦

Two weeks after the funeral, I remember sitting at the bottom of the staircase, watching Mama meet with the hotel and restaurant staff. She spoke from the floor of the restaurant, with everyone seated at the tables around her. "As of today, Sisko's hotel and restaurant are back open for business. I'll be taking over Miss Octavia's role as the hotel manager. Does anyone have any questions?"

Right then, Grandpa and Dad came down the stairs. They didn't say anything to me as they passed and walked into the restaurant. I could see that Dad looked upset. "What's going on?" he said.

Grandpa James was quiet as he sat at one of the empty tables with his son.

"Joseph," Mama said, her face all business. "I need you back in the kitchen tonight, and Mister James, I'd like you to resume your maître d' responsibilities, please."

My dad looked just like Elias or David right before they protested something. He opened his mouth, but before he could say anything, Grandpa put his hand on my father's shoulder and spoke instead. "Yes, ma'am," was all he said.

Mama smiled and clasped her hands together as she seemed to let out a sigh. "Great! All right, everyone, thanks for coming. Let's get back to work!"

My grandfather turned to me and gave me a wink. It was the first time in two weeks that I'd seen a glimpse of the man I knew. Watching what Mama did and how my grandfather reacted gave me an idea to help bring him back all the way.

✦

After Grandma passed away, we stopped spending Saturdays together as a family. I'd been watching Grandpa for about six months after the funeral, and it was like he was wearing a mask. At family dinners and outings, I would see a semblance of the engaging and funny man I remembered, but in those private moments, when he thought no one was watching, I would see the sadness in his eyes. How much he missed his wife, how alone he seemed. He started to say he was tired all the time and made excuses for why he couldn't be with the family. It was like he was disappearing before our eyes, but I was the only one who could see it.

Before dawn one Sunday morning, while everyone in the house was asleep, I knocked on my grandparents' bedroom door. I thought he'd be sleeping, but he answered right away. Grandpa James took one look at me, the fishing poles and gear I had, and he chuckled. "What's all this?" he said.

I grinned. "You're taking me fishing, Grandpa!"

"Ben…" My grandfather looked at me, and I could tell he was trying to figure out a way to say no.

I had rehearsed what I was going to say to him in the mirror for days, but when the moment came, my stomach turned in knots. I'd never really tried to convince an adult of anything before. "I already packed everything, Grandpa, including sandwiches. The car is charged, and I left a note on the fridge that we're going fishing, so all you have to do is say yes and get dressed!"

Grandpa James let out a low whistle. "Thought of everything, haven't you, Ben?" He looked off into space, deep in thought for a few seconds. "All right, we'll go, but you don't ask again until next month."

"Yes, sir!" I said, smiling.

✦

Out the window of the electrocar, the horizon was just starting to change from a deep black to the blueish hue that reveals sunrise isn't far away. The high beams punctuated the empty road and the steady hum from the electric vehicle's wheels was the only sound between us.

I always treasured the drive to Lake Pontchartrain. Usually I'd be in the backseat with the fishing gear while Grandpa would drive and Grandma Octavia would ride shotgun. I'd listen as she would tell me how their first date was a disaster at the lake. She'd say, "Your grandfather annoyed me, on our first date all he did was talk about food and music, but I couldn't stop thinking about him afterwards. That's how I knew I was in love."

But now I wasn't in the backseat—I was the one sitting next to my grandfather. We were almost at the lake, and he'd barely said a word the entire time, and I knew why. "I miss her too, and I've missed you, Grandpa," I said.

There was a long pause before he spoke, slowly at first, almost to himself more than to me. "You're smarter than your father, or I was at your age," Grandpa said. "We keep things inside. I'm sorry I taught your father that, but I'm glad he didn't pass it to you, Ben. You feel things and then do something about it. I see so much of Octavia and your mother in you, which is a good thing."

The car slowed until it came to a full stop. The battery indicator flashed, and then the dashboard and headlights flickered several times as they struggled to stay on, before losing the fight as everything in the car died.

My grandfather put a reassuring hand on my shoulder. "It's okay, Ben. This old jalopy probably just has a bad battery connector." Grandpa James smiled and gave me a kiss on my forehead. "I'll take care of it," he said.

My grandfather got out, and there was just enough light now to see that we'd made it to the lake, and we were alone. He walked around to the front of the car and raised the hood, blocking my view. After a pause, I could hear him fidgeting with something. "Yeah, just as I thought, bad connector. I'm gonna need to—" I heard what sounded like a growl and then a thumping sound.

Like something had fallen.

I called out for him, but all I could hear was the wind and the birds that began to wake with the morning light. As I opened the door, I could feel my chest tighten with fear. I called out again as I slowly walked around to the front of the car. He was on the ground, on his back. His body was in a position that told me that, for some reason, he'd fallen backward. It was clear from his face that he was in pain.

He was gritting his teeth, squeezing his eyes shut, and gripping his left arm as if all the pain was coming from there. I rushed over to him, and when I touched him it was like I brought him back from wherever the pain had taken him. He looked at me and forced a grin that was more of a grimace, and then whispered through his agony, "Phone, right jean pocket."

I pulled the slim smartphone out of his jean pocket. But before I could call for help, I could see the NO SERVICE indicator. I tried anyway, but nothing happened. I remembered Grandpa laughing once that having no service by the lake made it his place of solitude.

He must've seen the look on my face because he smiled again. He said, "It's okay, Benjamin. Everything is going to be all right."

There was something in the way he said it that made me cry. I wrapped my arms around him as best I could and just held on tight. He stopped holding onto his left arm and instead pulled me even closer to him. "You're a good boy, Benjamin, and you're going to be a good man. I want you to live life every day, don't wait. Like Grandma said, you can do anything you put your mind to, and you will. I know it!" He kissed me on the forehead, but this time, he kept it there for a long time, like he wanted to put all of his love in it. "Go back in the car, Ben. Help will be here soon."

"No, I don't want to," I managed through the tears.

Grandpa James sat up a little and I don't know if he was still in pain or if he was just hiding it but his smile was easy. "It's all right, I'm just going to rest out here for a bit. Get in the car, take the phone and call home if you get service. But stay in the car, Benjamin!"

There was something earnest in my grandfather's voice, and I didn't want to fight with him and make him feel worse. I used my sleeve to wipe my eyes, "Okay," I said as I got up. "I love you, Grandpa."

My grandfather leaned back on his elbows and breathed a sigh of relief. "Good boy, I love you too," he said.

They found me five hours later. I never visited Lake Pontchartrain again.

✦

You know Jake, I think of all of the advancements of humanity, of all the things we've accomplished and overcome over the years. Climate change, racism, poverty, disease. But humans still have a hard time dealing with death. Perhaps it's because, despite all we have achieved, it is still a great unknown. Perhaps because while it reminds us how precious the gift of life is, it also reminds us how vulnerable we are. The death of a loved one. That trauma, that grief can manifest itself in many different ways, son.

I've seen it in others, and in myself.

I'm not sure there's ever a clear path out of grief, Jake, but I do know that love and time are essential to make every day a little bit easier.

CHAPTER FOUR

REBELLION—2340

I WAS EIGHT YEARS OLD BEFORE I REALIZED I LIVED IN THE TWENTY-FOURTH CENTURY.

I know that may sound strange to you, son, but when you're homeschooled, and most of the people in your world all live under the same roof, it's a lot easier than it sounds. Sure, I'd see shuttles all the time, but how different is that from seeing a hovercopter in the twenty-second century?

After my grandparents passed away, Mama and Dad had their hands full, raising us kids and running the family business. Mama got us up in the morning and homeschooled us. Then in the afternoon she ran the hotel while a sitter watched us. And now that Dad was the restaurant's head chef and manager, he would get up even earlier, cook breakfast for us while we slept, and then go off to work. Most nights we'd see Mama, and the sitter wouldn't have to stay late, but it was rare when Mom and Dad were both with us for dinner.

In the midst of all this, I started to realize I had more time to myself than ever before. Being the oldest of four, everyone just kept less of an eye on me than Judith and the twins.

As a kid, I wasn't allowed into the hotel, so of course, I'd sneak in every chance I got. The staff usually turned a blind eye to my excursions. The simple fact was that they were far too busy to tell on the boss's kid. When they did take me back home, it was usually because I was talking to the guests. Sometimes, before getting caught, I'd see a glimpse of a Vulcan or a Tellarite and just walk up to them and start talking. Like my mom at her age, I would find myself wondering what strange places these people came from. I'd go home and tell Judith what I'd seen, and of course, JJ would tell Mama everything. So after a barrage of questions from the two oldest Sisko kids, Mama started teaching us about First Contact Day, aliens, and the Federation. It was all wildly fascinating and a lot of fun to learn that these people that looked so different from us came from other worlds, with cultures that were vastly unlike ours and yet, in a lot of ways, the same.

What I didn't realize was that in all those lessons about alien biology, alien languages and alien history we never really covered human technology. Sure, Mama taught us about starships, shuttles, and warp drives, but she never taught us about replicators, transporters, and communicators—that technology just didn't exist for me.

Then on one of my secret trips to the hotel, I was in the lobby sneaking a caramel from the candy dish at the front desk. Next to the front desk against the wall was a small stage, I'd seen it lots of times before but never really paid much attention to it. The clean lines and circular discs on its dark floor always seemed out of place in the hotel. The thing had become nearly invisible to me, so I was amazed when it hummed to life. The circular discs lit up and a curtain of streaming light appeared right above the platform. A man, woman, and a boy not much younger than me appeared from the curtain. They were all carrying luggage. The family stepped off the platform and stood right next to me. My heart was racing. My mind was reeling, I couldn't stop staring at them. There were real people in front of me that hadn't existed just a few seconds ago.

The man glanced down at me while the concierge was busy checking them in. Dumbfounded awe must've been all over my face. "First time seeing a transporter?" the man said. He chuckled and gave me a pat on the head. The boy stuck out his tongue. As the family walked off to their room, I stood there, frozen in my introduction to the twenty-fourth century.

A transporter. That's what the man had called the magical device.

Reese, the concierge, leaned over the front desk and looked down at me. Reese was only fifteen, with eyes that gave them a grown-up look even though they weren't. The teenager was my babysitter from time to time, but now in their oversized blazer and glasses, it felt like we were friends. "Hey, Ben," they whispered. "We have another one in the back. You wanna see?"

I didn't understand, Jake. This magical thing, this transporter had been here the whole time, and no one had said anything. Not my grandparents, or Dad, not even Mama.

I nodded.

✦

The hotel loading dock was a place I'd heard about before but had never seen. The hotel was already off-limits, and I knew if I were ever discovered back there, there'd be no end to the punishments I'd receive. The loading dock had two bays for electrotrucks to unload their goods onto. Off to the side was a transporter platform twice the size of the one in the lobby. Reese and I walked over to the console next to the platform. "This controls the transporter," they said. "It breaks down anything, turns it into energy, and then sends it wherever and then reforms it. Yesterday we got a shipment of beef for the restaurant, from Japan."

I knew Japan was far, far away, another continent, and my head was just beginning to understand what a transporter could do. There was no way I wasn't going to try it out. "I want to take a trip," I said excitedly.

Reese's eyes widened and their face went a sickly pale. "Benjamin, I—I can't. If we got caught, Mrs. Sisko would fire me!"

Usually, I was the one pleading with an adult for something, and I knew Reese wasn't exactly an adult yet, but it felt good. I remembered Mama's lesson on Vulcan logic, so I thought I'd try it out. "But we're already here, and I promise you I won't ask again, and you know I won't tell anyone because then I'd get in trouble!" I held up my hand in the Vulcan salute as an added incentive.

Reese laughed out loud, then remembering where they were, started to whisper. "Put your hand down," they said. After a few moments deep in thought, the teenager smirked. "All right, one trip, I pick where and then we never do this, or talk about it, again. Deal?"

My newfound partner outstretched their hand, and I shook it without hesitating. "Deal!" I said, as I started towards the platform.

Reese caught my hand. "Hold on, mister, we can do it from right here— besides, all transports from the pad are logged."

I watched Reese take off the Sisko's badge from the lapel of their blazer and wave it over the console. The computer board lit up and Reese started talking out loud as they tapped on the screen. At first, I thought it was to me, but then I realized this was a way of reminding theirself what someone had taught them. "Okay, the transporter is already paired to the badge, so I just scan the target area, make sure it's clear, confirm, and… we're taking a trip!"

The console lit up and, my partner was smiling and slapped the badge back on their lapel. I was about to ask a question when Reese placed one hand on my shoulder and used the other to double tap the badge. I heard a hum, felt a tingle like static electricity, and then found myself surrounded in an ocean of blue light. I could still feel Reese's firm, reassuring grip on my shoulder. For the second time in my life, I was exploring a strange new world. And unlike my experience when I first learned to swim, I liked this, a lot. A second later, the light faded, and I was in my room with Reese.

"That was amazing!" I shouted.

Reese quickly put a finger up to their lips and motioned for me to keep it down. "Yeah, I'm sure it was," they whispered. "A deal is a deal, right, Ben?"

I was disappointed, but I remembered Dad once told me my word would be the only currency I'd ever need, and I was starting to understand what he meant. "A deal's a deal," I said.

The concierge let out a sigh of relief. "Oh, thank goodness," they said. Reese tapped their badge and absentmindedly looked up while speaking, I followed their eye-line, but no one was on my ceiling. "Reese to front desk, my break is over, can you just beam me back?" the teenager said to no one.

A half second later a response came from the badge. I could hear that it was Brian, who had taken over when Reese left the front desk with me. "Sure, no problem, Reese. Hang on a sec," he said.

Now I had a million more questions than a few seconds ago, but it started with one: "How can you talk through the badge? I thought it controlled the transporter?"

Reese looked mildly annoyed at me, then seemed to remember how much I didn't know. "Wow. Your parents really never told you any of this stuff, huh? Yeah, it's also a communicator. They come in different shapes and sizes, but with one, you can talk to anyone anywhere on the planet. Later!" With that, my babysitter and newfound educator stood straight and tall, stiffening as if they were about to be measured for something, and disappeared in a cascade of blue light.

As I stared at the empty space that Reese filled just a second ago, I could feel a sadness I thought I had left behind returning. But now it was wrapped in something new.

Anger.

All I could think about was how useful a communicator and transporter would've been six months ago when Grandpa James died.

✦

My parents had been lying to me.

As I lay in bed that night, Jake, I couldn't sleep. Mister Bayou stared at me, now more a confidant than a protector. My world had always been my family, the restaurant, hotel, and what I knew about New Orleans. I never thought I needed much else. But there was another world out there, filled with wondrous things like transporters and communicators. And the world I knew was starting to feel much smaller. I told all this to Mister Bayou, who like a good friend, listened patiently. But looking at my stuffed confidant, I thought maybe that was the problem. I had never felt like my parents were treating me or my sister and brothers like babies. They always talked to us in much the same way they spoke to adults, and answered our questions in the same way as well. But they had been lying to me. To all us Sisko kids. At the very least, maybe they thought that we had to be spoon-fed knowledge. Only a little at a time, and never too much. If they knew all these wonderful things existed and used them for the hotel and restaurant, why didn't the family have them? And what had Grandpa said to me that last day we went fishing?

"Don't wait. Live life every day."

So I got up, got dressed as quietly as possible, and waited.

✦

I learned quickly that the best time to do anything "questionable" in the house of a master chef and hotel manager is late at night—the later the better. By trial and error, I came to learn two in the morning was the best time. By two, it's so late that everyone is asleep, and it's before my father would get up to start the restaurant, which was usually around four. If I wanted to get some ice cream or shrimp from the restaurant's kitchen, I did it at two. If I wanted to go to the hotel lounge on the fourth floor and stargaze—two. And if I wanted to "borrow" a Sisko's badge so I could use the transporter—definitely two in the morning!

At some point before World War III a door was installed on the first floor between our house and the hotel. This was when it was a jazz club instead of a restaurant, and the hotel was usually booked by musicians playing at the club. The musicians could go from their hotel rooms, downstairs through the door, and be backstage. When the club ended and the restaurant began, it became a great way to deliver room service. What I loved about it was that the door only locked—or could be opened—from the restaurant's side, our side.

Usually, when I did this, I'd just sneak up to the hotel's "sky deck," which was a fancy lounge on the roof. There were huge telescopes and a self-serve ice cream machine up there that I loved. But tonight, I was quietly making my way to the front desk. I would never do this the week before, during, or after Mardi Gras. No one ever slept then. But now, in September, most of the guests were asleep or in their rooms.

The Sisko's badges were right where I expected, behind the front desk in a cabinet with a simple latch on it. I'd seen the hotel staff go into the cabinet and grab badges from there hundreds of times, but I hadn't realized the power that the little name tags held. I grabbed the first one I saw, which looked identical to the others. A gold metal badge with *Sisko's* in large letters and *Hotel* smaller underneath. I'd never held one before. The badge had some weight to it, and I realized that was because it was much more than it appeared.

I closed the cabinet and moved quietly down the hall past the linen and break rooms to the loading dock, unlocking the necessary doors as I went and reminding myself I'd have to do the reverse on the way back. The two loading bays for the electrotrucks and dock itself sat outside, basically a large alcove that connected to the back of the hotel. When I opened that last door, the dock was dark and quiet, with the humid Louisiana night a sharp contrast to the temperature-controlled hotel. I walked over to the transporter control and was surprised by the motion-activated lights. I shot a glance to the back of the second floor of our house, but everything remained dark.

Waving the badge across the transporter controls, I watched it snap to life exactly like it had before, which made me smile at this small accomplishment. As the scanning, targeting, and transporter sections lit up on the console, I found myself imitating Reese's walk-through out loud. "Okay, okay, the badge is connected to the transporter, so I need to scan the target area first." I suddenly realized that was a problem because, from the console, it looked like I couldn't scan much farther than around the house. And now that I thought about it, if I did figure out how to go really far away—how was I going to get back? After thinking though my problem for a few moments, I came up with a solution that made me smile. I input the target area, made sure it was clear, confirmed transport, and watched the transporter console change from amber to green. "Yes!" I heard myself say louder than I should have. Now there was nothing left to do but to take my trip.

With the badge firmly in my hand I ran full out for the edge of the raised loading dock. Just before reaching the edge, I jumped. I knew there was only about four feet of nothing between the raised dock platform and the ground below, so I wasn't worried if I got it wrong. But in that second of flight I felt something I'd never felt before.

Free.

I double-tapped the badge, and before my feet touched the ground I was swallowed up in an ocean of blue light. The next thing I knew I was standing just a few feet away from the transporter control, right where I'd started. I got down on the ground and must've laughed for a good five minutes straight! I thought about doing it again, but I was afraid my laughter would have wakened someone in the hotel or my house. So I retraced my steps, locking everything up, putting the badge back where I found it (but taking a caramel from the candy dish), snuck back into my room, and began planning my next adventure.

✦

Over the next few weeks, I learned the price of being invincible.

The day after my late-night "trip" I jumped every time Mama called my name. I just knew somehow, someway Mama or Dad would discover what I'd done and I'd be punished. But one day without any retribution turned into two and then three.

Once I was sure I'd gotten away with my first adventure, I became bolder. Soon after, I went back to the hotel in the dead of night, and this time the height of the docking bay wasn't enough for me. I set the transport destination for where I was near the transporter console, but I needed to find higher ground to leap from. Then I realized I had the perfect place. Creeping back into the hotel, I quietly walked up the staircase to the second floor. Looking back down at the ground floor, I felt a twinge in my stomach, which was half the fun.

Without any more hesitation, I jumped down the flight of stairs in the hotel, and was saved by the transporter.

Or so I thought.

When I reappeared from the successful transport and landed a few inches above the ground next to the console, I heard a cracking sound as I landed on my right arm. A half second later, streams of pain shot up my arm, and I cried out as I immediately realized what I'd done wrong. The transport worked, but I was still falling as if I'd jumped from the top of the stairs—I had nothing to break my fall! I wanted to cry but held it back because I knew getting caught would just make everything much worse. So I pushed the tears back and screamed into my hand that was covering my mouth so I wouldn't make a lot of noise, and then put everything back as best I could. My arm felt like it was on fire, but I could still move my fingers which I figured was a good sign. By the time I left the hotel and made it to my parents' bedroom, I was in tears. I told Dad and Mama I was trying to slide down the banister and fell. I couldn't look them in the face when I told them the half-truth that I knew was an outright lie.

My parents never questioned me. They just called the doctor and told me everything would be all right. Judith hid behind Mama, her little face mirroring Mama's worry. The doctor arrived, a young woman with reddish blonde hair, and blue eyes that made her look incredibly serious. Introducing herself, she then flipped open a small box and waved it over me. After a moment of this, she ejected a cylinder from the bottom of the box and pressed it to my neck. A hissing sound escaped the small cylinder, like a snake was injecting me with its venom, but I started feeling better immediately. "What's that?" I asked.

The doctor looked over at my parents, a sense of puzzlement playing across her face, then back to me as she smiled and reached into her shoulder bag. "Medical devices, a tricorder, and hypospray. This," she said, holding up the small disc she'd taken out of her bag and began waving it across my arm, "is a bone regenerator. There, how does that feel?"

I cautiously bent my arm back and forth, testing for pain, but there was none. "Great," I said, astonished.

The doctor chuckled, "You fractured your arm, young man, but you're fine now. Just don't go sliding down any more banisters!"

After that night, I was filled with mixed emotions. On the one hand I was eager to sneak back to the transporter. Now that I knew this new future I lived in could heal broken bones with a wave of a mechanical magical wand, I really didn't have to worry, at least not very much. On the other hand, I knew that if I kept this up, it would only be a matter of time before I was caught.

✦

One night I went to the loading dock, and a big-rig electrotruck was sitting in the bay. Sometimes while enroute to some preprogrammed destination, the automated trucks would park themselves in our loading dock to recharge overnight. The mammoth vehicle was backed into the loading bay slot with its driverless carriage facing outwards and the back end charging away. I knew the rig would be gone in a few hours and this would be my only opportunity. It was nearly twenty feet from the roof of the truck to the tires. This was higher than anything I'd tried. I figured if I climbed to the top, ran the length of the rig, and then jumped up at the last second, I might actually get close to a full twenty feet in the air before coming down. But this time, after nearly breaking my arm, I decided to have some insurance when I landed. I first beamed a mattress from the linen room to my usual target spot, so when I was transported to my target area I would have something to cushion my "fall." After setting, and affirming my transport for this exact spot, the console lit up in confirmation.

I used the technician's mini ladder on the side of the truck to climb to the top. Looking over the side, I felt my stomach tighten. I was so high it almost felt like I was looking out the window of my room. But I looked at the badge in my hand, and I knew I had my own personal parachute.

I was living life. This was going to be fun.

I ran down the length of the truck and leaped. I was sure I was at least twenty feet off the ground before gravity took over. I double-tapped my badge and waited for the tsunami of comforting blue light to swirl around me, and usher me to safety.

Nothing happened.

I double-tapped the badge again, and again, but nothing. It was too late. Unlike the other jumps, which were filled with exhilaration, time now seemed to oddly expand and contract around me at the same time. I had mere seconds before I slammed into the pavement, but those seconds seemed to stretch on endlessly. I could feel the cool crisp night air on my face, hear the cicadas' nightly rhythms all around me, taste the bile that was threatening to push up from the tightening knot in my stomach. In that last instant, with the ground rushing towards me, I twisted violently, trying to turn and land on my side. Without any mattress under me, I was hoping a broken arm that could be magically fixed would break this fall. But I was scared and flailing, I turned too much and landed on my back. If there was the sound of bones breaking, I didn't hear it. In the distance, far, far away, I could hear someone screaming.

After a moment, I realized the person screaming was me.

Like before, at Lake Pontchartrain, I could feel myself submerged, drowning, but this was an ocean of pain that had no surface to swim to. I could feel myself being pulled, and dragged into a deep and unforgiving darkness. I looked up for anyone and anything that might help me, but all I could see were the jewels of stars overhead in the night sky, and as my eyes started to close, I wondered if I would ever see them again.

CHAPTER FIVE
RECOVERY—2340-2341

I KNEW I WASN'T DEAD WHEN I WOKE UP.

There's no sense of time when you're unconscious. When I opened my eyes, I still expected to see stars above me, but instead I saw the faces of my parents. It seemed like Mama had been quietly crying, but when I awoke she started sobbing outright. My father's face was wet, and he tried to force a smile. "We thought we'd lost you, son," he said.

I'd never been in a hospital before, but now, somehow, it was clear to me, that was where I was. The room had white walls with blue trim, and there was a window where I could just make out some of New Orleans' skyscrapers. My left arm had a cuff with a tiny screen that I realized was monitoring my heartbeat. A thin blue sleeve on my right arm had tubes attached that ran into the wall. When I tried to sit up, an energy field that only left my arms free shimmered, covering my body from the neck down to my toes like a perfectly fitted warm blanket. But this blanket didn't allow me to move a millimeter.

Moving my head around, I noticed an electronic panel above the bed was clearly monitoring my body. Then it hit me.

My head and arms were free, but I couldn't move anything else.

I tried to speak, but my mouth felt as if it was filled with sand. I swallowed but had so little saliva that it hurt. I was about to try to mouth something to my parents when a familiar face entered the room. The same doctor who had healed my arm at our house smiled as she came in. "I see our little daredevil is awake," she said as she gave a reassuring look to Mama, who was smiling now as well.

The doctor stood on the opposite side of my bed from my parents and glanced up at the console above me. She then reached into her oversized white hospital jacket, pulled out a hypospray, and placed it on my neck. The medication (whatever it was) worked quickly in my system. I could swallow without it hurting and felt like I could finally speak. "Thanks," I said.

The doctor took a moment to take me in. Then she took out a penlight and began checking my eyes. "You're welcome, Ben. I'm not sure you remember me. My name is Doctor Pulaski. I took care of your arm," she said.

I nodded, mostly because I was still trying to catch up with what happened, and I wanted to hear what she had to say.

Satisfied with whatever she had seen, she put the penlight away, took a couple of steps back, and stuffed her hands in her pockets. "You gave us quite a scare, young man. When you came in, your legs, arms, and back were broken. We had to put you in a medically induced coma while we accessed and repaired the damage. You've been out for three days." Doctor Pulaski smiled again as she looked over at my parents, and it felt to me like she was trying to make us all feel better. "The good news is that we've repaired your arms and legs, but you've fractured several vertebrae in your spine, and have some neural damage. That's going to take more time to completely heal… about six months." The doctor sighed. "The bad news is you're going to have to stay immobilized in the stasis field during that time so your vertebrae and spine can fully recover, Benjamin."

I looked over at Mama and Dad. I had so many questions, but the most obvious one came to mind. "How will I go to the bathroom?"

Doctor Pulaski chuckled, "Well, ironically, because you'll be completely immobile, we're able to use a special medical transporter to beam waste out of you." Her demeanor changed, taking on a more serious tone as she walked over to the side of the bed my parents were on and stood by them. "I won't lie to you, Ben, six months nearly immobile like this isn't going to be easy, especially at your age. But I know you can do it, and when everything is healed, you'll be as good as new!"

The doctor turned to leave, but before she did I noticed she made sure she looked Mama in the eyes while she put a reassuring hand on her arm. "We're going to do everything we can to make his stay here as comfortable as possible, Mrs. Sisko, I promise."

As my doctor left the room, Mama came over and gave me a kiss on the forehead. "You'll be healed up and back home before you know it, Benjamin." As my mother tried to console me my father was still standing back with his head down.

When he finally spoke, his voice was barely above a whisper. "You could've died if I hadn't found you, Ben. From the looks of things this wasn't the first time you'd been playing this… game. And trying to beam off the roof of a rig that ships materials that scramble transporters? It's no surprise your transport didn't work. You're lucky to be alive. Why'd you do it, son? Why?"

Even though I wasn't feeling any pain, the anguish in my father's voice and Mama's eyes was unbearable. I turned my face to look out the window as I spoke. "I—It was exciting, and Grandpa said—he told me I shouldn't wait, I should live life."

"What? I don't understand," he said. "What did Pop tell you?" My father's voice was cautious, as if he were venturing into some uncharted territory.

I could feel the tears on my face sliding onto my pillow. I hadn't cried since that night with Grandpa James, I told myself I wouldn't now, but thinking about him and saying his name out loud, I couldn't hold it back. "That day… at the lake, he told me not to wait, to live life every day. When I found out about the transporter, it felt like that was what I was doing."

Dad was standing next to Mama now and I could see him carefully considering his words. "There's a difference between excitement and fulfillment, Benjamin," he said finally. "Sometimes people spend their whole lives chasing excitement because they're not fulfilled. Doing things that thrill you and make you feel like you're alive is different from having experiences full of life. Pop wanted you to live every day fully, son, not foolishly."

My father held my hand and my mother's. "I think we've had enough excitement. How about from now on, we work on fulfillment? Deal?"

I nodded. I could feel the love and patience in my father's explanation. At the same time I felt like I had come through something, and maybe now, I could see the world a little clearer. I wiped my tears, and said, "Deal!"

✦

Late one evening, a Vulcan doctor I'd never seen before came into my room. He stood over my bed, silently reading my chart. I couldn't help that his pointed ears made me feel uneasy: didn't monsters have pointed ears? After a few minutes of silent reading, he looked up at me tepidly.

"Benjamin Sisko?" he asked.

"Yes, that's me," I replied cheerfully.

The Vulcan put the PADD back in the slot at the foot of my bed, and folded his arms behind his back. "Your chart says you are immobilized and haven't walked in months. You have even had a birthday while here. How does that make you feel?"

"Are you serious?" I asked.

"I am," the Vulcan said dryly.

I looked at him for some sign of humor or anything to break the tension. When I didn't see any, I answered the question. "Well, sometimes I dream I can fly, but most times I feel like I'm gonna go out of my mind!"

"Precisely. That is our determination as well." The Vulcan moved from the foot of the bed and stood over me. "We believe you will benefit from a mind meld." The doctor reached out with his hand toward my face.

"A mind-what?" I'd heard that a couple of weeks ago a Vulcan doctor had used a mind-thing to help a kid having a seizure. Well, I wasn't having a seizure, and didn't want one. I grabbed the doctor's wrist with my hands. "No thanks," I said forcefully.

The doctor easily used one hand to pin both of my arms, and with the stasis field on, I couldn't kick or even squirm out of the way.

I was helpless.

The Vulcan pressed his thumb, index finger, and middle finger onto my face. I could feel my mind starting to go blank, like I was falling a great distance, and in that distance, I could hear him whispering calmly. "My mind, to your mind. Your thoughts, to my thoughts."

I woke up screaming.

I heard a voice whispering in the darkness. "It was the Vulcan again, right? Did you punch him in the face like I suggested?"

The voice had kept me company for the last three weeks. A few days after

I arrived, the hospital staff had beamed Ralph into my room, bed and all. Someone had thought it would be a good idea to put a human that couldn't walk and a Tellarite that couldn't see in the same room together.

"No, Ralph, I'm sorry I didn't really have the opportunity to punch the Vulcan in the face. I was a little busy trying to keep him from scrambling my brains!" I lifted my head and could see Ralph halfway sitting up in bed, leaning on his elbows. His eyes were bandaged, and as he faced my direction, his furry face, pig-like snout, and tusks cast a more menacing image in the shadows than he realized.

Ralph jerked back as if physically struck by my words. "Listen, hu-man, you're the one having nightmares about brain-sucking Vulcans. My dreams are filled with real baseball and real pizza!"

Ralph was older than me by a few years, and thought he knew everything—simply because he was older. What he really was, was annoying. I found myself making the same faces at the Tellarite that Judith and the twins made at me. I said, "Baseball, maybe. But c'mon, who dreams about pizza?"

Excitedly, Ralph sat up in bed completely. He crossed his legs, eager to get into a conversation. "I do! Not that replicated cardboard they say is pizza. I mean *real* pizza with the grease and gooey cheese, oh, and maybe some pepperoni! Even after that wild Conigliaro pitch fractured my face and broke my eye, what did I want to eat when I woke up? Real, oven-baked pizza!"

I sighed. "Yeah I know the story, you've already told it to me a thousand times. Can we get back to my nightmare, please?"

The Tellarite scratched his fur and abruptly dropped his smile. "Yeah, sure. This is your what, fourth time having that dream?"

"Fifth," I said.

"Look, kid, I got hit in the face with a one-hundred-mile-an-hour pitch. One eye was destroyed, and cells from the other eye had to be harvested, cloned, and implanted in the bad eye, so for all intents and purposes, I'm blind until both eyes heal. Am I still thinking about that pitch? No! I'm planning my next up at bat." Ralph chuckled, but with his snout, it sounded more like a snort. "You really are paralyzed. You're so worried that you can't walk you got a Vulcan visiting you in your sleep. You need to make peace with the fact that you can't get out of bed. Start thinking about your next time at bat!"

I didn't have a big brother, but I imagined if I did, having one would probably include moments like this. I thought about Ralph's words for a few minutes before I finally spoke. "I don't know a lot about baseball, but from what I do know, your analogy makes some sense," I said, finally.

Eager to change the subject now, I asked, "So, do you know what're you gonna do when your eyes heal? Like for a job, a career, I mean? Please tell me it's not baseball."

Ralph chuckled in a way that felt off. "No. My dad is on the Federation Council. He talks to everyone, he helps people communicate, and helps them help each other. I've seen him go places and get things done that even Starfleet people can't do. About two years ago, I told him I wanted to do what he does. He was so happy…" Ralph's voice trailed off.

Even with the bandages over his eyes, it was clear he was seeing and reliving something in his past. I tried to fill the silence. "Okay, that's a good thing, right?"

Ralph sighed. "Yeah, it was. I entered the Federation junior dignitary program. I was having a great time, studying and learning all the hard work it takes to become an advisor, an ambassador, and a politician. And then, one day, my Dad took me to an authentic pizza shop in New York, and I was hooked…" Ralph trailed off again, but this time he pulled himself back from wherever he was. "Sitting in that small shop, eating and reading about the history of pizza on your planet. All the different locations claimed they had the best, so I tried them all, and they're all great! That was when I saw it so clearly. I still want to do what my dad does, but smaller. I want to open the first pizza shop on Tellar Prime and connect with people my own way."

Everything Ralph was saying was exciting, but there was no excitement in his voice, no enthusiasm. He sounded almost defeated. "What did your dad say when you told him?" I asked.

"I haven't," Ralph said.

"What? I don't understand. You're the one talking about planning your next at-bat. Doesn't this count?" I asked.

I couldn't see Ralph's expression in the darkness of our room, but it was clear he was annoyed. I just couldn't tell if it was with me, or himself. "Yeah, I know, I know, all right? It's just that some pitches are harder to swing at than others."

Now I was sure of what I heard in my friend's voice. As smart and confident as Ralph was, he was scared to tell his father about his dreams. And I wasn't sure if he ever would. I changed the subject, again. "So you never told me why your parents named you Ralph? Isn't that a very hu-man name?" I teased.

I could feel the mood lighten. This time the Tellarite snorted loudly as he laughed. "It's short for Raphael. Since I was born here on Earth, my parents thought a human name should be part of my heritage."

"Ralph, the way you love baseball and pizza, I think everyone knows you're about as human as we come."

✦

Jake, there are going to be times life is going to throw you a curveball, things that you will not see coming and just won't be able to comprehend fully at the time. Events like that can cripple and destroy you, or they can reveal who you are.

About a week after our discussion, Ralph's eyes had healed enough for him to go home. I was alone again in my room and thinking a lot about what he had said to me.

I was alone, but it was more than that; I was helpless.

I had gone from being able to run and play and go anywhere I wanted one day, to being confined to a bed, unable to walk, unable to feed myself or even use the bathroom on my own.

When the twins were born, Mama taught me how to change their diapers, and it was a little scary to see how helpless and dependent they were, how dependent we all are as babies. I never wanted to be like that again—no kid does—and now here I was. The first few days after Ralph left, it took everything I had not just to scream and cry out of anger and fear.

But I didn't. I hadn't told anyone about the dreams except Ralph, but after he left I told Mama during one of our many video calls. For a moment, I could see her brow tighten and her eyes squint with worry but then it was gone, replaced with her familiar smile. She told me she'd have something for me when she next came to see me.

My parents came to visit me every day. At first, they came together, but then I asked them to visit separately, except for Sundays, which made me feel like I was still participating in our family weekends. Being in the bed, it was just easier for one person to visit at a time. I also asked my parents not to bring my siblings. I knew they were already crying a lot because of what had happened, and I didn't want to make them any sadder coming to see me. To my surprise my parents agreed. I'd see my sister and brothers during video calls— sometime when I called on the hospital PADD they'd be in the background, other times they would pick up the call. I'd answer every question the twins had or chat with Judith until she'd get tired of talking to me and just put the PADD down without giving it to anyone.

My father would come to see me Mondays, Wednesdays, and Fridays. He'd always bring too much food for me from the restaurant, mainly because I couldn't stomach the hospital food. I'd never eaten replicated food before, and you could tell it wasn't real. After one bite, I had had enough, I couldn't get it down. The texture, taste, even the aromas were all just off.

More than anything, it was bland. My father had a few arguments with the hospital staff and then he said he would just prepare all my meals for me. Ultimately they agreed that now wasn't the time to change what my body was used to, but that my father would need to prepare meals that matched their dietary specifications.

Tuesdays, Thursdays, and Saturdays belonged to Mama. My favorite day of the week in the hospital became Thursdays. After I'd told her about my nightmare with the Vulcan, that very next day was a Thursday, and she showed up with a large bag, from which she took out a small gift. Without unwrapping it, I already knew it was a book. Before I learned about starships and warp drives, books were my vehicle of choice. The ultimate starship, a book can take you places warp drive can never reach.

"Well, open it." Mama smiled.

Without hesitation, I tore off the paper and saw an a title that surprised me: *The Autobiography of Christopher Pike.* There was an old Starfleet insignia, and a faint sketch of the *U.S.S. Enterprise* blended into the cover. When Mama started teaching us about the Federation and Starfleet she started with the *Enterprise.* The history of ships named *Enterprise* went all the way back to sailing ships. Captains of ships named *Enterprise* had been responsible for helping humanity go to the stars and build the Federation. "Which one is Pike again?" I asked.

My teacher-mom gave me a *we-went-over-this-in-class* look. "Captain Christopher Pike is after Captain Robert April and *before* Captain Kirk,"

Mama said.

"Right," I replied, remembering the rhythm I had used to pass her *Enterprise* captains test. "After April, before Kirk," I sang to myself.

"His science officer was a Vulcan, Mister Spock. I think you'll find this an enjoyable and logical read."

I was scared of the Vulcan doctor that visited me in my nightmares, but Mister Spock was different. He was Kirk's Spock. Learning about his exploits in school, I became engrossed. Half Vulcan, half human, he had been involved in so much history on both worlds, and still was. I smiled back at Mama, then gave the Vulcan salute and used the catchphrase everyone knew was Mister Spock's favorite. "Fascinating," I teased.

Mama held up the large gift bag, "I got you something else, but you're going to have to sit up for this one."

We both knew I couldn't sit up. The stasis field inhibited all motion inside the field, leaving only my arms, neck, and head free. I reached for the PADD attached to the side of my bed and used it to rotate my bed by ninety degrees, standing the bed and me upright. I tapped another command in and a tray table slid out from the side of the bed and in front of me. "What is it?" I asked.

Mama reached into the gift bag and pulled out a second wrapped gift nearly as large and wide as the bag. "I think you're going to like this," she said.

I tore the wrapping off and realized she was right. "*U.S.S. Octavia Butler,* NCC-2258. *Ambassador* class," I whispered.

The model was an exact replica of the Federation starship. I'd seen pictures of starships before in class, but this was different somehow. Holding the model and looking at the image of the starship on the face of the box, I could feel its purpose to protect and power to defend, like I could tap into its intensity. The sleek design of its saucer section and nacelles radiated speed. I opened the box and gazed at the dozens of pieces that beckoned for me to assemble them and create a work of art.

It was beautiful.

Something happened to me in that moment. It wasn't so much a decision, at least not yet, but it was the beginning of an intent. An unwavering, perhaps even single-minded focus, towards Starfleet and starships. After a few moments, I realized my mother had been silently watching me, her eyes filled with the same kind of joy I'd seen on her face on Christmas mornings when we all opened our presents.

"You know your grandmother was named after Octavia Butler," she said.

I looked at the name again, etched across the hull of the vessel. I knew starships were named after people and places of significance, but I didn't know this one. "Who was she?" I asked.

Mama's face softened. "A pivotal author of the twentieth century. Your grandfather was named after James Baldwin, another legendary author. That's how your grandparents met. They were in a bookstore. Grandma was looking for a book by Baldwin, and your grandfather was looking for a book by Butler. They were in the same aisle and saw each other."

I looked at Mama. "Why did you and dad name me Benjamin?"

When I asked her that, for a moment, she turned away to the window. Back then, I thought it was because the question made her emotional, but now I understand just how deep the simple question went and how fraught with pain the answer must have been. Mama turned back to me with a smile. Every hint of the truth that she held in her heart had disappeared. "Your father isn't a writer, but he always believed that words have power and names have strength. Since the days of the Bible, Benjamin has always been a name that represented strength, courage, and integrity. The way you've been dealing with everything, your father and I can see you're everything we hoped you would be, and more, Benjamin."

I was about to ask another question but Mama just kept staring at my head. "What?" I asked.

"Your hair is really growing. I didn't really notice it until you moved the bed," she said.

I could feel what was coming. "I know Mama, I can get it cut after—"

"Move the bed so that you're lying down and your head is facing me."

I opened my mouth to protest but thought better of it. Instead, I just did as I was told. After a few minutes of positioning and repositioning, the bed was now lower than usual and Mama sat at the top of my bed, braiding my hair. I winced as she separated and parted my hair, then slowly wove it into a braid.

"So mister laughfeyette, do you know why your middle name is Lafayette?" she said.

When it was just Mama, Dad and me, she would call me her little laughfeyette because she could make me laugh for almost any reason. It was usually contagious and before I knew it, we were all laughing for some silly reason. I chuckled. "Something to do with baseball, right?"

"Well, baseball died out on Earth a long time ago. Captain Lafayette Hood was the astronaut that was the commander of the first domed city on Mars. He loved everything about baseball so, on the day the dome was complete, his team played the first baseball game on Mars. When the other domed cities were built they started the Mars Baseball League. After a while, people down here started saying Mars baseball wasn't real baseball because of the gravity. And before you know it, teams started back up here to play against Mars. All because of Lafayette Hood, so don't forget you're named after someone who never quit believing in baseball. And because he believed in baseball, it came back," she said.

"Well, now I understand what Ralph meant when he talked about real baseball," I said.

Mama stopped braiding my hair and leaned over so I could see her face. "I forgot to tell you, Ralph and his family came by the restaurant a few days ago. He can see a little now, and was upset pizza wasn't on the menu."

We both laughed.

Mama leaned back in the chair and continued her work on my hair. "Your father made him pizza, and all was forgiven. He said he might even come back!"

Listening to Mama's voice, I was struck by how it reminded me of those times she would read to me at night all those years ago. Even though I was older now, our friendship felt the same.

She said, "When I visited the model shop, I noticed they had deluxe *Enterprise* models. Everything from the NX-01 to the *Enterprise* -C. If you finish this one by next week—and do everything your doctors tell you—I'll bring you one every week. But only if you promise to work as hard on your physical therapy as I know you will on the models."

I made that promise, and not long after that, Vulcan doctors stopped visiting me in my dreams.

CHAPTER SIX

EDUCATION—2341-2342

MY VERTEBRAE COMPLETELY HEALED, ALMOST AS IF NOTHING HAD EVER HAPPENED.
But my treatment also stimulated bone growth, so oddly, I was taller as well.
Not much, just the inch or two I would have gained normally over the same
time. But because it was all at once when I stood up, I noticed—and so did
everyone else when they saw me standing on my own for the first time during
physical therapy.

"Oh, my baby. You're so tall," Mama had said, beaming. As for my father,
I still had to look up at him, but I was definitely gaining on him. In another
few years, we'd be eye to eye. He didn't comment when he saw me standing.
Instead, he just shook my hand and slapped me on the shoulder. Seeing myself
through my parents' eyes I realized I wasn't just taller, I looked different,
sturdier, older. After six months of lying flat on my back in bed, I had another
month of physical therapy before I could leave the hospital. Learning to walk
again, stretching, intense weight training. I was stronger as well.

For the entire seven months, I was never around more than two or three
people at a time. Most of the time I saw my parents individually, and I usually
saw Doctor Pulaski and my therapist one-on-one as well. So on the day I
walked out of the hospital unassisted and onto the street, I was overwhelmed.
People were everywhere—sights, sounds, and smells coming my way at the
speed of life. I had to stop on the way to the electrocar a few times and just

shut my eyes and take deep relaxing breaths. The counselor at the hospital had suggested beaming me straight home and easing me in to stimuli over a few weeks. But I found, for now, I'd lost my appetite for the transporter. Today, I'd live life by taking the long way home.

I sat in the back seat of the electrocar with the four boxes of personal items I had accumulated in the hospital. After all that time the four boxes were filled with only three things: a few books, like Captain Pike's and one on the Federation; several get-well cards, including a really large one from Reese; and twenty-two model starships.

I'd amassed my own little fleet. Some of the model ships were designed in such a way that you could build them deck by deck. I had installed warp cores, run warp coils for the nacelles, and stocked the bays with tiny shuttles. With a few I'd gone beyond the specifications, making my own improvements on the ship designs. Swapping out saucer sections and nacelles, giving one ship more speed and another more firepower. No matter what I imagined, I felt it paled in comparison to the ships that were really out there soaring between the stars, patrolling and protecting the Federation.

In the front seat, my parents were so excited I was coming home. Dad had cooked the family's favorite jambalaya-a-la-Sisko, a rare treat reserved only for birthdays and, apparently, a return from the hospital. The night before, my parents came to the hospital to tell me that they'd made the decision to let go of the hotel. Mama said that without Grandma and Grandpa, it was too hard for her to manage the hotel and for Dad to run the kitchen, and hold the family together. Dad said that Feinberg Books, the global seller, wanted to rent the hotel's first floor and that the Federation was interested in using the other floors for visiting dignitaries. They were smiling and talking about how this was such a blessing that would benefit the family. But I've always thought they blamed themselves for what I did. That if they hadn't been so busy, working so hard, I wouldn't have been able to sneak off and do what I did. I know that wasn't true, I knew it wasn't their fault, but I didn't say anything because I also knew I'd never convince them otherwise.

As I looked out the car window, New Orleans was bursting with life. Kids were playing on the sidewalk, and ground taxis weaved in and out of traffic. Mardi Gras was only a few days away, and everyone looked like they were rushing to go somewhere. We stopped at a light, and on the corner a girl, not much older than me, was playing the violin. Next to her was a man around the age Grandpa would've been, seated in a fold-out chair, playing on a keyboard. His long, weathered fingers moved across the keys with ease, and the young girl smiled at him as she swayed back and forth, the jazz from the piano and violin intertwined as the notes lifted into the air.

A group of people had gathered to listen to the music, some of them swinging to the rhythm of the music, others simply with their eyes closed. At the girl's feet was her open violin case with isolinear memory chips scattered inside. As people peeled off from the admiring crowd, they would stoop down and pick up a chip to take with them before they left.

This wasn't new to me. Living in New Orleans, I'd always seen moments like this. But something was different this time. I felt like I was inside this one, sharing it, living the moment with them. I could see from the expression on the young woman's face, she was doing what she absolutely loved.

She was free.

I didn't know if the man playing with her was her grandfather, but I imagined he was. Maybe he had told her to live her life, to follow her dreams, and was helping her to do it. As our car started again, I watched them for as long as I could, listening until their music dimmed and was finally swallowed by life in the city. I stared at the starships in my boxes, and I wondered if they would ever find their way out again.

My dad was looking at me through the rearview mirror. "You know, Ben, I think this would be a great time for you to start shadowing me in the kitchen. I was around your age when my father started to—"

I couldn't stop thinking about Ralph and the fear in his voice when I asked him about telling his dreams to his father. I didn't want that to be me. I caught my Dad's eyes in the rearview mirror he always used instead of the HUD display. "I want to go to Starfleet Academy, so I can become an engineer to design and build starships."

Mama turned around in her seat, her eyes wide with excitement. She studied me, sizing up my declaration. When we Siskos made a statement, we learned to be responsible for our words, because words lead to actions, and actions have consequences. It was the first time I remember seeing in Mama's eyes the acknowledgement that I was becoming an adult.

Mama nodded in agreement, I think more with her own thoughts than me. She said, "Well alright then, it looks like we have some work to do, Mister Sisko! Looks like we're going to have an engineer in the family, Joseph!"

My father stared at Mama for a moment, then turned his eyes back to the road. We drove the rest of the way home in silence.

✦

I felt like a stranger returning home. Everything was familiar, but I was different.

I'd lost Grandma Octavia, lost Grandpa James, and that night on the loading dock when I closed my eyes looking up at the stars, I lost a part of myself too. That Benjamin Sisko was gone, and he wasn't coming back.

I had walked through the door of my home a thousand times before, but now it felt strange. In many ways, it could've been any other day—Mama opening the door ahead of me while I carried my boxes in, and my father was parking our car behind the hotel like we'd done countless times before—but I'd never seen him like this.

He still hadn't said anything to me.

I was putting the boxes down in our first-floor vestibule when I heard the thumping of bare feet racing down our wood staircase. I turned just in time for Judith to run into me. "Benzy!" she screamed. I bent down to accommodate her, and she wrapped her little arms around my neck.

My sister looked so different. I'd see glimpses of her on video calls, but she would never stay still long enough for me to take her in. Now I could see I wasn't the only one that had changed. Judith looked so much like the pictures of Mama when she was young, soft brown eyes with the same button nose, and a laugh that was as warm as Mama's but all JJ, it was uncanny.

"You're big," I said, giving her a kiss on the forehead.

Judith hugged me even tighter and let out a muffled "You too!" from around my neck.

Mama walked up with my twin brothers in tow. David and Elias were paying more attention to the ice cream cones they were holding than me. Even though they were twins, it was becoming very easy to tell them apart. David was physically bigger than Elias. If it involved running, jumping, climbing, and swimming, David would do it until he was really good at it and then do it some more. Elias, on the other hand, was more interested in food and the kitchen. At dinner, he would always want to know about every ingredient we were eating. Where did it come from? Why did it have the name it had? Who created the dish we were eating? My father would answer his questions, but when he didn't know, he and Elias would investigate, together. It was really clear to everyone that somehow, someway, David and Elias were going to wind up doing something in sports and cuisine, which really excited Dad. The real mystery was JJ. No one knew what Judith Josephine Sisko's passion was yet—including her. We all had to just wait and see.

✦

A few nights later, I woke up to voices coming from downstairs. I looked over at Mister Bayou on my bookshelf, now more memento than confidant, but he didn't know what was happening. I couldn't make out what they were saying, so I slipped out of my room to listen. When I reached the staircase, it was clear the voices were my parents', and they were doing something I never heard them do before.

Arguing.

It wasn't just their voices, but the tone in them that I could hear loud and clear. "This life was good enough for my father, and it's good enough for me. Once he understands, he'll want to stay," my father was saying.

I couldn't help myself from slowly creeping down the stairs. I stopped when I saw my parents were flipping the chairs onto the dinner tables, something done every night before mopping the floors. Usually they did this chore together, choosing tables close to each other—tonight, they were at opposite ends of the room.

My mother was angry. I'd never seen her face look this way and it shocked me. As she talked, her tone changed from anger to pleading with my father for him to understand. "He wants more, Joseph, you can see it in his eyes, and you should want more for him!"

My father was about to respond when he saw me. "Go to bed, son," he said. I could see on his face how he had tried to take the emotion out of his voice when he spoke to me.

Mama seemed to be trying to put aside some of her own feelings as well. "Listen to your father, Ben. I'll be up in a little bit."

I ran back to my room. My entire life, I had never seen my parents disagree about anything, and now they were arguing, about me. I don't know for how long I'd been crying when I heard a knock at my door.

In our house, the rules were that adults could lock their doors, kids could not, but everyone would respect the desire for privacy. My parents always knocked and then waited before they came in. When Mama walked in, she was holding something behind her back. I really didn't care what it was; I couldn't stop thinking about why they were arguing. "I'm sorry," I said to Mama.

Elizabeth Sisko looked at me sternly, "No, we're not doing that, Benjamin. You're not going to blame yourself for something that's not your fault!" Mama sat down on the bed next to me, taking what I could now see was a gift from behind her back and placing it on my desk next to the bed. After thinking about it for a moment she lay down facing me and wiped away my tears. She said, "Do you remember when I told you I never met my parents because they died while they served in Starfleet when I was very young?"

I nodded. "I remember."

"Well, it took me a long time to make peace with that. Your father has some things he needs to make peace with, do you understand?"

I nodded like I understood, but I really didn't. What I did know was that I loved and trusted my father and believed that would be enough. "What did you get me?" I asked wiping away the rest of my tears.

Mama passed me the wrapped present as I sat up. "Open it."

I tore off the paper to reveal my new best friend—*Mr. Scott's Guide to the Fundamentals of Starships and Engineering*. As I thumbed through the book, it was clear this wasn't for kids. This covered everything from starship design to warp field theory. I wrapped my arms around Mama and gave her a big hug.

✦

The next morning there was another knock at my door. "Come in," I said hesitantly.

I was at my desk going through the book Mama gave me when my father walked in. It was early in the morning for the house but late for him. From the stains on his kitchen whites, he'd already been working for a few hours. When he saw what I was reading, he looked a little surprised, but without saying anything, he sat on the bed. We sat like that for a minute or so in silence before he finally spoke. "I want you to know, Benjamin, I'm not upset with you. I'm actually proud that you've made a decision about your life and your future."

My voice just above a whisper, I asked, "Then what's wrong?"

His pain was clear on his face. "The decision you've made, son, means a life in Starfleet, which means a life away from Earth, away from New Orleans, and away from your family. But it's not just that. It means a life away from your culture, away from your history, and away from everything that matters."

I was going to say something, but thought better of it. My father looked like there was some invisible weight on him, and I realized I needed to let him speak uninterrupted. "Ben, there was a time not long ago in Earth's past when a group of people were taken from their homes, enslaved, brought to faraway lands, beaten, and forced to work. Their history and culture were lost to them when this happened. Years later, after the period of slavery ended, this same group of people were treated poorly, criminalized, and intentionally kept from opportunity. All of this was done to them simply because of the dark pigment of their skin, simply because they were black. This happened all over Earth. Some groups of black people that were enslaved were brought to this continent, and this area which was once called America. While all this was happening to them, and even after slavery, our ancestors showed incredible strength, spirit, and perseverance. They did the best they could to hold onto their culture and history, and build new lives for themselves and their families in places like Harlem, Chicago, and here in New Orleans."

Dad could see the confusion on my face. He said, "It's true, Ben, it happened, for over four hundred years."

I let out a nervous chuckle. "But I don't understand," I said. "That's not possible—that's over four centuries. Dad, how could one group of people do that to another for something that's normal, like skin color?" After a moment of thought, I added "That's too stupid to be real."

I could see that my father was surprised by my reaction. "You need to see something," he said.

✦

We're both very fortunate, son.

We've both been raised in societies without oppression. We don't know what it's like to be condemned or ostracized because another group decides to declare you different or inferior. Sadly, there are people on worlds in the Alpha Quadrant that know all too well what that feels like. Humans on Earth used to be one of them. It's taken us a long time to let go of the pettiness and fears of the past that were holding us back from grasping our future.

And even though we're not like that anymore, I often wonder how much, or perhaps how little, it could take for us to turn on each other again. That's why the lessons of the past need to be remembered to safeguard the future.

✦

I'd never seen this part of New Orleans. This street was completely unfamiliar and many of the buildings and storefronts didn't look like I expected them to. They were from another place and another time. There were so many people around us. Before I realized it, we were deep in a crowd of men and women of all ages. I thought I was too old now to hold my father's hand, so I stayed close to him, trailing behind him, keeping him close. The other adults towered over me. None of them paid any attention to us.

Their focus was on something else, someone else.

Dad and I shifted toward the front of the crowd, both of us eager to see what everyone else was looking at. I could see now that the crowd was actually two large groups that had formed on either side of a walkway leading up to the steps of a school. Walking from a car and between these two crowds were four very tall men in suits. From the way they behaved—one pair in front and one pair behind—it was clear they were escorting someone. As the escort approached, the crowds stirred into a frenzy. The women and men started pointing, yelling, and screaming.

"Go back to where you came from!"

"We don't want your kind here!"

"Two, four, six, eight, we don't want to integrate!"

The crowd shifted, and before I knew it, I was separated from my father amidst a sea of enraged adults. I was pushed to the front of the crowd as the focus of their ire passed right by me. From the emotion in the crowd, I expected to see some kind of monster, but all I saw was a little girl. She was a little younger than Judith, probably about five or six, wearing a white dress with ribbons in her hair. She was walking in the middle of the four-man escort, eyes fixed straight ahead.

And then it hit me. She was black, like me.

It dawned on me that everyone in the crowd was white. I found myself searching the faces, desperately looking for someone, anyone that wasn't full of this viral hatred. Thankfully, I found a few in the crowd that weren't like the others. They didn't scream at the little girl and looked almost ashamed by what was happening. But those faces were far too few, like scattered life-preservers of fairness and hope floating along a sea of rage and hatred. The emotion of the crowd intensified, like an inferno reaching its peak. Some of the men and women tried to spit on her, and some succeeded, but she just kept walking.

She walked up the steps with her escort and into the school.

As soon as the school door closed, the crowd and the school disappeared. I was back in the exhibit hall where we started, and no longer on the holographic street. My father was several feet away. A gentle feminine voice started to speak. "Thank you for initiating the Ruby Bridges exhibit hologram at the New Orleans Remembrance Center. If you would like more information on Ruby Bridges, please touch any picture at the exhibit. If there is a specific historical instance of racial injustice you would like to examine, you may do so at any of the fifty thousand Remembrance Centers worldwide. And please, remember to never forget!"

My dad put his hand on my shoulder as we walked out of the exhibit. As we left, I watched the hologram crowd reappear, this time around an Andorian man and woman.

As we sat down on a bench just outside the exhibit, my head was swimming with questions as I tried to process the events I had just witnessed. My father sat next to me, silently, patiently waiting for me. "It was really like that back then?" I asked.

My father had a pain on his face I'd never seen before. It started behind his eyes, but it lived someplace much deeper. "Honestly, Ben, as bad as that was, it was much worse before and after that," he said.

I felt sick.

I couldn't get the images out of my mind, now my own internal center of remembrance. Replaying the faces so full of hatred for a child that, to those people, was a monster simply because of the color of her skin. "And this happened worldwide? Why did they treat black people so badly?" I asked.

Dad sighed, and I could see this was a question he had struggled with for a long time. He stared down at the tiles on the floor as if searching for an answer. "I'd love to sit here and give you an easy answer, but there's not a single or simple answer to that, son. Partly it's because the subjugation of people of color was a way to amass wealth and power. And partly because some people can only feel tall when they do everything they can to keep others on their knees."

I looked at the other remembrance rooms in this section of the center. I started to understand now why the vast rooms had transparent walls. So everyone could see what was happening.

And never forget.

"Well, it's not like that now. How did it get better?" I questioned.

My dad got up and motioned for me to follow him. In silence, we walked out of the Racism and Remembrance wing and into the Hall of War and Remembrance. A display above the entrance read *Two billion four hundred million dead*. The hall had videos of protests and burning buildings.

"What's not in these displays is just how bad it got, Ben. During the Second Civil War and Eugenics Wars, racism was rampant, and law enforcement fell apart. Sundown areas started appearing in cities all over the world. If anyone that was characterized as impure was found in these areas after sundown, they were beaten and sometimes killed. During all this, and World War III, New Orleans was one of the places that became a refuge for anyone that was labeled different, especially people of color."

I followed my father over to an area on the floor labeled *World War III*. As we stepped near the letters, multiple screens appeared, hovering around us, each with a massive city held in its frame. Each screen played a variation of the same moment. There was a bright flash over or in the city, followed by an explosion that reached out with raw destructive power eviscerating everything in its path. Screen after screen played out the same moment until they all went dark. A single screen appeared, showing a satellite view of the Earth as the nuclear missiles hit and the fires burned worldwide.

My father said, "You asked me how it got better. When World War III finally happened, over two billion people were killed. We were destroying ourselves as a species, son. At that point, racism had caused the world so much pain and suffering that we finally faced the reality… finally faced up to the fact that we needed to do better. A few years after that, humanity learned we weren't alone in the universe. That discovery gave the world a common goal—to travel to the stars—and humanity banded together like never before."

I shook my head. "Dad, I don't understand. If going to space brought everyone together, why don't you want me to go?"

My father started walking towards the exit, and I fell in next to him. "No Sisko has ever left Earth, Ben, not because we can't, but because there's something more important right here. Preserving our history and our culture. When I was about your age, my father brought me here to the Remembrance Center, and before that, his father brought him. Your identity, who you are, and who you become is more important than anywhere you can possibly go. So much of our ancestors' history and culture was lost, erased when they were brought here as slaves. We need to hold onto our family's history and culture that we've created, Ben."

We walked out of the Remembrance Center and stepped back into New Orleans City Park, where the sun was setting. I could see the discomfort on my father's face as he struggled to find the words he hoped would help me understand. "These days, too many people are always so caught up in something. They're always looking for the next thing or person to tell them how they feel or what to think. Always some new technology or comfort that they can lose themselves in. They forget who they are. That's why we don't deal with those things in our home, Ben, and it's why I don't want you to go to Starfleet Academy. I believe, just like my father, my grandfather, and my great-grandfather, that this is the only way to protect our family's history and culture and ensure we have a rich future, here on Earth. I only hope, son, that you understand how important this is."

I could hear it in my father's words, his need for me to understand what he was saying.

He was pleading for me to stay.

The sun was setting fast, and twilight arrived. Neither day nor night, some stars were already appearing in the sky. I looked up and realized there was no right or wrong, just two different points of view. "I do understand now why we stay here, Dad, I really do, but that's why I have to go. I'm not going to forget where I came from or lose myself out there, because I'll be taking everything we are, everything we love, everything you and Mama have taught me, and everything I've learned about myself, out there with me. I know who I am. Starfleet feels right. They are out there doing what you and Mama, Grandpa and Grandma always taught me to do—help, and not hurt. I want to be a part of that. I *need* to be a part of that. That's how I want to do what Grandpa said, and live *my* life." The words tumbled out of me so fast I realized they'd been right there beneath the surface for a long time, just waiting for the right moment to emerge.

Change has never come easy for my father. To people that don't know him, it may look like he's just stubborn. But that's not it at all. I've never seen Joseph Sisko make a decision that didn't come from a place of deep thought or love. And once a decision is made, my father never, ever second-guesses himself. He always tells me that doubt is crippling to a head chef. He says: *You're the foundation. You're the one making the decisions and setting the pace. If you doubt yourself, your kitchen and your crew will fall apart.*

My father was quiet for a long time but then just like I'd seen him do a million times in the kitchen, he made a decision.

"Well then, I guess we better get you ready for this Starfleet Academy."

And that was that.

CHAPTER SEVEN
NEW WORLDS—2342-2346

JUDITH CRIED WHEN SHE LEARNED I WAS GOING TO STARFLEET ACADEMY, and even though they still deny it today, when David and Elias saw her cry, they started crying too. When Mama explained to Judith that I wasn't leaving for a few years, she settled down almost immediately. "Well, I guess that's okay," she said.

Once everyone got on board with me going to the academy, it quickly became a family affair. Mama decided that we should all visit Bozeman, Montana, for First Contact Day, and visit the launch site of the first human warp flight. Until that time we had taken a few family trips, but it was always somewhere in New Orleans or Louisiana, someplace we could travel to by electrocar. On this trip, we took the transporter. This was the first time my father had been in a transporter, and my first since my fall. Neither of us was particularly eager to get on the pad. When he saw me step onto the platform, he followed. But, that didn't stop him from asking questions constantly up until and even during beaming, which he told us wasn't as bad as he thought it would be after all.

Mama had already taught us in school about Zefram Cochrane, the first human to develop warp drive on Earth. We knew all about him and his historic meeting with the Vulcans that eventually led to the creation of Starfleet and the Federation. But we didn't go there for any of that.

We went to see the *Phoenix*.

After I left the hospital, I continued to build model starships. Working on a model while in a partial stasis field had taught me patience, and focus, but it also slowed everything down for me. It was the same for me at home, and now that I think about it, Jake, it felt a lot like what you told me writing feels like for you. Something that when you did it just felt right, felt comfortable. I knew it would be a long time before I'd get to build the real thing, so I put together hundreds of models and studied the design specs on all of them. When I put together the *Phoenix* model, I was surprised at how simple, yet elegant Doctor Cochrane's design was. The ingenuity of taking a nuclear missile and its silo, and retrofitting them into the first warp-capable ship and launchpad was nothing short of genius.

The *Phoenix* in Bozeman wasn't the original, of course: that was in the Smithsonian Museum. This one was a replica that, like the original, could reach warp one. But it was also a ride for the visitors.

We all stood in line for what felt like hours. When it was finally our go, it was just us inside the ship—six seats behind the empty pilot's seat. I sat closest to the front and pilot's seat with Judith across from me, then behind us were the twins, and behind them our parents. When the launch sequence started, and the silo door opened, the entire ship vibrated with power. A hologram of Doctor Cochrane appeared in the pilot's seat. He sounded almost as excited as I was. As the engine ignited and the *Phoenix* began to rise, hologram Cochrane slipped a music disc into the console, and our tiny cockpit came alive. Judith was wide-eyed, and I could hear the twins laughing behind me. I felt a slight pressure on my chest as we raced skyward. I knew from Mister Scott's engineering book, without inertial dampeners, we would have been barely able to move.

I was so busy studying the console from behind holo-Cochrane, I was startled when the cockpit windows went dark. I looked up to see the countless points of light I had been dreaming of, the ones I thought I'd never see so long ago, and now I was among them. We were in space.

Through a corner of the cockpit window, I could see the Earth. She looked so beautiful and yet fragile, suspended against the black of space. This little blue ball held the hopes of and dreams of so many people throughout the galaxy.

Like me.

Cochrane started talking again, and I could hear a metal grinding coming from both sides of the ship. This was the warp nacelles unfolding. From somewhere deep inside the *Phoenix*, I could feel power being unleashed, the nacelles hummed to life, and an instant later, we were at warp. The stars became extended points of light that ushered me into a new world.

Behind me, my family gasped in astonishment, but I was quiet, calm. Everything just felt so natural to me, and then before I knew it, it was over. The elongated silver streaks of light once again became stars. The *Phoenix* casually turned around, and now a speck of blue could be seen in the distance. My father broke the silence with a whisper more to himself than anyone: "That's us, that's Earth. It's so beautiful."

On the return trip, everyone was quiet, even Judith. We all just wanted to take in every single second of this experience. As soon as we left the ride, the twins said they wanted to go again. Judith stood in front of everyone with her hands on her hips. "Why can't we go on trips like this all the time?" she said.

Hesitantly Mama turned and looked at Dad. "From the mouth of babes," she said.

My father looked at all of us and then broke into one of the widest grins I'd ever seen. "I try never to argue with women named Sisko," he said.

Judith giggled, David and Elias started screaming in excitement. I hugged Mama tighter that day than I ever had before. "Thank you, Mama," was all I said.

She gave me a kiss on my forehead. "I wanted your first time in a starship to be in the *Phoenix*, and with us," she said, smiling.

✦

For as long as I can remember, Judith has always loved Mama's dreads, touching them, asking questions about them, and wanting to grow her own. When Judith was little, Mama told JJ she could do whatever she wanted with her hair, but she should find something that was just hers.

As much as I loved Mama, and I know she loved me and loved my brothers, her relationship with Judith was unlike any other. It wasn't that Judith was her favorite—Mama always said we all were her favorite, of course.

But with Grandma gone, they were two women in a house filled with men. They had their own language, and their own energy. They were fun to watch together. Sometimes they'd look at each other and just start laughing—usually at something one of the Sisko men had done.

Dad and Mama moved up to the third floor and gave the second-floor bedrooms to us. Judith and I had our own rooms, and the twins shared the third bedroom. Not that any of that mattered to Judith, who was usually upstairs with Mama anyway. Most of the time, it was because Mama was braiding her hair. I remember the day Judith came downstairs with her hair braided into Bantu knots. She just looked different, more confident, and I realized she'd found something that was just hers.

✦

After the trip to Bozeman, Mama decided to integrate travel into our homeschool curriculum. For three days, twice a month, the Sisko family would beam to a location on Earth and learn all we could about the place while enjoying ourselves. Mama called them *Learning Vacations*, but the best thing about our family trips was that the Sisko kids always picked the destination.

Judith got to go first, and it was little surprise to any of us that she wanted to visit the place where Bantu knots originated. So just like that, the family was off to Africa. What started out as three days wound up being three weeks. One or two nights a week, Dad would beam back to the restaurant for a couple of hours to look in on things, but he always made it back before bedtime. It was a little strange at first to feel a familiarity with someplace I'd never been before, but so many things about Africa felt more like being reminded of a history we'd forgotten instead of learning about it for the first time. Because of Judith's hair curiosity, the whole family learned that Bantu knots originated from the Zulu tribe centuries ago. In many parts of Africa, whether you were male or female, hair was not just part of your cultural identity, but your spiritual identity as well. After we learned this, the twins asked for twists, and Mama braided my hair into cornrows for the first time. I remember looking at myself in the mirror that first moment after she was done, and it was like I was given a glimpse into how I would look as an adult.

Jake, I never told you this, but your mother and I discussed having another child. We both wanted a girl, a little sister that you could be a big brother to. I think a lot about what it would have been like raising the two of you alone after your mother died. Mama tried to teach me to braid hair, but I was never really good at it. Whenever I tried to braid Judith's hair, she always complained that I would hurt her and that her braids never looked or felt right. Now, with Kasidy pregnant, you may find out what it's like to be a big brother to a girl after all. If Kasidy has the baby before I get back, son, I'm going to need you to take care of them both and let them take care of you. Do better than your old man. Learn to braid hair. And one day, when you're braiding your own child's hair, you will thank me, I guarantee it!

Reminiscing about Africa, Jake, has me thinking about my African art collection and that Yoruba mask on the wall in my quarters. I know you've heard me say it before, son, but much of that collection is over two millennia old. Put it in storage for me. Safeguard it. Except one thing: I want you to take the Yoruba mask. It's yours now, Jake. Put it somewhere in your quarters where you can always see it. And there's something else I want you to do, something I'm sorry I never did with you. When your brother or sister gets old enough, I want you and Kasidy to go to Earth and take a trip to Africa. As humans and black people, it's our birthplace, and our heritage.

✦

Whenever it was Elias's turn to pick the location for the family location, it was always to visit a restaurant. Our resident junior chef was no longer interested in Cajun cuisine, but had gained a growing interest in everything dealing with extraterrestrial food. On one trip we went to Dubai. For weeks before, Elias had become fascinated with Vulcan food, and he had learned the best Vulcan restaurant was in Dubai, where everything was authentic, nothing replicated. When we got there my little brother became a different person. As soon as we all sat down in the restaurant, Elias announced he was ordering for the family. Plomeek soup, with forge pasta, and jumbo mollusks sautéed in rhombolian butter and redspice. For dessert, we had "Vulcan's Forge" ice cream.

At one point while we were waiting for the food, we noticed Elias wasn't at the table. He'd gone to the restroom and never come back. Dad went looking for him, and then he too didn't come back. When the food finally came out, it was Elias and Dad that brought it out. They had both been in the kitchen talking to the Vulcan chefs. It turned out that Elias was becoming passionate about extraterrestrial cuisine. The more exotic and further off world it was, the more it captivated my little brother's interest.

I think Dad was a little saddened that Elias was losing interest in the history and culture of New Orleans cuisine, but at the same time, he was excited that his son had been bitten by the food bug. After that it felt like Elias took the place I used to have with Dad in the kitchen, or at least the place my father wanted me to have. But we all saw Elias's passion as a budding xenocultural chef. He was always the Sisko that would become the next professional chef in the family.

✦

David always chose vacations around sporting events. Mom and Dad tried to get him to choose an exciting beach or an historical city, but they learned pretty quickly that just wasn't David. Of all of us he was always the most physical, always the best runner, the strongest jumper. My brother used one of his vacation choices to take us all to a Parrises Squares game. It was a smart move, because he'd asked before and Dad had always said no. The game is notorious for players getting injured, and Dad didn't want David to get any ideas in his head. But telling him no did just that. When we all finally went to see a game, David was riveted, and literally sat on the edge of his seat for the entire two hours. For a month after the game, not a day would pass that David wouldn't beg to join a Parrises Squares junior league. Mama and Dad made a deal with David—since he also liked baseball, they'd sign him up for the little league, and when he got older he could try out for a Parrises Squares team.

Of course, the hope was that by the time that happened, David would be so far into baseball or something else that he would no longer be interested in *Paralysis Squares*. I don't know if you've ever heard that term before, Jake, but back then that's what a lot of people were calling the game. But, of course, their plan backfired. David started training and grooming himself to be a multi-sport athlete. As a baseball pitcher, he excelled, developing a powerful arm at a young age that just got better and more refined over time. As the older brother, I remember when I first started playing catch with him when Dad wasn't around, or was busy. At first it was easy, just the two of us and some baseball gloves. But I started to wear more and more protection as David's arm got stronger. Even though I wasn't really into baseball back then, I was impressed with my little brother. He was packing heat with a fastball that, even with padding, knocked the wind out of me a few times.

It wasn't long before David started pitching for the New Orleans Cajun Comets. And not long after that, he tried out for and was accepted to the local Parrises Squares team. When one season ended, he'd have a little downtime with some training, and then before we knew it, the next season would start. It was in those blocks of downtime between seasons that I got to spend time with my little brother.

David has always been very quiet; Elias is the same way. Maybe it's something they share because they're twins. But what they don't talk about, they express in other ways: David in his performance on the field and Elias in his cooking.

✦

Unlike my brothers, Judith has always expressed herself. But JJ usually does it through her music. Even her baby gibberish sounded like she was stringing together a melody. Everyone would always talk about how beautiful her voice was. When JJ was very little, Grandma Octavia would sit my sister on her lap as she played the piano, and Judith would do her best to sing along. As she got older, the two of them would sound wonderful together. Sometimes I would even join in. When Grandma passed away, Judith stopped singing, and so did I. After that, whenever someone would ask JJ to sing something, she would just start crying.

So everyone stopped asking.

One day we were on vacation in Paris. We were coming out of the Louvre, and a group of people were watching an older woman sing the song 'This Little Light of Mine' to a little boy that was in the crowd. We stopped to watch, and out of nowhere, Judith grabbed my hand and pulled me to the front of the crowd with her. She started singing, and as she sang she gripped my hand tighter and tighter. It was amazing to hear her beautiful voice again. I joined in, but Judith's voice had become so full, so strong, I stopped and just listened.

Then the woman that had started singing stopped and was listening too. She was a famous singer and a few years later she gave Judith her big break that started her onto the path of the vocalist she is today.

You know, Jake, it's not lost on me that I'm talking to you about moments in my life while I'm with a species that is outside of linear time. They can't separate the past from the present or the future. Hindsight is as alien to the wormhole aliens as non-linear thinking is to us. I know the Bajorans consider them to be all-powerful, but I think we linear beings have gotten the better part of that deal. We can learn from our mistakes as well as cherish the moments that will never come again. This is all lost to the Prophets in an eternal infinite of the now. Those times with Dad and Mama, David, Elias, and JJ, are some of the happiest moments of my childhood, and some of the most precious memories of my life.

CHAPTER EIGHT
RULES—2346-2350

ONE EVENING THERE WAS A KNOCK ON MY DOOR and both Dad and Mama came into my room. Usually whenever I did something wrong, Mama would be the one to come and talk to me then, if it was really bad, Dad would come in afterwards as well. But this, this was unprecedented. I was lying in bed reading comics, but I got up and sat on the edge of the bed. Mama sat in my desk chair while my father leaned against the closed door. "We have something we want to talk about with you, son," he said.

Mama said, "It's about your Starfleet entrance exam, Benjamin."

For the past few weeks I'd been taking the preliminary entrance exam, even though the admission age was sixteen and I was only fourteen. Mama told me taking the exam early could only help me improve when I took the actual test. Now I understood why both my parents were here. This was their way of breaking it to me gently that I had failed. Mama gathered her thoughts before speaking again: "You've tested extraordinarily well. So much so that the academy has offered you the opportunity to apply early."

I was stunned. The knot that had begun to tighten in my stomach disappeared. I jumped to my feet, hands in the air, screaming in excitement! The dream that had started with model starships in a hospital bed was truly about to begin. I felt invincible and that future, my future, was set. I was already thinking about the starships I would design for Starfleet when I noticed that neither of my parents were smiling.

Mama said, "We don't think you should do it, Benjamin."

I lowered my arms, and sat back down, trying to hold onto the excitement that was already bleeding out of me. "Why not?" I asked.

Dad came off the wall and sat down next to me. "You're too young, Ben, and you don't know the things you don't know. If you take the test, you'll probably pass, and you'd be entering a world that's extremely demanding, both physically and mentally."

I needed my parents to believe what I knew. I told them, "I can do this, I know I can."

Now my father was shaking his head. "That's just it, Ben. We know you can too. But I've seen it with young chefs. They take on too much too soon, get to where they want to be, and then burn out." My dad put his hand on my shoulder. "We don't want to see that happen to you."

Now Mama took my hand in hers. "We want you to go to high school here, and then apply for the academy when you're eighteen. We're leaving it up to you—the choice is yours—but if you trust us and give it four more years, Starfleet won't know what hit them."

I could see this wasn't some trick to get me to stay home, that they hadn't come to talk to me out of fear of me leaving—it was from a place of love. But at the same time, I wanted to go to the academy, badly. I wanted to prove to them, and to myself, that I could do it, that I wouldn't burn out, and that one day they would travel in a starship of my design.

But, Jake, there was also a part of me, that voice that we all hear when we're at a crossroads. That part of yourself that knows the difference between what's right and what you want to do. I couldn't see everything they were telling me, even though I knew they believed in me. A nagging part of me felt like they were saying I wasn't good enough yet. As I thought about my options, and the deals I could make with them, I realized one thing was certain.

I trusted my parents.

Once I realized that fact and held onto it, it was easier to let go of the urgency and disappointment I felt. "It's not that far away—2350 is going to be a good year," I said, smiling.

✦

As I entered Booker T. Washington Public High School, it took me thirty seconds to realize my parents were right.

I didn't know what I didn't know.

Right away, it was clear to me that as great as my life had been up to that point, I'd been sheltered, more than even I realized.

Since before World War III, everyone referred to the school as simply BTW. The high school was one of the last and oldest prewar schools on Earth, having first opened in 1942. It had been renovated and expanded upon many times in the last four hundred years, even with new buildings and technology, but it smelled old. That odor was familiar to me even when nothing else was. No matter how many times my parents remodeled the restaurant and hotel, there were times I still smelled the same unmistakable stink of old wood grafted with durasteel and new paint.

Over the centuries, the school had become one of the best in New Orleans, which meant everyone wanted to send their kids there. And even though it was a public school you had to take an entrance test, which meant only the best and the brightest went there. And I was among them. I suddenly wondered if all my homeschooling could stand up against everything the twenty-fourth century had to offer. This was the first time in my life that I remember needing to prove myself, not to anyone else, but to myself.

The school was really a campus with several buildings interconnected by garden paths and transparent aluminum walkways overhead. Each building covered a different part of our curriculum: music, arts, sciences, and history. The main building was the hub of the campus. Home rooms, the cafeteria, and gymnasiums were here. This was where everyone started every day. I was shocked to see a sign that read *NO BEAMING BEYOND THIS POINT*.

About two thousand kids went to BTW, and it seemed like they were all crammed into the main lobby. Checking out the other kids, I realized two things. The first was that most of these kids were human, but many weren't. Living next to a hotel and over a restaurant, I thought I'd seen a lot of different aliens, but there were species here I'd only read about. The second was that I was the only student with a backpack. Every class provided PADDs, so the students' profiles followed them from class to class. A few kids had their own PADDs, but the teachers didn't let them use them. So no one really carried anything.

Except lucky me.

"Don't you have somewhere to be, Mister Sisko?" a familiar voice boomed from behind me.

I turned around to see Mister Collymore watching me intently. Nearly as wide as he was tall, with bronze skin and chiseled features, Mister Collymore was a saxophonist that would often stop by the restaurant for dinner and stay to play a set or two just because. According to the name tag on his suit, he was also the principal of BTW, which was news to me. I'd known this man for years, and watched him play the sax with a skill unlike anyone else. I'd always just assumed he was only a musician; it had never dawned on me until that moment that he or New Orleans was or could be anything else other than food and music. Seeing him in a professional demeanor I'd never seen before made me realize that New Orleans was a lot bigger than I thought it was. "Yes, sir!" I said, and I found myself standing straighter as I did.

Something behind me caught Principal Collymore's attention, so he was already looking ahead as he answered me: "Well, I suggest you get there then." Before he moved off, he stopped for a second and looked at me, his gaze softening slightly. "Welcome to BTW."

✦

I remember how relieved I felt by the lunch period that first day. I admit it was more than a little strange getting used to being in a classroom and not being taught by Mama. Several times I found myself expecting—maybe even hoping for—her to come in and take over the class. I now had a different teacher for each subject, and they all expected different things from me.

Sit up, Mister Sisko.

Pay attention, Mister Sisko.

Actually, that's incorrect, Mister Sisko.

I was quickly learning that how I interacted with my teachers was almost as important as the work I did in their classes.

My favorite was Ms. Tisdale in advanced xeno literature. By the fourth time I raised my hand, she started calling on me only when no one else could answer the question. At the end of the class, as I was leaving, she said to me, "Good job today, Mister Sisko, but it's going to be a tough year. Learn to pace yourself."

"Yes, ma'am," I said.

✦

The lunchroom was crammed with kids that, just like me, were relieved to get some free time to unwind and decompress—if only for a short while. The room was filled with laughter, the occasional shout, and the collective sounds of hundreds of hungry teenagers. But, there was no kitchen, no cooks, no trays of hot steaming food, no delightful aromas being carried through the air to whet your appetite. There were several lines, but they all led to food replicators.

When my father gave me my lunch that morning, he had mentioned that all schools, even schools in New Orleans, utilized replicators to feed their students. But what he was trying to tell me didn't really register until I saw it for myself. A large room with tables, chairs and computers that made food out of nothing. To everyone else this was normal, but it was strange to me. That was when I had an epiphany.

I was strange to everyone else.

I first started getting looks when I didn't get in line for one of the replicators, but I didn't think much of it. I was a little disappointed, because I hadn't made any friends yet. I had talked to a few other kids, even chatted with a few I knew from my neighborhood, but nothing real enough to sit next to anyone. So I found an empty table and sat by myself. I unzipped my backpack and pulled out my lunch.

That was when the whispers started.

Crabcakes, Cajun rice, grilled vegetables and a thermos with raspberry lemonade. My lunchbox reheated my food to perfection, and as soon as I took the lid off the sweet aroma of the crabcakes filled the entire lunchroom.

I was feeling a little self-conscious but my appetite took over. I decided if the student body of BTW wanted to watch me eat a customer favorite at Sisko's they were welcome to do so. I was deep into my third crabcake when a shadow appeared over me. I looked up to the sight of several kids in front of me. An Andorian boy was at the front, holding a food tray. From his size, he was most likely a sophomore or senior, his sleeveless T-shirt highlighting his blue biceps, obviously intentionally. One antenna was pointed towards me while the other responded to any sound in the room that rose above the cacophony. I'd only read about, but never met, Andorians before that moment. He was imposing, but more than that his blue skin, white mohawk and antennae were also intimidating. "I'm Flex," he said with a smile.

"Is that a nickname?" I asked curiously.

"No." he answered flatly as he put the lunch tray down and sat down across from me. I noticed the other kids with him stood even though there were available seats at my table. They reminded me of pets trained to sit on command, but instead these were trained to stand.

I outstretched my hand. "Ben Sisko, nice to meet you," I said.

Flex stared at my hand like the thought of him taking it, or touching me for that matter, was absurd. After a moment, I put my hand down. Flex's lunch tray had some steaming greyish-green mass that smelled so bad it immediately suffocated the aroma of my crab cakes, and made my stomach turn in the process. Looking at this "food" I realized I had no idea what Andorians ate, so I tried my best to keep my composure and not give any offense. Flex followed my gaze down to his food and looked up at me with a smile that didn't quite reach his eyes.

He sat back in the seat, getting comfortable. "I hear you've been homeschooled your whole life, never worn replicated clothes or ever eaten replicated food."

I wasn't sure if it was from the food or the Andorian's words, but I started to feel uneasy. I decided to lean back in my seat and try to look as comfortable as Flex did. "That's right on all counts."

The kids behind their leader started to chuckle, reminding me that they weren't just some weird background wallpaper. Flex flashed another rehearsed smile, and folded his arms. "Well, we want to welcome you to BTW. This is Gavesh, a Xindi Insectoid delicacy." The Andorian pushed the tray toward me. "Have some," he said with delight.

I could feel a tightening in my chest, but kept my eyes on Flex instead of the tray. "No thanks, I've already had lunch," I said.

Flex made a point of tightening his muscles as he slowly rolled his neck in a circle. As he did so his antennae followed the motion, then pointed toward me as if they were sensors locking in on a target. "I know you think you're so much better than everyone, but you're not. Here's how it's going to go, Homeschool: you're going to eat all of this or we're going to have problems." The Andorian smirked. "The choice is yours. So which is it going to be?"

I didn't understand the rage on the young Andorian's face or the delight in the faces behind him. Looking at Flex and his entourage, it was clear high school was a strange new world to me, one I couldn't navigate by just being smart or spitting out well-memorized facts. There was a social structure that was cruel and excluded anything deemed different, and other. I knew I didn't want to be a part of it.

But I did have a choice to make.

✦

I came home early from school.

Now that we no longer owned the hotel it was a lot harder to come into the house unnoticed. My father was still as busy as ever, but my mother was the issue. Before, at this time in the afternoon, Mama would be busy managing the hotel, but now she could be anywhere in the house.

There was nothing I could do, so I opened the front door, slowly. I heard sounds coming from the kitchen—my father and Nathan prepping before the restaurant opened, but my mom and siblings were nowhere to be found. Most likely everyone was up on the third floor, as usual. Without hesitation, I started racing up the stairs to my room and safety. I was halfway up the staircase when I heard Mama's voice. "What on earth is that smell?"

It was too late; I stopped when I should've kept going. My mother walked over from the restaurant's seating area, and gasped when she saw me. "Ben! What happened?"

I stood there for a moment, imagining how I must've looked to my mother. The black eye hurt, but not as much as the grey-green goop that soaked my shirt and pants. With every move I made, the Xindi Insectoid delicacy nauseated me. I slinked back down the stairs and told my mother everything. She was patient, and when I was finished took a long moment before finally speaking. "So you walked all the way back home," she said.

"Yes, ma'am," I answered.

My mother tilted her head and gave me a look that told me she wanted the truth, whatever it was. "Did you fight back?" she asked.

"Kinda," I murmured.

"Where's your bag?"

Until that moment I hadn't even realized I didn't have my backpack with me. "I dunno, I think the Andorian kid took it," I said looking at the floor.

Mama held my chin and turned my face to get a better look at my bruise. "So, what do you want to do?" she asked.

I was fighting to hold back the tears and anger that was welling up inside of me. I'd had a long time to think this through on the walk back home. "I know the school has a no transporter policy, but if you talk to them they'll have to let me beam straight to my class in the morning and then beam back for lunch."

I'd never seen disappointment on my mother's face before, but it was clear she was. That hurt far more than the black eye and shame. In a flash, it was gone, and my mother's face had softened but was still resolved. "Okay, Benjamin," was all she said.

I turned and started to go back up the staircase. Mama let me get halfway up before she said anything: "Where are you going?"

The tone in her voice was so light I didn't understand the question. I looked at her, then towards my room and back again. "I'm going to clean up and go to my room," I said.

Mama looked at me with a glare I'd never seen before. "What you're going to do, Benjamin, is use those public transporters that were put in across the street last month, go back to school, find that Andorian boy, punch him in the face, and get your bag back."

I stared at my mother.

Mama walked up the stairs to where I was, and then walked me back down to the door, and opened it. "You may not understand this now, Benjamin, but if you let this bully push you around, you'll be living your whole life the same way. Violence isn't condoned in this house, but sometimes you need to speak to people in a language they can understand before they can hear you." My mother found a clean spot on my forehead and kissed it. "Sometimes you have to get in good trouble. Don't come back in this house without that bag, son."

I could tell from the look in my mother's eyes that she was serious about everything she'd just said to me. My whole life my parents had guided and helped me to make the best decisions I could. We both knew that she could step in and take care of this for me, perhaps not in the way I asked but in a way that would make it easier for me. She knew I hadn't created this problem, but she also knew I needed to deal with it. Completely on my own. I nodded, and walked out of our front door

...and onto Bajor?

The infinite white landscape of the Celestial Temple disappeared. Captain Benjamin Sisko spun around and onto the street of a sprawling city with buildings carved out of centuries-old stone. The midday sun blazed as Bajoran citizens went about their daily lives, uninterested in the presence of this new visitor to the city.

A massive obelisk stood in front of Sisko.

"Wait, I was talking about school, when I was walking out the door... years ago." Sisko turned around again, slower this time, as he tried to gain his bearings. "But this isn't back home growing up, or even Booker T. Washington High School. I don't understand. I was sending a message to Jake. This is Bajor? How is this possible?"

Sisko circled the pillar, tracing the runes carved into the stone with his fingers. "The Bantaca spire. The stone looks clean, freshly carved. Is this B'hala rebuilt?" he asked aloud, to no one.

The Starfleet captain stopped, closed his eyes, took a deep breath, and rested his hand on the giant obelisk. "The temple chimes, the burning bateret leaves on the wind." His eyes flashed open with understanding. "No, this is Old Bajor. This is the ancient city of B'hala. I'm at least twenty thousand years in the past."

Something immense passed overhead, casting a shadow over Sisko's field of view. As he looked up into the afternoon sky, B'hala fell into an eerie twilight as the structure overhead blocked out the sun over the city.

Screams filled the street.

"What the hell is that?" Sisko whispered.

The object covered not just B'hala City, but from its size and the distance, perhaps all of the continent.

It was like nothing he'd ever seen before. Not a lifeform or a vessel: the entity appeared to be some sort of hybrid. With its smooth, diamond-shaped skin-like hull, the vessel looked more like an immense manta ray than a ship. Its elongated pectoral wings flapped slowly up and down as if it were immersed in the depths of some vast unseen ocean. The hull itself seemed to expand and contract as if the ship were mimicking a very familiar action.

Breathing.

Then a starburst appeared in the sky. A vortex of energy and color swirled in an eruption of light, opening a familiar doorway. Sisko watched the wormhole open with disbelief. "Why is it in the Bajoran sector in the past?" he asked.

From the vantage point of B'hala City, the wormhole filled nearly all of the Bajoran sky. As large as the mysterious creature-ship was above B'hala, it became a silhouette against the backdrop of the Celestial Temple. Thousands of specks began pouring out of the wormhole like grains of pollen being ejected into space. As the specks approached Bajor, their configuration was unmistakable. Insect-like design, elongated, wing-like nacelles with an unmistakable lavender power signature.

Dominion ships.

Sisko looked up and whispered to himself. "This is where you sent them?"

The ship-creature opened its mouth and made a sound that was somewhere between a mechanical alert and an organic shriek. The immense manta ray stopped moving, and began to vibrate. An instant later, the creature-ship broke apart, not in some explosion, but in a purposeful way. Like some form of cellular mitosis, it began to divide. First, into two vessels, each half the size of the immense original. And then the process was repeated again, and again, and again until thousands of manta ray-like creature-ships blanketed the Bajoran sky over B'hala.

As the wormhole closed, both armadas engaged over the city of B'hala. Bajoran citizens came out onto the street alongside Sisko, looking up, pointing, and holding their children tightly. Terror and confusion on their faces as the two armadas fought for victory and the future of Bajor.

"It is time, Emissary," a voice next to Sisko said.

Ben turned to see a woman standing next to him. Like him, she was looking up at the raging battle above them. Sisko stared at the woman for a moment. "Sarah?" he said, finally.

The prophet known as Sarah Sisko continued to watch the struggle above them. "There is much to learn. Many tasks still lie ahead for the Sisko."

"Now?" Sisko said, not bothering to mask the anger in his voice. "I was talking to my son, to Jake. Trying to leave him a message, trying to—" He stopped and took a breath before continuing. "No. We don't need to do this right now. It's not linear, right? If the past, present, or future are all the same to you, there's truly no difference. Then we can do this tomorrow, or have done it yesterday. Right?"

Sisko moved so that he was no longer standing next to Sarah, but in front of her. "I understand I'm here because you want to teach me, guide me, but I need to talk to Jake. I need to talk to Kasidy. I need to talk to my family first. They need this, and frankly, so do I."

Sarah took her eyes off the engagement above and looked at her son. "Sometimes you need to speak to people in a language they can understand before they can hear you." The wormhole prophet that was also once Sarah Sisko reached out and held her son's face in her hand. "The Emissary has spoken."

CHAPTER NINE

MOVING DAY—2347-2350

I HAD JUST BEAMED HOME FROM SCHOOL ONE DAY WHEN I SAW HER. The public transporter was across the street from my house, and right next to a house that had been vacant on our block—until that day. Usually, when people moved into the neighborhood they just gave the coordinates, and beds were beamed into bedrooms and sofas into living rooms. But this family must have gotten their coordinates wrong because pieces of furniture kept appearing on their front lawn. I was standing in the street watching this when a girl carrying a very thick, very heavy oakwood chair walked by me. "Hi, I like your afro," she said, as she flashed a smile that left me breathless, then scuffled with the chair into the house.

I'd never met anyone that reminded me of a season before, but with her gray eyes, coffee complexion, and long hair tied back into a knot, she felt like a warm summer's breeze on my face. I was in a stupor as I sleepwalked across the street into our house. I was about to go up to my room when I realized I was being an idiot. A few weeks before that, Neffie Beumont had shot me down when I asked her out, but I thought of my father's advice: "Ben, there comes a time in every man's life when he must stop thinking and start doing."

I had a plan. I may have improvised it in the moment, but it was a plan.

I dropped my backpack where I stood and ran into the restaurant's kitchen. Dad wasn't there, but Nathan was washing collard greens in the sink. I must've looked crazed because he started laughing as soon as he saw me. "Where's the fire, Benjamin?" he said.

As I walked towards the freezer in the back of the kitchen I called over my shoulder, "What's on the dessert menu for tonight? Any pies or cakes?"

Nathan turned off the running water and began drying his hands. "Yeah, we got a few king cakes and some sweet potato pies we made fresh this morning. Say, what's this about?"

A king cake would be perfect! I opened up the freezer and walked straight to where Dad kept the desserts: second aisle, middle shelf. I had raided the kitchen for ice cream and desserts as a kid so many times I could have found it blindfolded. As I gently pulled out a chilled king cake, I shouted back to Nathan, "Some neighbors are moving in across the street. I thought this might be a nice way to say hello and get them to come to Sisko's."

I carried the New Orleans delicacy to the freezer entrance, where Nathan was standing in the doorway with his arms folded. His tall thin frame wasn't usually intimidating, but silhouetted in the freezer doorway, he managed it. I'd known Nathan my entire life, he'd been the sous chef at Sisko's forever, but he'd been family longer than that. In so many ways, Nathan and my father were like brothers, laughing and arguing but doing everything, even when they disagreed with each other, out of love. Unlike most of us in the house, Nathan never said much, because he didn't need to. Everyone knew Nathan's body language said more than the man ever did. If he liked you, he'd be smiling and laughing around you, and if he didn't, you wouldn't even know he was in the room. "What's her name?" he said with a smirk on his face.

As good a sous chef as Nathan was—and, other than my father, he was the best I'd seen—he was also a great judge of character. Whenever one of us Sisko kids had tried to get something by him, he'd call us on it right away. We called him our uncle because it was true. I knew there was no way I was going to get anything by him. "I don't know," I said. "That's what the cake is for."

Nathan laughed so hard that I thought he was going to bust something. "All right, all right," he said, flashing his heartwarming grin. "Yes, sir, that's how you do it. Always be a gentleman. You never go over to a young lady's house empty-handed, it's disrespectful."

My eyes widened, "Should I take over some flowers too?" I asked.

Nathan gently took the cake from me and walked over to the pastry station. "No, that's too much," he said flatly. "If you actually get a date, then you can bring some flowers, and give them to her mom. Let me just box it up for you and send you on your way, Mister Sisko."

✦

By the time I got back outside, there was no more furniture on the lawn. Either the new family had brought it all inside or figured out the right coordinates. So I rang the doorbell. And after I rang the third time, I began to picture myself walking defeated back across the street, into the freezer, and staying there.

Then the door opened.

To my surprise, I recognized the guy standing in front of me. We were about the same height—I was almost six feet, and he only had a few inches on me—but he had probably twice my muscle. He was a senior at BTW and on the basketball team. As a sophomore on the wrestling team, every now and then, I found myself traveling in the same circles as juniors and seniors. I'd never spoken to him before but he was a good player, known for hitting threes. His nickname was something like Downtown Danny, or Donald. He took one look at me, holding the box, and had me completely figured out. "Zo, it's some boy for you," he said and closed the door.

From inside, I heard the same beautiful voice that had entranced me earlier, but now she was screaming and full of frustration. "Damian! Why are you always so rude?"

The door opened, and the first thing I noticed was that her hair was no longer tied back in a knot. Now, it was a free mass of silky curls that beautifully framed her gray eyes. She was already smiling, which felt like a good sign. "Hi again," she said in a voice that was even softer than the first time she said it.

Luckily, since I was holding the cake, I didn't have to overthink if I looked awkward or what to do with my sweaty palms. I knew the best thing wasn't to think at all. "Hi, I'm Ben Sisko. Welcome to the neighborhood," I said.

My new neighbor started to take the box from me. I gently held onto the cake and looked into her eyes. "If you're not doing anything next weekend, I was wondering if you'd like to go to the Zero-G park with me," I said.

This summer's breeze that had eased into my life took the box from me, but stayed close. "Sure, I'd like that, Ben," and then she gave me a sly smile as she took a step back and started to close the door. "You were trying to be so smooth you forgot to ask my name. It's Zoey, Zoey Phillips."

✦

I remember, Jake, when you were dating Mardah. My sixteen-year-old son was dating a twenty-year-old dabo girl. Oh no, I was not going to allow this to continue. But seeing the two of you together, and then talking to, Mardah at dinner, it was clear you two were learning from each other, growing because of each other. Sometimes people are only in our lives for a short time and we need to reflect on who we became because of them.

When you have a young child, Jake, don't be too hard on them; remember your old man had an open mind when you were dating a dabo girl. Young love always feels like it's forever, even more so when it's temporary. Without those first relationships, we'd never build longer, more sustainable ones.

✦

Watching Zo dance was always different. Sometimes it felt deeply personal, even spiritual when her freestyle would blend seamlessly from a pirouette into a contemporary hip-hop rhythm. Other times she would leap into a jeté and come down tap dancing.

I remember one of the last times I watched her dance, it was on Andoria for the Federation Day Celebration. Zoey was one of the principal dancers with the New Orleans Dance Legacy group. The group preserved all forms of dance from Earth and performed throughout the Federation. I stood in the shadows backstage, and as I watched my girlfriend I realized this time there was just something different about her. This was the first time she was performing as a principal, but it was more than that. There was a confidence, an audacity in her moves that had been a long time coming. "Discipline is rewarded, Ben. Win or fail you always get stronger," she'd said.

Dating Zoey had started out with me being smitten and feeling very lucky she decided to go out with me. Now, after dating for three years, we were both eighteen and on the edge of adulthood. Independence was becoming the rule instead of the exception for both of us. It had been well over a year since we'd had a chaperone when going out. Both our families were confident they'd raised adults that understood the consequences of their choices.

But I learned so much more than personal freedom from Zoey. There was a difference between hard work and discipline. My parents had taught me the value of diligence, and I was comfortable with putting in the work needed to get the results I wanted. But discipline was doing something every day when you didn't—couldn't—see the goal.

Before Zoey I felt like I'd been running sprints, and she showed me how to run a marathon.

Whenever I would complain about working out with her at five in the morning before school, then meeting her at five in the evening for her to teach me fundamentals of ballet and balance, she would just give me a kiss and say, "Discipline is what keeps you from being more of a distraction than you already are in my life, Ben, and it's going to make you a great wrestler."

Of course, she was right on both counts. Before Zoey I literally had no balance. None whatsoever, you could nudge me, and I'd fall over like a top-heavy tower. Once she convinced me to let her start teaching me ballet, everything changed. My gait altered, I became more confident, and I started winning my wrestling matches not by chance but by choice. And she was right, I was a distraction, convincing Zo to blow off that second hour of training to go out with me almost every week. She would always go out with me and then still put the time in, just getting up earlier or staying longer the next day.

Because we were in love.

When the performance ended, the Andorians rose to give Zoey Phillips a standing ovation. As soon as the curtain descended the final time, the artist that had danced the performance of her life disappeared. Zo ran off the stage and leapt into my arms, exhausted, yet happy. Her face was brimming with emotion, and her eyes full of love.

✦

On the shuttle back to Earth, Zoey held my hand in silence. I knew she was exhausted, but there was something else. After a time, Zo leaned her head on my shoulder. "You're very lucky, Benjamin. Your career can run your whole life. I've only got about another ten or fifteen years of performances like tonight in me, twenty at best," she said.

"What are you talking about?" I said, shocked.

Zoey kept her head on my shoulder and squeezed my hand a little tighter. "Ask your brother, he'll tell you. Athletes, dancers, we wear down our bodies quicker than everyone else. Then we start to replace parts to try to maintain the quality of our performance, but it's never the same after that."

I realized we were talking about something more than her recital. In a few weeks I'd be off to Starfleet Academy, having passed the test easily. Zoey and I had worked out a preliminary schedule that allowed us to see each other at least once a week, but now all of our plans were starting to feel hollow. "Zo," I said slowly, "what's going on? What are you saying? I love you."

Zoey smiled. "I know, but are you in love with me enough to do anything to make this work, Benjamin Sisko?"

Her words hit me hard. I had never thought about my love for Zoey in that way. But the moment she said it, I had to admit to myself that something in them rang true.

Zoey took my face in her hands and kissed me passionately, deeply, fully. After she kissed me, she looked me straight in the eyes, and it was clear a door had been closed. "I love you, Ben, more than I think you understand. I love you so much I'd do almost anything for this relationship, but I'm not going to be with someone that isn't ready to do the same for me."

Her words angered me, but I remained silent. Somewhere deep inside, she had touched upon a truth. I loved Zoey, but it took me time to understand it was a love that couldn't survive the future, because I didn't love her enough to do what was necessary to make a future with her. What I felt for Zo paled in comparison to what I felt about Starfleet. That wasn't just a love, it was a *dream* I'd been nurturing for almost ten years. I never compared the two, saw no point to stack one love against the other—but Zo knew better. She knew she'd make compromises with dancing to be with me, but when it was my turn and it came between her and Starfleet, she didn't stand a chance.

And as painful as it was, I had to admit, she was right.

The next day I woke up and realized I lived across the street from someone I still cared for deeply, even though our relationship was over. In the weeks before I went off to Starfleet Academy, we tried to be cordial whenever we saw each other, but somehow that made it worse. Not long after that she got accepted to the Harlem Dance Theatre and her family moved.

I never saw Zoey Phillips again.

CHAPTER TEN
ACADEMY—2350

WE BEAMED INTO THE STARFLEET ACADEMY Family Arrival and Departure Center Atrium holding hands. I didn't want to, none of the Sisko kids did, but Mama didn't give us a choice, and now I'm glad she didn't.

The Atrium is traditionally used for families to say goodbye to departing cadets. Everyone in the space was doing the same as us, getting in one last hug, one last goodbye. The twins had run off immediately after beam-in, more interested in the giant rotating Federation symbol hovering over the water fountain at the atrium's center than their big brother. Judith, like Dad and Mama, was at my side, but she was transfixed by the vast circular symbol etched into the floor and the lettering wrapped around it that we stood nearly in the center of. She tilted her head in that way I know you've seen her do when she's thinking through something. "*Ex Astris Scientia*. Latin, right?" she asked.

Nearly everyone on Earth, and on Federation worlds, recognized the familiar Starfleet Academy logo—triangular red, gold and black, with a representation of the Golden Gate Bridge in its center and the Latin words *Ex Astris Scientia* on the side. But few knew it originated from the United Earth Space Academy logo created before the founding of the Federation. The very same logo we were gazing at on the floor. That circular emblem also depicted the Golden Gate Bridge but in gold, red, blue, and white, the first colors assigned to command, security, science, and medicine in Starfleet.

There were four more Latin phrases, one in each corner of the symbol. I pointed in the upper left and went clockwise around the circle. "*Ex animo, spes.* From the heart, Hope. *Ex Astra, Scientia.* From the stars, knowledge. *Ex anima, exploratio.* From the soul, exploration, and *Ex intellectu, amicitia.* From understanding, friendship."

When I finished, Dad outstretched his hand to me, and when I took it he pulled me in close and hugged me tight. "I can't think of a better explanation for why you're here, son." As my father was hugging me, I felt Judith's arms wrap around me, and then Mama's.

As I nestled my face in my father's shoulder, out of nowhere I heard Elias shout, "Group hug!" And then I could feel his and David's arms join the family sendoff.

✦

Starfleet Academy was the dream that very quickly became a nightmare.

Jake, I had spent so much of my life working towards getting into the academy. I'd envisioned what my first day and my first week would be like. The friends I'd make, and the great experiences I would have at the beginning of my journey. But that week taught me a valuable lesson: in life, if you work hard, you may get what you set out to achieve, but it's rarely in the way you planned for it.

Fifteen minutes after saying goodbye to everyone I was assigned to room 47-C. I'd be sharing the room with Cadet Laporin, a Benzite. I'd never met a member of his species before and was really excited to get to know him. I walked in and the room was more spacious than I had expected, but that didn't really matter. Laporin had already unpacked and moved his bed and desk by the window, the only one in our room, which had a fantastic view of the academy grounds and the Golden Gate Bridge. My bed and desk were right next to the door.

Laporin was at his desk, with his back to me. His hairless, smooth, blue-grey skinned head took no notice of my entry. I couldn't be sure, but he seemed to be reviewing something on his desktop PADD. I dropped my bags down on my bed, walked over to him and outstretched my hand. "You must be Laporin. I'm Ben, Ben Sisko. It's great to meet you."

He swiveled in his chair to face me, his appearance remarkably more cetacean than I expected. With a double bone plate skull, Benzites appear to be wearing a mask over their own face. The breathing apparatus that extended from his uniform to directly under his chin emitted a steaming vapor of his homeworld for him to breathe. I looked past my roommate onto his desktop PADD and was surprised at what I saw.

My picture and public information at Starfleet Academy.

Laporin stared at my hand for a moment, then looked up at me. "Benjamin Lafayette Sisko, you come from a place called New Orleans, presumably because something was wrong with the old one. Everything in this room, like everything in my life, has a place designed to facilitate my success in Starfleet Academy. To avoid any confusion I have assigned you a place in this room. If you respect the boundaries I have set, I am sure we will get along."

He turned back around, and my face disappeared from the screen on his PADD. Now that he had said what he needed to, I had no doubt I had also disappeared from his thoughts as well. This wasn't high school, and I didn't need Mama to tell me a bloody nose and busted lip would've probably worked wonders for Laporin's first contact with me.

But violence wasn't the answer. This was Starfleet Academy, not high school.

Somehow I'd gotten it into my head that Starfleet was this utopia where everyone worked together and helped each other because they were the best version of themselves. But I had it backward. We may have all been the smartest, the highest achievers or most ambitious from wherever we came from, but none of us really came to the academy at our best. It was the rigors of living and working together, of learning with people from different worlds and diverse civilizations that changed us all and put us on the path toward our better selves. And I was going to help Laporin get there even if I had to drag him kicking and screaming the whole way.

I just needed to speak to my roommate in a language he could understand.

✦

I've always found it ironic that for a species that strives to reach new frontiers, humans still have some habits that hold us back. As much as we applaud those who lead and those who think outside the box, many more are also comfortable staying within their circles of comfort. Even though humans and other species had learned to let go of so many prejudices, we still held onto one of the most common: condemning someone or something simply because they're different from us.

During my classes and nearly every interaction, I started to notice a pattern. A series of questions that defined me as "the other," even if those asking didn't consciously realize it.

How do people live in New Orleans? Isn't that like living in the past?

Did you make your own clothes?

Why would you waste all that time cooking your food?

Every time I'd enter a class or walk down a hall, I could feel eyes following me, examining me, scrutinizing me. It got worse when I sat down with a group of cadets for lunch at the academy mess hall. We'd just finished a ten-mile run and I wanted to fit in, so even though I'd never eaten anything replicated before, I ordered what everyone else did. Apparently, it was a traditional first-after-run meal—egg white burritos with green juice, extra green.

Five minutes into the lunch, I threw up everything I'd eaten.

After that, the whispers started and I stopped eating on campus altogether. I'd power through my classes, and at the end of every day use my transporter credits to go home. I'd show up in the living room in time for dinner. Dad and Mama didn't say a word, and neither did I. They probably thought I was just homesick, and they were right, I was, but it was more than that. Even though we talked about everything, I felt like this was something I had to figure out on my own. Still, it was good coming home for a couple of hours every night, and seeing everyone. There's something about being home, close to those you love when other parts of your life are falling apart, that gives you strength, reenergizes you.

As the first week at the academy came to an end, I knew something had to change. For one thing, I was running out of transporter credits; the allotment of credits were for one month and I had nearly used them all in a week. So after dinner on my last night I went to the restaurant freezer. I took a temp-controlled fridge bag we use for deliveries and started stuffing items from the stock shelf into the bag. I was nearly done when I heard laughter behind me.

"Have you thrown up already?" Nathan said.

I turned to see Nathan where he always seemed to be, in the doorway, catching me in the act. The man was uncanny. I looked at my shoes instead of my uncle. "In front of everyone, couldn't keep it down for five minutes," I whispered.

Nathan gave me one of those low, long whistles full of empathy. "Yeah, same thing happened to me. You gotta start slow with that machine food, Ben. Toast, oatmeal, stuff like that, give your body time to adjust." Our sous chef walked into the freezer to get a better look at what I was putting into the bag. "What are you gonna make?" he asked.

I zipped up the bag and slung it over my shoulder. "I've got a few ideas," I said.

Nathan broke out laughing again, "Starfleet ain't ready."

✦

Luckily, the next day was a Saturday. Unlike my roommate, I skipped my morning run, using the time to make some engineering adjustments to my desk. I didn't know how to build starships yet, but I grew up in kitchens and my father made sure there wasn't a person in the Sisko household that couldn't fix anything there. Thinking about it now, I realize that the first time I actually started taking things apart and putting them back together was with my dad in the kitchen, and it's probably what started me on the path to wanting to be an engineer. After rerouting the power flow to the desk and replicating a few simple parts, the surface of my desk now doubled as an induction stove.

By the time Laporin came back from his run, I had a stock pot simmering a Sisko favorite on my makeshift creation. I could tell my roommate wanted to ask about it, but he was halfway into our room, before he stopped and inhaled the air around him, instead of the atmosphere coming from the disk attached to his chest unit. "What is that delicious aroma?" he asked.

I looked over at Laporin from my "assigned place" by the door in the room and smiled. I could see in my roommate's eyes that he wanted to sample whatever was creating such a delicious aroma but thought better of it. I went back to cooking, remembering my father's words: "A distracted chef is a sloppy chef." To my delight it was becoming clear that everything my father had drilled into me for years wasn't in vain. The dish I was cooking looked, smelled, and, more importantly, tasted like something you'd find any week on the menu at Sisko's.

Laporin walked over to the replicator station in our room. I could tell he was hungry even before he ordered a plate of food. As usual, the replicator hummed to life, but it delivered the Benzite a plate full of self-sealing stem bolts. My roommate's head snapped around so fast towards me I thought it was going to pop off. He turned back to the replicator and began to order in a frenzy, but it didn't matter. No matter what kind of food he requested, the replicator gave him the same thing.

More stem bolts.

Laporin switched to beverages, but the results were similar, except with hot sauce. The Benzite was livid. "This is your doing, isn't it?" he demanded.

I got up, went to the replicator and ordered a glass of water, and smiled at my roommate. Once the water appeared, I took a sip and went back and sat down at my assigned space. "I'm an engineer, what do you think? Buckle up, you're going to have a long year," I said.

It wasn't long before our doorbell started ringing. When I answered, a young female human cadet with curly red hair stood in front of me. She only reached my shoulders, but she seemed shorter, with her head bent over her open tricorder. Two other cadets were standing behind her, a Vulcan and human, both male. Without looking up the redhead asked, "Ben Sisko, right? You're cooking real food in here aren't you?

I nodded. "Yeah. Jambalaya, it's a New Orleans cuisine," I said.

The cadet finally looked up at me, her smile as fiery as her red top. "I knew it! Smells wonderful." She jerked her head at the two behind her "I told them an aroma like that doesn't come from resequenced protein, it had to be the real thing." The young woman held out her hand to me, "Oh I'm Susanna Leijten, my friends call me Suz. This is Charlie Reynolds, and Mister Emotional there is Solok."

Charlie had a handshake that damn near crushed my hand and a smile so genuine that it made up for it. I gave Solok the traditional Vulcan salute and was surprised when he just stared back at me, so I put my hand down. After a moment I realized my fellow cadets were staring expectedly at me, waiting. "Would you guys like to come in, try some?" I asked.

Suz pushed past me, and was already heading over to the replicator by the time I followed everyone into my room. "Gee, Sisko, I was wondering when you were gonna get the hint. With sensors like that I hope you're not going into command," she said.

"No chance of that," I said. "Engineering is my dream."

I looked over towards the window and Laporin was sitting at his desk glaring at all of us inhaling as much vapor from his small disk as he possibly could as he watched us. I nodded towards my roommate. "Everyone, this is Laporin. Laporin, everyone."

With my introduction, my roommate just turned his back to us.

Charlie looked around the room at each of us and then chuckled. "Red alert!"

As Suz replicated four bowls with spoons, she looked up at me. "What's with the stem bolts and hot sauce?"

"Oh, long story." I replied.

Solok pulled out his tricorder and was analyzing my desk stove. "A fascinating dual purpose of the desk. Fortunately for you, the academy allows for adaptability within cadet living quarters, or I would be bound to report your... contraption."

It was clear from the start something about me just rubbed Solok the wrong way. We've all met someone like Solok before. Real or imagined, purposeful or not, the offense doesn't really matter. What matters to them is they believe it and they have no interest in a resolution. So, as an engineer to be, I decided I wasn't going to feed any negative energy into this particular engine.

Charlie must have saw the look on my face, because he came over. "Don't pay any attention to our resident Vulcan. He told us he's still not sure First Contact with humanity was a good idea, so he joined Starfleet to acquire data."

"Tell me you're joking."

"I wish," Charlie said.

Suz started to fill the bowls, and pass them out. The room fell into a silence after that and as I looked around I realized it was because nearly everyone had a bowl and was eating—even Solok. Between bites Suz finally handed me a bowl. "I've never tasted anything this good, Ben. Thanks for putting up with us barging in like that," she said.

I walked over and placed the bowl Suz had given me down in front of Laporin. The Benzite looked up at me, absolutely stunned. He took the bowl and actually smiled for the first time. "Thank you," Laporin said.

"No problem," I responded.

As I leaned on Laporin's desk, I was surprised how quickly Suz felt like a friend and how her energy just made me like her. Solok? He put his bowl down when our eyes met. At the same time, my roommate was nearly halfway through his bowl. "I'm just happy everyone likes it."

Suz's eyes widened, and she pointed at me with her fork. "Now I'm going to do you a favor: take some of this jambawhatisit when you go see George, and tell him Suz sent you!"

It dawned on me how in the span of just a few short minutes, the misery of the last week began to evaporate. That was the moment when I truly started to feel like I belonged at Starfleet Academy—when I first made friends.

"Sure. Who's George?" I asked.

✦

The Federation is made up of nearly two hundred species, and roughly eighty percent of them have hair or fur that needs to be maintained on a regular basis. Enter George McCray's barbershop and salon, one of the few civilian-owned establishments on Starfleet Academy grounds. In a lot of ways, McCray's was where I felt the most comfortable at the academy, probably because it felt so much like the barbershop I went to for years in New Orleans. The old-style padded leather chairs with a pump pedal at their base for the barber to raise or lower the chair. The smell of freshly cut hair, that's the same regardless of the species. The sounds of clippers, actual scissors trimming a hairline, and energy field shears doing detailed work. But it was more than just the smells and sounds of the equipment, it was also the people.

Nearly everyone at the academy and everyone in Starfleet visited McCray's at some point. George's one rule was when you walked in, you left your rank at the door. It was a place where you could talk and voice your opinion without reprieve or reprimand. Starfleet has the serious business of keeping the quadrant safe, and McCray's has always been a safe space for cadets. Sometimes you'd see a cadet and an admiral sitting on the same couch, both waiting for their barbers. The salon side was no different. A family-run business, George's mother, Ella, and her team, handled everything from hairstyles to manicures and pedicures.

The first time I met George, it was about two weeks after meeting Suz, and I did exactly what she told me to do. I walked into his shop with a food-stasis container filled with jambalaya. When it was finally my turn to get a cut, instead of going over to the barber assigned to me, I walked over to George. It wasn't difficult to spot him. Pictures of George with VIPs in his chair were all over the shop. My favorite was one of him with Ambassador Spock. Unlike other Vulcans I'd met, there was just the slightest hint of enjoyment on the Starfleet legend's face. The picture was one of the most recent on the shop's wall. George looked the same: tall and thin, with light brown skin, curly hair, and eyes that seemed to reflect his relaxed composure. George wore his barber's apron over a buttoned-down dress shirt with rolled-up sleeves. His crew cut blended nicely into a closely trimmed beard. The dress shirt and beard gave him a sense of style that was different from anyone else in the shop and certainly stood out against Starfleet uniforms.

As I approached, he was just finishing up with a client. He waved me off before I could open my mouth. "I'm sorry, kid, but I don't see walk-ins anymore. You gotta be on my client list," George said.

As I was about to speak, the client in the chair that George was finishing up with interrupted. "Where're your manners, McCray, can't you see the cadet brought you something? What do you have there, son?" he asked.

Now that I was squarely in front of both of them, I could see George's client was none other than Admiral Owen Paris. Even though I was in the shop and didn't need to snap to attention, I could feel my spine straighten in the admiral's presence. I smiled politely to both men and handed over the container. "I'm Benjamin Sisko. It's something I made. I'm friends with Susanna Leijten and she thought you'd like it."

The admiral chuckled as he pulled off the barber's cape and got out of the chair. "I've been to Sisko's and if this young man cooks anything like his father, you're in for a treat, George. Nicely done, Mister Sisko. Here, have a seat. I say that at least earned you a haircut from the best in the shop!"

As I sat down and watched the admiral leave, my new barber was very quiet behind me. As I'd done a thousand times before in barber shops, I looked into the mirrors along the wall to watch my new barber. George had opened the food stasis container I'd given him and was sampling the hot food. "Hey, this is real food," he said, followed by, "Hey, this is good, real good!"

George turned me around in the chair and told me the admiral was right, anyone that could create the magic he'd just tasted deserved a cut from him. Up until that time I'd had a short afro for years—the one Zo had admired the first time I saw her—and I didn't plan on changing that, even though I was in the academy. George disagreed with me. "You should go shorter, let me do a fade. You're entering a new and exciting time in your life, and you should be reminded of that when you look in the mirror."

His words felt right so I agreed, and for the next thirty minutes as he cut my hair, we talked about everything. I learned that Suz interned at the salon last summer so she could learn the ins and outs of the academy before she officially joined. I talked about my family and New Orleans and how my emotions for both goes into what I cook. I told him about my love for engineering and building starships since I was a kid in the hospital, how it felt like a calling more than anything else. I learned I was the first cadet, not to mention officer below lieutenant, he had in his chair in over five years. The business had actually belonged to his father, Baker McCray, but when he died five years ago, George McCray took over the business to keep it going. Before that George was a DJ hosting some of the most elite parties in the Alpha Quadrant. Now that he was back home he still hosted, but only on or close to Earth, and the parties were always exclusive.

As George finished my cut, he did what I imagine barbers have been doing for centuries. He turned me around to face the long wall-length mirror, took a medium-sized handheld mirror off the counter where he kept his barber's tools, then stood behind me so I could see the back of my head and the sharp clean lines of my new fade. Putting the mirror away, he took a brush and wiped away the excess hair from my shoulders and the back of my neck. George took the barber's cape off me in one swift motion, then I got up and shook George's hand. He held mine in his grasp. "Come back in a couple of weeks for a shape-up, I'll put you on the list." Then he added with a smile, "and if you teach me how to cook like that, I'll let you come to my parties. You never know who you'll meet."

✦

When I was a kid, Jake, I was never really one for working out. Sisko men have always been tall and healthy, so I always took my own fitness for granted. Thankfully, that all changed when I met Zoey, and it didn't make sense to stop when I got to the academy. Many of my fellow cadets had a better lung capacity, denser bone structure, and more muscle strength because of the diverse environments on so many different worlds they came from. When a Vulcan has three times the strength of a human, fitness becomes essential. But it wasn't only that: engineering professor Elhmer Ohring would always remind us that when a life support system fails or the artificial gravity goes haywire, personal fitness will be the first tool of an engineer.

So I worked out in the academy gym, at least I tried to. The gym was so crowded during the day, every day, it became nearly impossible to get a decent workout in. Humans, Betazoids, Trill, every species that had to worry about fitness did, and they were constantly in the gym. I began to understand why so many cadets just went on morning runs instead. However, a few of us were stubborn and figured out that the gym was usually empty between four and six in the morning. After a few weeks I became a regular among the early risers. We didn't know each other's names, communicating with head nods and occasionally spotting each other with free weights.

One morning I was in my second set of a bench press when the cadet that was spotting me raised an eyebrow and smiled. "You can definitely do more than that," he said.

I breathed out as I pushed up and put the bar back on the rack. I was benching one-hundred-and-eighty-five pounds, a weight I'd never gone over. Like me, the cadet was a regular in the gym in the mornings. From time to time, I would ask him to spot me on weights because we were about the same height, but he was a lot wider than me and definitely had more muscle on him. "You think so?" I asked cautiously.

My spotter had already grabbed two more free-weight plates and slapped one on each side of the barbel bar. "How much did you put on?" I asked.

The cadet took both of his hands and gripped the center of the bar. "Don't think about that, doesn't matter. I got you, and you got this!"

I did my best to put the weight out of my mind. I pushed the bar up and off the rack on my own, testing the extra load. My spotter maintained a firm grip on the center of the bar, just in case. I brought the bar down to my chest, but as I began to push back up, I could feel the added weight working against me. "Geeez, how much did you put on?" I gritted out.

My spotter ignored the question. "Push!" he demanded.

I started pushing up, and I could feel the cadet helping me, just enough to get the bar up, but not so much that he was doing all of the work. I breathed out and pushed the bar all the way up and started to rack the bar when my spotter stopped me. "One more!" he insisted.

This time I didn't think about it at all and brought the bar down in one smooth, swift motion. I was halfway back up before I could feel the weight working against me. Once again, my spotter added a little help to get me to the all the way up. "Last one!" the cadet commanded.

I could feel my muscles working hard now as I brought the bar down to my chest, but my spotter was right there with me, helping me control the descent. I tightened my grip and pushed up one last time. When I reached the top I had nothing left to give. The cadet quickly seized control and put the bar on the rack. "That was pretty good," he said, smiling.

I sat up from the bench and checked the plates added by the cadet. I couldn't believe it. "Two-hundred-and-twenty-five pounds?" I said, astonished.

The cadet flashed a knowing smile. "See, I told you could do more than one-eighty-five. I'm on the wrestling team. You should think about signing up."

This guy had just helped me to push myself harder than I ever had, and it felt good, real good. I was already taking the mandatory self-defense classes, but returning to wrestling sounded like it could be a great addition. "Thanks, you were right. And you know, wrestling's not a bad idea, I might just do that." I held out my hand, "Ben Sisko."

My spotter grinned and took my hand. "Cal Hudson."

CHAPTER ELEVEN

RENEGADE—2350

"THE PRIME DIRECTIVE IS A HYPOCRITICAL PRACTICE used by Starfleet and the Federation when it suits them." Tryla Scott said.

I remember looking across the lecture hall at my classmate in disbelief. Perfectly set brown eyes sat above high caramel cheekbones, creating a face that could be as cold as it was beautiful. Her dark curly hair was cut short on the sides and in the back, with a crop on top that framed her beauty and seemed to perfectly channel the fierce intensity that burned within her.

The year had just started, and Prime Directive 101 was the mandatory first class. Everyone already knew Scott. She simply didn't believe in keeping her opinion to herself, especially when she felt she was right, which was most of the time.

Even our Professor, Admiral Savar, was caught off guard, and for a moment, raised both eyebrows in disbelief at the young woman's audacity. Then after a second, the Vulcan composed himself, his face returning to an emotionless expression under a crop of graying hair. "A bold statement, Cadet. How do you support this supposition?" he asked.

"With facts, Professor: April and Na'rel, Kirk with the Organians and Klingons, on and on. Starfleet has a nasty habit of turning a blind eye to General Order One when it suits them. And that's not even the worst of it, sir. The mandate of the directive is to not interfere with the natural course of development of other cultures and civilizations, especially pre-warp civilizations. And yet, for hundreds of years, Starfleet has actively walked among other cultures by disguising ourselves to look like an unsuspecting species so we can study them up close." Scott didn't bother trying to mask the contempt in her voice. "Now we've even created duck blinds for more permanent residence on worlds we were never invited to. It's wrong." After a moment of reflection, Scott added, "Sir."

Savar stared at Scott impassively. "Exploration and meeting new cultures is the core purpose for Starfleet. The structure you rebuke, Cadet, has worked well for two centuries. How would you change it?"

Everyone turned to look at Scott. Savar had framed the question to put her in the hotseat, to come up with a better practice for investigating new worlds than what the Federation had been using for over two hundred years.

Scott didn't even hesitate.

"We have the best starships in the quadrant, sir. There's no reason we can't use our sensors from high orbit to gather information on species that are less technologically advanced than we are. We go down to planets without invitation because we can, and that's not respecting the boundaries of our neighbors, Admiral. That's hubris and taking advantage of our technological privileges over them. Where's the Prime Directive then?" The young woman leaned back in her seat and crossed her legs. "Most of the cultures we 'investigate' ultimately wind up becoming Federation worlds. Is what we're doing true non-interference, or are we just setting up a softer form of colonization?"

The room fell silent, but I had to say something.

"You're wrong," I said. "When the Prime Directive is overlooked, it is usually in an effort to mitigate a major crisis befalling a world, or to avert death and destruction, not to take advantage."

Scott kept her eyes forward and never even looked at me as she responded. "Right. Like we did on Rigel VII and Neural, just to name two planets. We seem to have acquired a knack for studying people and planets that can help us out. Isn't it funny how rare it is that we never seem to go to planets that have absolutely nothing to offer Starfleet or the Federation?"

Admiral Savar looked at both of us and then the class: "Well, this debate has been very informative, and emotional. Miss Scott, I would like you to expand upon your argument in a paper of no less than ten thousand words, and hand it in by the end of the week. Mister Sisko, I would like the same from you regarding your position."

After the class finished, I caught up to Scott. I wasn't happy about the confrontation or the extra work. "Thanks a lot," I said as I passed her desk.

Scott was still at her desk, stuffing PADDs into her backpack, and chuckled as I walked away. "We live to serve." She said it with the same contempt in her voice from earlier.

I stopped and turned around.

"If you think Starfleet is some evil empire, then why are you even here?"

Scott finished packing her backpack in silence and then stood up. She was taller than I expected. After a moment of just standing in front of me and looking up at me, she finally spoke. "I love Starfleet and the Federation more than anything else, and it is exactly for that reason I reserve the right to criticize them perpetually."

Her response was not what I expected. "You're paraphrasing a James Baldwin quote," I said, shocked.

Tryla smiled, and I immediately knew I was seeing a side of her few ever did. "Well, Mister Sisko, there may be hope for you after all," she said.

I realized I wanted to get to know this complicated woman. "Do you want to go get some lunch?" I asked.

"No," she said flatly. "But let's work on these papers together. I think it'll be fun."

✦

Knowing Tryla Scott and dating her were two entirely different things. At the academy, Tryla was known as this force of nature, powerful, intense, and unrelenting—a maelstrom you didn't want to mess with. Tryla never learned the social lesson of not always speaking your mind, and she did not suffer fools.

One afternoon we were between classes and decided to lay out on the grass under the old oak tree on the grounds. The spot was a favorite among couples, probably because it was one of those few places that didn't feel like the academy but was still very much a part of it. She lay under that tree with her head on my chest, and I asked her what she thought about what people said about her.

"People often mistake confidence for arrogance, especially when you don't fit their narrative," she said with her eyes closed.

"Tryla, I've seen you make professors squirm, especially when you know you're right. Sometimes you are arrogant."

She sighed and nestled into my chest. "Life is short and outer space is a cold, dark, harsh environment. If I'm going to spend my life working in space, I'm not going to hold back who I am for the benefit of others."

After five months of being together, I learned that even though Tryla came from Andoria and had embraced technology all her life, for all our differences, we had the same moral compass.

I liked that, a lot.

"Now I've got a question for you," she said, opening her eyes and looking into mine.

"Shoot," I said.

"Why engineering? Don't get me wrong, lover: when I become a captain, my ship is going to need an engineer I can trust and someone that will always think about the ship and crew before themselves, and that's you," she said.

In everything that had happened between us since we met, this was the first time she'd asked me about my career path. It felt like we'd taken another step towards something. I could see we both felt it.

"But…" I knew she wanted to say more.

Tryla sat up. Our faces were so close it felt like I could feel her heart beating. "But… it's a waste of material, Mister Sisko. You're built for more. Everyone here sees it but you," she whispered.

She kissed me deeply and then stood up, "I'm late for class. Dinner tonight?"

"Always," I said.

That was the other side of Tryla—once you were allowed within the eye of her maelstrom everything was fine, she was loving and nurturing in a way I had never experienced before. As she left, I thought about her words, and, if I'm being completely honest, something about what she was saying felt right—but my love for engineering got me into Starfleet and I wasn't ready to let it go.

✦

From the moment she opened the door, Mama didn't take her eyes off Tryla. Her initial reaction was colder than I expected. I'd been talking to my parents about Tryla for a couple of months, and with the end of our first year at the academy coming up, they suggested I bring her over for dinner.

Dad was easy to read. "The girl's probably eaten from replicators her entire life, let's have her over for a real cooked meal before you think about getting serious," he said.

"Too late," I told him.

Mama said even less. It was true that Tryla was only the second girl I'd had over to the house, Zoey being the first—maybe it was because Zoey was my neighbor and after a while, was over all the time, maybe it was my age—but when Zoey and I broke up all Mama said was, "These things happen, baby."

Now, Mama was taking my relationship with Tryla seriously, and I could see it was because I was serious about her.

If my girlfriend noticed my mother's scrutiny, she didn't say anything, which was unusual from Tryla Scott. It was also unexpected that morning when she asked me, "What should I wear tonight?"

In the ten months of being with Tryla I never asked, nor expected her to wear anything special for my benefit. I also knew better. So I was surprised at the question. "Whatever you want is fine. My parents are going to love you, because I love you, not because of what you're wearing," I answered.

Tryla kissed me on the cheek. "Okay, I'll see you tonight," she said.

I was anxiously waiting for Tryla at the academy transporter pad until, five minutes before we were supposed to appear at my parents' front door, she showed up.

And I forgot everything.

I couldn't take my eyes off her or the lavender off-the-shoulder summer dress she was wearing. A dress! As we stepped onto the transporter pad, Tryla smiled casually. "You're staring, Ben," she said as we disappeared.

Mama was also staring. At Tryla, at us together, at how she interacted with Judith and the twins— who loved her. My siblings were asking her questions about the academy and starships they never asked me. I asked my little sister about this, and she just beamed as she held Tryla's hand. "You just want to be an engineer, but she wants to be a captain!" Judith said.

After dinner Tryla excused herself to go the ladies' room, and not thirty seconds after she left, Mama did the same. My father and I locked eyes across the dinner table. "What do you think they're talking about?" I asked.

As my father got up he slapped me on the shoulder and chuckled. "It's not about dinner," he said.

Whatever they were talking about, when they came back fifteen minutes later, the ice had broken. They were laughing and talking like Tryla was an extended member of the family.

Which I guess she now was.

✦

About a month after dinner with my parents, our semester was finally over. By this time, Tryla and I were inseparable. A lot of cadets were taking advanced summer courses to prepare for the next academic year. But we decided to take the time off and spend it with each other. We wanted to build a foundation to our relationship and knew we wouldn't have the opportunity to work on us in our second year or after graduation.

For Tryla's birthday at the end of July, I surprised her with a vacation to her favorite place on Earth: Japan. My father had a connection with a Kobe beef distributor allowing us to stay in Minka homes throughout Japan. We stayed a week each in Tokyo, Kyoto, Nara, and our last week was in Shizuoka City. One morning, just before dawn, I woke to the sounds of crying. Tryla was out on the balcony, the majesty and strength of Mount Fuji enduring in the distance. In her purple and white kimono against the rising sun, she looked so breathtakingly beautiful and also so incredibly sad. I walked up next to her, and we stood together in silence for a long time before she started speaking.

"When my dad was a kid, he loved old samurai movies, so when I was old enough—which was really way too young—we started watching them together." Tryla used her palm to wipe away her tears as she laughed. "It must've been in the genes because I loved them! He told me when I was old enough to hold a katana, we would all take a trip here to learn all about them together." Tryla turned to face me. In that moment, I could feel her pain and her vulnerability. "But he was a lieutenant on the *Enterprise* at Narendra III. I was eleven when he died and left us."

This was the first time she'd ever opened up like this to me. Maybe to anyone. Tryla never really talked about her family. I knew the broad strokes, that her father had passed away and that her mother lived on Andoria, but she said nothing specific beyond that, and I never asked. Now that she was confiding in me, I felt closer to her than I had ever felt to anyone before. I wanted to say something to make her feel better. I thought of a million things I could say, but instead, I just held her hand and let her continue.

"At some point I got it in my head that Starfleet captains were the closest things to samurai. They defend the weak, protect the Federation, and have a code of honor beyond reproach. I told my dad I was going to become one, and that's a promise I intend to keep."

"That's beautiful. I know he's going to be proud of you when it happens."

"I'm not sure it will if we stay together, Ben."

There was a finality in her words, a sadness. "I don't understand. What do you mean?" I heard myself whisper.

"I love you deeply, completely. This relationship is becoming the most important thing in my life, it's changing me, and I can't let that happen. I told you when we first met I love Starfleet more than anything, and I'm not going to give up my dream to become a captain for anyone, not even you, Ben.

"It's over."

✦

Tryla left less than an hour after that, and I could see in her eyes, I was back on the outside. There was no point talking about it with her. She was right, it was over.

I was devastated, Jake. For the next week, I stayed in Japan. I was in a daze, stuck. I'd seen my future with Tryla and in Starfleet so clearly, and now I was uncertain about everything. Somehow Dad and Mama found out and kept trying to get in contact with me. I knew they were worried, but I needed time. Time to just sit and think about what to do next.

I had a couple of weeks before the academic year started. No matter how I tried, I couldn't see myself going back, being in the same class with Tryla, possibly training with her. I loved her, and a part of me always would, but I also loved Starfleet, and Tryla was right about one thing, I wasn't prepared to let my dream die either. I couldn't help but find myself thinking about Zoey Phillips, and irony. Zoey broke up with me because she knew I would choose Starfleet over her, and now I knew what that felt like when Tryla chose Starfleet over me.

Jake, there will be times in your life son when something will be so painful you will want to run away from it. But I want you to understand there's a difference between allowing pain or fear to cripple you, and realizing that sometimes you are so close to someone or something you need to step back to gain a new perspective. That's what I did with Tryla, and that's what I did when Jadzia died.

For my sophomore year, I had originally planned to do my engineering field study at the Utopia Planitia shipyards. Tryla was entering the command track, and her field study would be at different locations in the Sol system. This way, we could be together a couple of nights a week, stay together. Now I wanted to get as far away from Earth and the Sol system as possible.

I searched for places where I would be allowed to continue my engineering track and gain practical field study experience while not at Starfleet Academy. On such short notice for second-year cadets, there was only one option available.

Starbase 137.

CHAPTER TWELVE

STARBASE 137—2351

I WENT STRAIGHT FROM JAPAN TO STARBASE 137. Dad and especially Mama were troubled by this, but after a couple of chats over subspace, they forgave me. Dad said to me, "You're your own man now, Benjamin. Making your own decisions, what parent would be upset with that?"

The *U.S.S. John Lewis* took me to the planet Moser IV and Starbase 137, where I would be spending the next year of my life. When I was a kid, I built an earlier version of the starship before its retrofit. I told myself this was a good sign.

A half-size version of the familiar mushroom-shaped space station was in orbit over Moser IV, but this wasn't the starbase. This was just a Federation waystation where ships docked to unload supplies and personnel.

Moser IV was a Class-M world roughly the size of Earth, but about eighty-five percent of it was covered with water, and there were only two major land masses on the planet. What made Moser IV unique was that it was the only place in the known galaxy to have a planet-wide undersea sequoia forest. Some of these underwater sequoia grew to over nine thousand feet high—underwater. The wood from the trees was as strong as duranium and was starting to be implemented into the materials of starship and starbase design.

Starbase 137 wasn't on either of the planet's continents but in the ocean. The starbase was an ancient city that had been abandoned for centuries, carved entirely out of the same sequoia wood. Spread out across ten square miles, the city was found by Captain Philippa Georgiou and her First Officer Michael Burnham of the *U.S.S. Shenzhou*. After the city was deemed safe and not the property of any known species, it was claimed by Starfleet using Earth's ancient maritime law. A few decades after it was discovered, Starfleet began using Moser IV as a place to train engineers.

All of this was in the data packet that briefed me on the way to the planet, but none of this information really prepared me. Moser IV is the closest I've seen to having an entire ocean suspended in space. The first thing I noticed on the waystation was how easy it was to tell the personnel apart. Everyone coming from ships, regardless of their uniform or rank, didn't look as rugged and fit as the people that worked on the station. And since this planet's primary purposes were training, education, undersea logging, and tree restoration, that meant everyone that worked up on the waystation did a stint down on Moser IV.

That should've been my first clue.

There were seven of us on the shuttle down to the planet wearing cadet uniforms. I recognized three familiar faces. Fausto Singh, a brown-eyed baby face with ears so big everyone at the academy teased he could be an honorary Ferengi. Tanya Stolzoff—at six feet, with long dark hair and a swimmer's build, she was one of the tallest human cadets; she was a crack shot on the phaser range and a really good boxer. And Maritza Gonzalez. Everyone said Gonzalez reminded them of their little sister and it was true. She was short like a little pixie with a haircut to match, friendly and could fix anything in five minutes flat. They were on the engineering track like me, and I'd had classes with them. I could tell from the looks on their faces that they were surprised to see me and wanted to come over to talk. But I'd come all the way out here to get away from everything I knew, and I didn't want to make new friends.

The other three, I didn't recognize. A Vulcan female, a Bolian male and a human. The Vulcan and Bolian must've been at the Starfleet Academy annex on Psi Epsilon III, since I'd never seen them in San Francisco. The third, a human male, was clearly from the Starfleet Technical Services Academy on Mars. I knew this because of the square-shaped pip on his cadet uniform and the lack of a communicator badge. Being a place primarily for non-commissioned officers and enlisted personnel that chose not to attend Starfleet Academy, the Technical Services Academy did things a little differently. I noticed that when some of the

Elizabeth Sisko

▲ Young Ben in the New Orleans French Quarter with his treasured childhood friend, Mister Bayou. Image courtesy J. Sisko

The Sisko family, taken in the family restaurant, Sisko's. From left to right, Elizabeth, Elias, Joseph, David, Ben and Judith. Image courtesy J. Sisko ▼

BENJAMIN L. SISKO FB-010-993

STARFLEET ACADEMY
CLASS OF 2354

Ben's Academy graduation photo. Image courtesy Starfleet Command.

▲ Jennifer Sisko with baby Jake shortly after his birth in San Francisco. Image courtesy J. Sisko

Ben with the "Old Man", his friend, Curzon Dax, on their way to the *U.S.S. Livingston* in 2359. Image courtesy E. Dax ▼

The August 1973 issue of *Incredible Tales*, featuring Benny Russell's story, "Deep Space Nine: Epilogue".

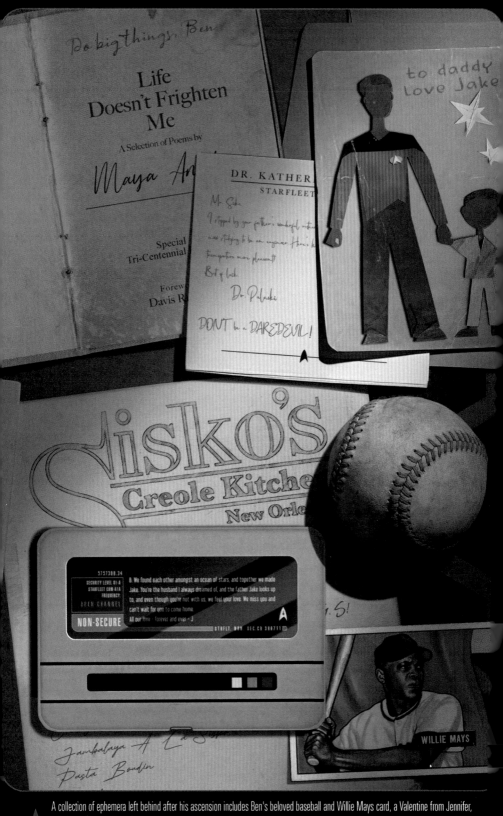

Do big things, Ben

Life
Doesn't Frighten
Me

A Selection of Poems by

Maya An

Special
Tri-Centennial

Forew
Davis R

to daddy
love Jake

DR. KATHER
STARFLEET

Mr. Sisko
I stopped by your father's wonderful restaurant
...was studying to be an engineer there's ...
Transporters more pleasant
Best of luck
Dr. Pulaski

DON'T be a DAREDEVIL!

Sisko's
Creole Kitchen
New Orle

5757308.34
SECURITY LEVEL 01-A
STARFLEET COM-41A
FREQUENCY:
OPEN CHANNEL
NON-SECURE

B: We found each other amongst an ocean of stars, and together we made
Jake. You're the husband I always dreamed of, and the father Jake looks up
to, and even though you're not with us, we feel your love. We miss you and
can't wait for you to come home.
All our love - forever and ever – J

STRFLT. NPA SEC.CD 306711

..., S!

WILLIE MAYS

Jambalaya A La Sa
Pasta Boudin

A collection of ephemera left behind after his ascension includes Ben's beloved baseball and Willie Mays card, a Valentine from Jennifer,
a Father's Day card from Jake, a brief note from Dr. Pulaski, and his treasured copy of *Life Doesn't Frighten Me*. Image courtesy J. Sisko.

"Make it a good life, Jake-O. Because I'll be watching."

Jake Sisko, with his baby sister, Sarabeth Jadzia Sisko, and her best friend, Mister Bayou. Image courtesy J. Sisko.

Here's to Trouble Free Tomorrows! Vic Fontaine

▲ Ben and the crew of Deep Space 9 relaxing at Vic Fontaine's Las Vegas Lounge. Image courtesy Quark

other cadets made eye contact with him, he'd just roll his eyes and chuckle, like they were beneath him. We'd all learn later that this was Stanley Kosinski.

As we passed through the atmosphere of Moser IV, the beauty of the world was breathtaking. Aqua blue oceans with green patches that stretched across the face of the entire planet. When the shuttle descended towards Starbase 137, I realized those green patches were thousands of sequoia trees sprouting up from the depths of the ocean. Their green crowns and brown trunks spread out along the blue ocean as far and wide as the eye could see. On final approach, the water was so clear that I could see that beneath the surface of the water was an entire planetwide forest of these beautiful yet stoic timekeepers silently marking the eons of the planet's history.

I was amazed by the pinwheel spiral design of the city. With a ten-mile diameter it was striking how closely the city resembled a spiral galaxy. I wondered if the architects of this wooden megastructure had these same thoughts when they created it so long ago. At the center of the spiral was a single solitary tower, at least twenty-five stories high. The tower was not only the hub of the city but the municipal command center. Each spiral stem was miles long with dozens of buildings from five to ten stories tall. Bridges connected each stem to the next, and between each lay parks and forests. It was clear millions had lived and thrived here once long ago. At the tip of each spiral tail was a vast docking platform for sailing ships and a landing pad for shuttles. Our shuttle landed on one of the outermost spirals, next to a series of buildings on the dock that were shipyards.

As we left the shuttle, there was a single individual waiting for us. We'd all seen his picture and knew his service record, but seeing the man in person was something entirely different. John Diviticus West stood on the landing pad, silent, full of expectation. For a man in his sixties, he was taller, more fit and muscular than I expected. He used his durasteel hand and arm to take a pull on a cigar. When West was twenty-two he was assigned to engineering aboard the *U.S.S. Paul Robeson*, when it was hit by a stellar core fragment. The ship was moments away from destruction, and he was pinned under debris. He did what was necessary, phasered off his own arm and kept himself going long enough to save the ship. Someone said that when West was stuck between a rock and a hard place he phasered off his arm. That's how he got his name.

The Rock.

Without any instruction we all fell in line, at attention, and waited. West took another pull from his cigar, blowing out the smoke as he slowly walked down our line. "You're all here because you want to be engineers," he said, stopping briefly to look each of us in the eyes. "I've seen it a hundred times before, some of you probably built model starships as children, others may feel you have a gift for building or fixing. I'm here to tell you it takes more than a dream or a gift to be a Starfleet engineer; it takes a hell of a lot of hard work and a way of seeing things differently. Fortunately, you've come to the right place for both."

West walked off towards a group of buildings on the dock. We all looked at each other. Tanya Stolzoff looked at us. "Do we follow him?" she said.

The Bolian answered, "I vote yes," and walked off after West.

"Makes sense," I said to the others. "Better to follow him than explain why we're all just standing here." We all caught up to West quickly, stepping into line slightly behind him as he walked.

The Rock made no acknowledgment of it as he began to speak. "These barracks will be your home for the next ten months that you're here with me." The three buildings that made up the shipyards complex were eight stories each. The first building, closest to us, looked to be administrative. But the other two were built at the edge of the dock with slipways that extended into the water so that whatever was created inside could be navigated right out of the dock onto the ocean. Nothing that I saw at this dock looked like it was for ships that operated in space.

The female Vulcan cadet must've realized the same thing, because she moved up alongside West and asked the question we were all thinking. "Excuse me, sir. If we will be living here, will we be transporting, or taking a shuttle up to the waystation daily for our engineering lessons?

Our instructor stopped, chuckled more to himself than anyone and then looked up at us. "Does anyone here have any nautical experience whatsoever or time at sea?"

No one raised their hand.

"It never ceases to amaze me. Everyone wants to work in space and yet hardly anyone has ever even been on the ocean. You know it doesn't really matter what planet you come from, before any species could find their way to the stars they first mastered their oceans." West walked over to the young

Vulcan who was now back in line again with us. "So, to answer your question, Cadet, no. It will be some time before any of you go back into space again. I am going to make sailors out of all of you, and teach you engineering from the ground up. It will be some of the most physically and mentally demanding work you've ever done, maybe will ever do."

West walked off into the administrative building, and this time we followed right in step. The ground level of the building had communal living quarters, sonic showers, and food replicators. In the center of the living quarters was a transporter pad, and an old style navy bell on the transporter console. West stood beside it. "In the next thirty days we're going to build an ancient Egyptian barge, and we're going to do it by hand with the materials and ancient tools discovered here on Moser IV. I'll be grading you individually as well as an engineering team."

The master chief activated the transporter pad, watching our puzzled faces as the device hummed to life. "If at any time anyone feels this is unfair, or too hard, they are welcome to ring the bell three times and leave. Be aware that doing so means expulsion from the engineering track, but not Starfleet Academy." West finished his cigar, putting it out in the palm of his durasteel hand. "Command, science, security, these are all essential within Starfleet. But the longer you work in space, the more you realize it's engineering that keeps you safe, keeps you alive out here. Engineering isn't for everyone. By the time we're done, I fully expect most of you not to be here, or to change to one of the other three tracks."

Almost on cue, the Vulcan stepped out of line, walked over to the bell, and rang it three times. The tones from the bell felt deafening in the silence of the room. Then she stepped onto the transporter pad. "This is most illogical," was all she said.

West worked the transporter controls in silence, and the cadet disappeared in the familiar shimmer of blue light. After another moment of silence, the Rock spoke. "Nothing I said changes. You're just down an engineer now, and you'll have to figure it out. We start at 0500 tomorrow. Goodnight, cadets."

✦

That next day none of us knew what to expect. At 0500 hours we walked into building C, which was about four hundred feet long and half as wide. A massive slot in the floor about twenty feet wide and almost as deep ran the length of the building and out onto the slipway. Two cranes also ran the length of the slot. Under the first crane was a stack of indigenous sequoia logs, at least fifty feet long and half as wide. In the back of the building at the beginning of the slot were about a half dozen workstations and a large meeting table.

West was at the meeting table, looking over a series of blueprints. As we gathered around the table, he began without bothering to look up at us. "On Earth in 1954, the original Khufu solar ship was discovered disassembled near the Great Pyramid of Giza. When archeologists reconstructed it, they learned the ship didn't need nails or any kind of adhesive. It used ropes to bind the timber together so tightly that she became seaworthy. The ship was a barge that was one-hundred-and-forty-two feet long and nineteen feet wide. Twelve oars were used for propulsion, ten at the bow and two at the stern." The Rock looked around the table. "We're going to build a replica of this Egyptian barge using the Moser IV sequoia and their indigenous cutting and woodworking tools. The only modern addition will be a kinetic sail to assist with propulsion. We'll be using my plan and work schedule." West sat down and lit a cigar. "Let's go over it. I want to be carving the hull before we break for lunch."

✦

Three weeks into building the Egyptian Khufu solar ship, Kosinski quit. Our self-proclaimed cadet team leader had been on the fence from the moment we started building the vessel. He said he joined Starfleet to be an engineer, not to build a replica of a five-thousand-year-old barge. At the end of our third week, we woke up in the middle of the night to a bell being rung. I looked up from my pillow to see Kosinski disappearing off the transporter pad. In truth, I was upset, but I understood why he did it. The work was exhausting. Sixteen-hour days, six days a week, with one day off. What made it bearable, even worthwhile, for me was that John Diviticus West was there with us every minute, and out of his intensity we were picking up skills and ways of thinking unlike anything in our first year at the academy.

Every day West had us go through his ritual. Plan. Perform. Patience.

In the morning, we'd plan the day to the minute and who would be working on what. Next to nothing was left to chance. Once we got to work, we'd perform what had been taught to us the day before. And every two days, we would switch tasks so everyone was cross-trained and could pick up where someone else left off. Slowly, begrudgingly, we were learning to become patient with the process. Yes, we were working hard against a ticking clock, but the six of us were starting to fall into a rhythm, and find our way through.

But now there were five of us.

Maritza sighed as she sat up in her bed. "I was tired of Kosinski's mouth anyway, we're better off without him," she said.

"We're not gonna get this done in time." The worry on Greth's pale blue face mirrored what we were all feeling. Like the rest of us, the Bolian had been working hard, but now I could see defeat in him. It had taken us two weeks to finish carving all of the hull sections out of the massive sequoia, and then another week to put those sections together cleanly to form a completed hull. Because we were working with trees as strong as durasteel, the process would've been completed in a day or two if we had used phasers, but we could only use the saws and tools of the ancient culture on Moser IV. After that, we interconnected all the pieces just as the Egyptians designed, but instead of using rope to tighten the pieces together and make the barge watertight, we used the Moser IV kelp to draw them together. The kelp from this planet had a tensile strength equal to duranium cable.

We now had a week to finish everything else.

At the academy or here, Singh never spoke a lot. He was definitely the most introverted of us, so when he said something it usually made us all stop and listen. "Ben, talk to West. Tell him we need more time."

I looked at Singh, and then around the room. "Wait, what? Why me?" I asked.

Singh looked at me like I was crazy. Tanya started to chuckle. "Seriously? You're the one that's keeping this on the rails, making sure we're all on the same page, Ben. It was never Kosinski," she said.

A lot of what we were doing reminded me of working in the kitchen back home. I had learned how to spot when people were out of rhythm or slowing down the team, and I'd given some advice. Now, it seemed these people were looking to me to talk to West for the group. "All right, I'll see what I can do," I said.

✦

"Request denied." West said without looking up from his PADD.

I stood there in his office, feeling small against the enormity of this man's presence and his past. I'd just made our best case for asking for an extension, and the Rock hadn't even bothered to look up at me. It was early, I hadn't slept since Kosinski left, and in thirty minutes our work day was about to start. "With all due respect, Master Chief, making five people do the work of seven is wrong."

West looked up at me. "In Starfleet, like in life, we don't get the luxury of choosing the challenges we face. We either rise or fail to meet them. If you can't handle the pressure of building a wooden ship in thirty days, how the hell are any of you going to handle being an engineer in a life-or-death situation? Better to find out now. Dismissed, Cadet." West returned to his PADD, and it felt like he forgot I was in the room.

As I turned to walk out, West lifted his head up again, looked at me for a moment. "And Mister Sisko, you're now the team leader!"

✦

"He's right," I said as I looked around the barracks at my fellow cadets sitting on their beds.

Tanya whistled. "That must've been some speech The Rock gave you, Ben."

"He said if we can't cut it, if we can't adapt, we don't need to be here, and he's got a point." I took off my combadge and held it in my hand. "We're in Starfleet Academy. A lot of people don't get this far, but we have for a reason. We all had the dream to get here, and this is what being here is all about, dealing with the unexpected. Whether it will be on a starship dealing with the unknown or here, now, building a wooden ship. We're engineers, and no matter where we are, we're never out of our element."

Singh got up off his bed, looked at everyone, and then turned to me, "You heard the man. Engineers, it's time to go to work." Singh slapped me on the shoulder as he walked out. Everyone followed his cue, slapping me on the shoulder as they left the barracks. Stolzoff was the last in line, and she stopped as she slapped me on the shoulder. "Now that was a good speech."

✦

With less than a week to go, the five of us finally hoisted the ship up and set it in the slipway for launch. It took a lot longer without using the antigrav cranes, but the Egyptians didn't have antigrav technology when they did it, so neither did we. Looking at our work docked in the slipway, I realized if we continued to follow West's assignment schedule we'd never finish in time. He had us learning everything together and then only paired people off once we had all learned the same thing. But since this was slowing everything down, I changed it, splitting us up into teams. Just like working in the kitchen, after a while I had gotten a pretty good feel for what everyone was capable of and excelled at. Stolzoff and Greth were adept at detail work, so their job was to finish the oars. Singh's and Gonzalez's task was to finish the cabin on the deck, and I took the job of supporting both teams. When they didn't need me, I worked on installing the kinetic sail.

When West learned I had changed the assignments, he didn't say anything. That was when I realized the assignment schedule had just been another obstacle the Rock had put in our way. West had taught us the benefits of planning, performance, and patience, but it was up to us to learn to adapt to anything at any time—that's how engineers came to be known as miracle workers in Starfleet. We had such a reverence for the man that we had never considered approaching him with our own options. After that, I vowed never to let someone's rank or title intimidate me. That last week, West stopped showing up and we understood the statement. He had taught us what we needed. Succeed or fail, it was all on us now.

We worked through the day and into the night of the last hour of the last day. It had taken us working round the clock without sleep for almost three days. With ten minutes left, Stolzoff and Greth had finished the oars, and I finished installing the kinetic sail. I checked their work, while they checked mine. Then we went and helped Singh and Gonzalez put the finishing touches on the cabin.

All of a sudden Gonzalez stopped what she was doing and yelled out. "¡Ay, Dios mio!" She looked around at us and started laughing. "How could we forget, we've got to name her!"

Greth didn't bother to look up at us as he kept working. "Master Chief didn't say anything about giving the ship a name, guys."

I interjected quickly, "That's because it's up to us. Maritza is right, after all the work we've put in, she needs a name."

Singh nodded. "Something that reflects what we've been through to get here."

Stolzoff said, "Yeah well, whatever it is, we need to make it quick. There's barely enough time to carve a name on the hull."

After each of us offered a couple names that the rest of us shot down, in the end, there was only one that we all agreed upon.

The *Defiant* rolled off of the slipway and into the ocean with minutes to spare. We all held our breath as our new ship was tested by the water beneath her. If our construction was off even by millimeters, or the kelp cable was not bound tightly enough, water would seep onto the deck, reveal our errors, and sink our ship. But one minute turned into five, and five into ten.

She held.

In the glow of Moser IV's moon we all yelled and screamed so hard and so loudly, I was sure they could hear us up on the waystation. While we were all at the ship's bow celebrating, the deck was bathed in the familiar blue transporter light. When it subsided, West was standing on the deck with a cache of equipment laid out behind him. The Rock took a lighter and a cigar out of his uniform tunic, lit the cigar, and put the lighter away. "Congratulations, cadets, really good work," West said.

We all formed around West. "Thank you, Master Chief," I said.

Stolzoff stepped up so she was in front of West, but she was looking at me. "I won't be staying. My family has always been in Starfleet security. When it came to my turn, I thought I wanted to try something different, but I see now that security is where I belong. It just didn't feel right quitting before we finished this." Stolzoff outstretched her hand to me. Her smile was almost apologetic. "Good luck, Ben," she said.

I shook my teammate's hand and returned the smile. "Thanks for all your help, Tanya. We couldn't have done it without you."

When Tanya had finished saying her goodbyes to everyone else, West tapped his combadge. "Waystation, this is West. Beam up Cadet Stolzoff."

Tanya disappeared in the transporter beam, and just like that there were four of us.

✦

After seven months of living and working on Starbase 137, we had forgotten what a classroom looked like. Once we had successfully completed our thirty-day trial by fire, the master chief took a more personal approach with us. We began to shadow him, in essence becoming his apprentices, learning by doing. This, we discovered, was how West operated every year with cadets that came to Starbase 137. Giving them some godforsaken Herculean task, and whoever was left after the dust settled got the John Diviticus West engineering master class. On occasions when he was too busy, we would get passed over to his assistant, Lieutenant Cass Tovid.

Tovid, a Betazoid, had come to 137 three years earlier on the engineering track as a cadet and got an invitation from West to stay on. It was clear that the lieutenant saw himself as the heir apparent, even if no one else did. And it was also clear that he didn't care much at all for cadets that had made it this far to learn under West, even though he had once done the exact same thing. For the last week we'd been under Tovid's care. The master chief had lent us to him to help solve the starbase's problems with its Sequoia tree pick-and-plant program. As we stood on the bridge of the Starfleet barge with the lieutenant around the Operations table, it was obvious he wasn't happy.

"You four are wasting our time." Tovid's all-black Betazoid eyes had a habit of focusing squarely on me whenever he was displeased. He was about six foot one with chiseled features and smooth tanned skin that made him look like he had just come back from Risa. Completely black irises are a Betazoid trait that never bothered me, but with Tovid it was as if his dark eyes reflected what he was feeling deep within his soul. Being a Betazoid, he was also a natural telepath, and while being in Starfleet made it illegal for him to read the minds of others, it didn't prevent him from picking up surface thoughts and emotions. The lieutenant tilted his head as he looked at me and smiled as he stepped into my personal space. "Anything you want to say to me, Cadet?" he asked.

This time I smiled. "Not at all, please carry on, Lieutenant."

From the look on his face, I didn't need to be telepathic to read Tovid's mind when I used his rank.

The Betazoid Starfleet officer returned his attention back to the operations table. "The master chief thought you four could help solve our pick-and-plant problem, but you're just making it worse."

The sequoia reforestation program on Moser IV was probably the most important program on the planet. Starfleet engineers would dive to an area of the undersea sequoia forest designated for extraction, place an antigrav collar around the tree, use a special phaser to cut the tree down, and watch it float up to the surface, where the barge would lock onto it with a tractor beam and bring it aboard. The problem was that properties in the wood made it difficult to lock on with a tractor beam.

"We're almost there," Singh said. The cadet looked at everyone around the operations table. "The graviton attenuators we designed for the collars will work. Once we find the correct bandwidth, they will lock onto the gravitons in the tractor beam, establishing a lock."

Greth nodded eagerly. "Yeah, all we need is a little more time to find the right wavelength."

Tovid looked upset by the positivity around the table. "Well, time is something we don't have, we're burning daylight, and we're already behind schedule."

Gonzalez smiled, and I could tell she was doing her best to mask her real emotions in front of our Betazoid lieutenant. "Then just leave a shuttle up here with its tractor beam on while we go down and work on the attenuator problem. The barge can go to the other reforestation locations and this way we don't waste time. Everyone wins," she said.

Tovid stared at Gonzalez for a moment, and then returned the fake smile. "Great idea, but there's no need for all of you to go. I'm sending Sisko. He's the team leader, so we'll let Captain Dunsel lead."

✦

Since the first moment he laid eyes on me, Lieutenant Tovid rarely missed an opportunity to try to make me miserable. It was just one of those relationships where I rubbed him the wrong way. With him being a superior officer there was only so much that I could do. He thought sending me down alone would be a punishment, but the truth was that I loved diving. There was a world of awe and splendor in the ocean of Moser IV. The trees of the undersea sequoia forest swayed not from wind, but the ocean currents. Schools of luminescent fish playfully darted in and out of the crown of leaves, while larger whale sized lifeforms swam by unaware or unconcerned of my presence.

Thankfully, my Starfleet rebreather mask and wetsuit took care of my oxygen, temperature, and pressure needs, which allowed me to concentrate on my job. I swam down two hundred feet to a patch of the forest we sectioned off for reforestation. I wrapped an antigrav collar around a younger tree about eighty feet high and then went down to its base and began cutting the trunk with my phaser. After about thirty minutes, I finally cut through, and the tree began to list. I pulled out my tricorder, activated the antigrav collar, and watched it slowly ascend to the surface. With the tractor beam active on the shuttle above I began looking for the right frequency combination for the collar to lock onto the tractor beam. After about twenty minutes of searching for the right combination, my tricorder stopped reading the tractor beam.

The shuttle was gone.

I swam up to the surface. The log was hovering just above the ocean's waves, but both the barge and the shuttle were nowhere in sight. I tapped my combadge, but I didn't hear the familiar chirp. I tried again, but the same thing happened. Somehow my communicator was dead. "Sisko to shuttle, Sisko to Starbase 137. Is anyone reading me?"

There was no response, the sun was setting on the horizon, and I was twenty miles from the Starbase. I wasn't going to wait and hope the shuttle came back. There was really only one option.

I used the tricorder to locate the direction for the Starbase and began to swim.

✦

Nine hours later, in the dead of night, I crawled onto the dock. Some personnel nearby rushed over to me as I turned over onto my back and just lay there, exhausted. As I looked up a familiar blue head came into view. "Ben, we thought you were dead! We've been trying to reach you and looking for you for hours. Why did you leave the area you were assigned to work in?" Greth asked me.

I sat up and looked at my friend. "My communicator died. What do you mean, left the area I was working in?" It had been nagging at me the whole swim back to the Starbase, but now I was certain of it. "Where's Tovid?" I said as I got up.

Greth looked at me and he must've seen something in my face because he stepped back and away from me. "He's in the master chief's office helping him coordinate the search for you."

✦

When I walked into West's office, Tovid and the master chief were crowded over his operations table. Both men looked up, and the lieutenant rushed over to me. I didn't have any proof, and I never knew if I would, but as he approached me I saw all I needed on his face—sheer delight. That was when I realized he could feel my exhaustion, my frustration, my anger, and he was delighted. "Thank the sacred chalice, you're alive! We've been looking for you for—"

I hit him.

The look of shock on his face was so satisfying, I did it again, and again, and again. When West finally pulled me off Tovid I could hear myself shouting, "Did you feel that? How does that feel?" My hands, like the lieutenant's face and uniform, were bloodied, but through it all, he was smiling.

West shoved me in a chair, while Tovid was busy quoting academy regulations about conduct unbecoming of a cadet. The lieutenant spit out a mouthful of blood and then said, "You don't get to strike an officer and stay in the academy. Sisko, you're done!"

The master chief told Tovid to go wait for further instructions in his quarters. West's tone seemed to surprise the lieutenant and when he opened his mouth to say something, West beat him to it. "That's an order," he said flatly.

As I sat in the chair, West silently walked back behind his desk and sat down. He took a moment to look at me before he spoke. "He's right. Striking an officer is grounds for dismissal, Benjamin."

The space between us felt like an abyss. "He left me out there—probably tried to get me killed," I said.

West leaned back in his chair. "That's what you feel. Do you have any proof?"

I had thought it through on the long swim back to the starbase. It was very rare for combadges to go dead, but it did happen. And by now, I was almost certain the shuttle's logs would have shown it was at a different location than where I actually was. There was only one possibility left. I took out my tricorder, flipped it open, but the device had reset to its original settings. West chuckled. "The new OS went out last night. When you made it back to the Starbase, your tricorder picked up the new OS, and wiped the old data. Tovid thought of everything."

I looked up at my commanding officer and mentor. "You knew?" I asked.

West leaned forward, "I suspected. Tovid has a problem seeing anyone at the top that isn't him, but that just makes him a poor leader. Not a saboteur." West stood up, straightened his uniform and walked over to the ceiling-to-floor window that overlooked the city. From this vantage point in the spire, he had a complete view of Starbase 137. He stood there for a moment looking out at everything he had helped to build and maintain before he continued. "Once he learned I was going to ask you to stay on and ultimately take on a leadership role here, his demeanor grew worse."

I got up and walked over to West at the window. In the darkness, out on the ocean, Starbase 137 always felt a lot like it was floating in the depths of space. I looked out at the thousands of lights across the city. Each point of light was a person and place I knew. Somewhere along the way, somehow, this place had become my home away from Earth.

But there was still so much more out there.

I started to speak to West when he held up his hand, he could see what I was going to say to him was already on my face. "Don't bother, I get it, Mister Sisko. It was selfish of me to try to get to you before the stars did, but I see now I was probably about ten years too late anyway."

"What about Tovid? What I did?" I asked.

"Tovid set you up to fail. It looks to me like he either bet on you having an 'accident' out there, or that you'd be so upset he could make up a false narrative about an out-of-control temper. Unfortunately, Starfleet has more assholes in it than any of us care to admit." West turned away from the window and the lights and lives on 137. He faced me, and as he spoke, it was the first time I felt like I was listening to the man and not my commanding officer. "When I was starting out in Starfleet, someone helped me when I was in a tight spot, and Starbase 137 is my way of paying it forward. Find your way or your person to pay it forward, Mister Sisko, that's all I ask."

I extended my hand. "Thank you, I will. You have my word, Master Chief."

West took my hand. "You know, a lesser person would have said yes to my offer just to make sure they stayed in the academy. I respect that's not who you are. I'll take care of Tovid; he won't be a problem. But he won't be the last either. Starfleet is a wonderful institution, but it's not without those that come to it for selfish reasons. You're going to be a good engineer, but you can be an even better leader if you give yourself a chance."

As I shook the master chief's hand and thanked him, it hit me just how lucky I was. The pettiness and jealousy of one person had nearly destroyed my dream and career before it even started to take flight. It was in that moment that I began to realize what lengths some people would go to obtain what they believed they deserved.

CHAPTER THIRTEEN
PROTOCOL—2353

AT THE BEGINNING OF EVERY YEAR ALL CADETS have to go through an orientation session. So much can change in between semesters. New policies, procedures, and rules on campus and annex grounds. Sometimes sections are closed while new wings are opened, buildings go under renovation to accommodate a new member species entering the academy, changes in the overall curriculum need to be addressed. This meant every cadet, new and returning, had to attend the forty-five-minute orientation.

About fifty of us were sitting in one of the smaller lecture halls waiting for our orientation liaison when all the electronic equipment died. The lights, screens, and even the ventilation system stopped. Our personal PADDs and tricorders, everything just stopped working: without a window in the room, we were in complete darkness. Emotion swept through the chamber. I heard a scream from the lecture hall next door, which wasn't good. Someone shouted that the doors were locked, for a second the room was lit with the familiar blue hue of a transporter, and then three people close to the door were gone.

We were trapped in a box, and someone was beaming us out.

I could hear everyone shuffling about, and a few arguments started. I stayed in my seat and tried to assess the situation. There had been no announcement and no help, which meant what was happening was probably academy-wide and the administration was either unwilling or unable to help. The room lit up again, and now the students in the top row of the hall were gone.

I was roughly in the middle of the lecture hall and was about to make my way down towards the blackboard when someone trying to climb down from the row above kicked me in the back of the head. The blow was followed by a polite, and remarkably calm voice that I recognized. "Oh, I'm sorry, are you all right?" she said.

There was no mistaking my friend Susanna Leijten's voice. "I'm fine," I said. "I'm guessing you're not in the mood for a beam-out today?"

Suz feigned a chuckle but now I could hear the edges of stress in her voice. "Best case scenario this is the Crisis Protocol, worst case…" Her voice trailed off to a place I didn't want to consider either.

A little-known fact outside of the academy is that, since the early days, there has always been an exercise devised to force every level of cadet to work together, from freshman to senior. The exercise started back in the early 2150s when Starfleet Academy was still the Space Academy. It was the year after the Xindi Incident, when members of the Xindi species sent a prototype sphere weapon to Earth as a test for a full-scale weapon. The sphere carved a swathe with its particle beam from Venezuela to Florida, killing over seven million. After that, Starfleet created the annual exercise and dubbed it the Xindi Protocol. Several years later the name was declared derogatory towards the Xindi species and became simply the Crisis Protocol.

The idea of Crisis Protocol is that it could happen without warning at any time to the entire student body. When you realized it was happening there were only two rules: no names and no rank. Most intelligent species live in a structured society, which usually means a hierarchy. And as much as Starfleet Command holds true to the chain of command, it recognizes that sometimes the best ideas don't come from the top.

I searched in the darkness, found Susanna's hand and reminded myself not to use her name. "Should be easier to get down to the front of the class together," I said. She squeezed my hand in response. As we both started feeling for the row below us, the row of students closest to the blackboard were beamed out.

We were being penned in from the front and back now, with no way out.

"That's not good," Suz whispered.

The room broke out into a full panic. People started moving in every direction for whatever reason their personal logic dictated. I realized that, because I hadn't been on Earth in a year, I only recognized a few voices in the room. Most were probably new cadets, which explained the panic. I was just lucky Susanna had hit me in the head, or we wouldn't have found each other. As people moved to the sides of the room, the beam outs lost their orderliness and began picking off cadets individually. The one thing that we took for granted every day was now being used against us and taking us out. "Deactivate your combadges. They're using them to lock on!" I shouted to the room as I double-tapped my communicator, deactivating it. Someone in the chamber disagreed and said it was Starfleet trying to rescue us. More arguments broke out, someone started crying. Another voice, this one a strong male voice from somewhere near the top of the hall stairs, agreed with me: "He's right, we've got to deactivate our badges!" Throughout the room, there were a few deactivation chirps from badges, but not nearly enough.

I could hear somebody climbing up from the row beneath us with purpose, almost like they could see. The individual climbed up and stood right in front of me, putting a hand on my shoulder. "It's a rotating EM pulse on a high-frequency band. It's blanketing everywhere. Give me your tricorder, I think I can find it!"

This voice came from a young man: I could make out his outline from the wisps of light coming from the other cadets being beamed out. He was shorter than me, and there was something odd about his face. How did he know I had a tricorder? Where was he getting his information from? I had a million questions for him, but time and my curiosity were luxuries none of us could afford. The random beam-outs seemed to be getting closer to us in the center of the hall. As the transports increased, there were enough slivers of blue light to see Susanna's soft features and short hair. We weren't supposed to use names, but we shared a knowing smile when our eyes met. I could see we were on the same page. "If that's true, I know someplace it's not blanketing," Suz said.

"Wherever the beaming is coming from," I added as I offered my tricorder to the darkness, and the young man took it without any effort. From the intermittent light of the beam-outs, I could see now there weren't many of us left in the lecture hall, maybe twenty, divided into a few groups.

There wasn't much time.

"Can you configure the tricorder to emit its own EM pulse?" I asked. "Let's send back a message."

The young man removed something from his face and connected it to the tricorder, which lit up faintly. "I'm on it. Luckily, this technology is compatible, and EM pulses don't work well on bio-electric energy."

In the low light from the tricorder the young man looked like he was working by touch alone, as if he were blind. Which gave me an idea. I took off my combadge and began to work inside the device. Unlike industrial or commercial communicators, the devices used by Starfleet are designed to be adaptable within emergency situations. This meant that badges could be reconfigured by making a few changes to internal switches on its circuit board. We'd been taught how to do this by touch, but I never thought I'd be doing it on academy grounds. "I'm reconfiguring my badge for distress, that should get someone's attention!"

Suz followed suit and opened her combadge casing to fiddle inside. "I'm reconfiguring the communicator chassis to emit a wide range mayday on the Starfleet subspace channel once it's outside the EM pulse. Between the two of us, someone will figure it out!"

The young man disconnected the device from the tricorder and placed it back over his eyes. "Okay, we're good to go. Tricorder has a two-minute charge. Your badge signals will go out, then the EM pulse, until the tricorder gets shut down, destroyed, or runs out of power. Give me the badges and stand clear!"

I reactivated the supercapacitor kinetic cell in my combadge right before I turned it over to my new friend. Suz did the same and then the three of us quickly moved away from the jury-rigged tricorder with our combadges attached, just in time to watch the efforts of our makeshift plan disappear in a transporter beam.

Then we waited.

The three of us held hands in the darkness for what seemed like an eternity. After a few minutes, the hall lights and screens flickered back to life. I looked around the room, and there were more of us than I thought. But I noticed that everyone that was still in the room wasn't wearing a communicator. An announcement over the PA system told us that this had indeed been a Crisis Protocol exercise and assessments would be delivered later.

I looked at the two faces smiling back at me, one old friend and one new. I held out my hand to the young cadet that had just started his first year. I was happy he'd found us during this exercise. "I'm Benjamin Sisko, welcome to the academy," I said to the young man.

As we shook hands, Susanna slapped the newbie on the shoulder. "Susanna Leijten. Just call me Suz—and don't worry! Every day won't be as boring as today," she said with a wry smile.

The young man's laugh was immediately infectious. "If that was boring then I'm definitely in the right place! I'm Geordi La Forge. You two were the only ones moving with purpose, and you had a tricorder, made you easy to see. That saved us," he said.

It was clear now that Geordi was wearing a VISOR. I'd seen a few before, but nothing as sophisticated as his. "No, Geordi, you saved us." I said as I put a hand on his shoulder.

Suz was shaking her head with a knowing smile, "You're both wrong," she said. "We saved each other. Teamwork. That's what Starfleet does!"

✦

Being here, Jake, in the Celestial Temple, I've been thinking a lot about that day. It's never easy to trust someone or something you don't know. Part of the appeal of Starfleet when I was a kid was always hearing it was a place of trust and goodwill. An institution within which you would be safe to explore not just the stars but to pursue your dreams. And to everyone on the outside, the Federation and Starfleet have always been institutions of refuge and known as places those in need can seek help and kindness.

I think you can see, Jake, from some of the stories I've told you, the reality is often different from the brochure. But my experiences at Starbase 137 and this one reminded me that, for most of the people wearing this uniform, we believed in the same ideals and principles, and they could be trusted.

That's what I want for you.

No, this isn't the old man trying to convince you to join Starfleet again. That's not the path you chose, and I respect that. Actually, thinking about it, in many ways, you chose a harder path. Instead of joining an institution over two hundred years old with an infrastructure and powerbase that reaches throughout the quadrant, you opted to forge your own career. But I still want you to share that with people who believe in the same things you do. I know you love writing, Jake, and reading your work, it's been clear to me for some time that you're not just good, but have a gift for it. But being a writer can be terribly solitary, even isolating, and there's a strength that comes from being a part of something larger than yourself. It helps you to see different perspectives—everything you're going to need for that novel that I know will be the first of many. Maybe it will be working for the Federation News Service, maybe someplace else. What's important is that you keep yourself open to new ideas, new experiences, and new relationships.

When it's right, you'll know.

CHAPTER FOURTEEN

HOME—2354

IT WAS THE MORNING OF MY _KOBAYASHI MARU_ TEST, and I felt like it wasn't just four years that culminated in this day, but every day since I was that little kid lying in stasis in the hospital putting model starships together.

Today meant everything.

It's hard to get used to sonic showers when you've bathed your entire childhood with water. The sonic showers are supposed to have a frequency that not only cleans but relaxes, but after thirty minutes, I felt neither clean nor relaxed.

I was too nervous to feel anything. Except nervous.

When I got out of the shower, my desktop PADD had an active alert, and my combadge was chirping. Both were telling me that someone from off campus was trying to get in touch with me. I got dressed quickly and was about to tap my badge when my doorbell chimed.

My stomach tightened.

I pressed the control for the door and it slid open to reveal Admiral Paris. Judith was standing next to him, staring at the floor, and it took her a long time before she looked up at me. When she finally did, I could see that her eyes were red and filled with tears.

"Mom's gone," she whispered.

✦

Judith and I watched our father working in the kitchen like it was just another day. Nathan clearly shared our concerns, but was not saying anything. "How long has he been like this?" I asked.

Judith said, "Right after the doctor left, I heard him crying upstairs. Then he came down here and started cooking, said he was going to open tonight."

JJ's voice sounded tired, and weak. I looked at my little sister and realized that, now our mother was gone, she was the only woman left in the Sisko house. I also understood why my father wasn't just grieving, and in shock, but why he was upset. I'd read the doctor's report. Mama had had a stroke, something that was rare and not usually fatal today. But even though Mama lived in the twenty-fourth century she still ate like it was the twenty-first. I instinctively knew my father was having a terrible time trying to reconcile that something he loved may have been responsible for the death of someone he loved. His entire adult life, cooking was the only thing he'd ever done, the only profession he'd ever known.

At the time, I couldn't imagine losing someone I loved because of my profession. All I knew was that my dad was hurting, and I wanted to help.

I walked into the kitchen and put an apron on over my cadet uniform. "Where do you want me, Chef?" I asked.

I could see a moment of hesitation and sadness in my father's face and then something shifted and he gave me a faint smile. "Those clams aren't going to clean themselves, son."

✦

Being in my old room felt strange. I recognized everything. Mister Bayou was looking worse than I remembered, but it felt like he had belonged to someone else. And he did because I was different. In this room, dreams had been put into action, but now I was on the other side of them. For four years, I'd been living my dreams and turning them into a life, but now all of that was coming to an end.

Somehow, it felt fitting that those dreams should die here.

JJ came into my room, and sat on my bed. "What the hell are you doing?"

I chuckled. "What happened to the rule of knocking first? That's just out the window now?" I asked.

Judith just stared at me.

She wasn't playing my game, so I got serious. "It's already a done deal, JJ. The academy said I could delay my final test for up to a year, but that will only make things harder. I pick up my stuff tomorrow. Best to have a clean cut now and be done with it."

"You don't have to do this, Ben," she replied.

There was a sadness and exhaustion in my sister's voice that was all too familiar, but it was almost too much for me to bear. "I'm the oldest, JJ. It's my responsibility. You guys are on the cusp of so many exciting things, you deserve every opportunity. Nathan and I will help Dad with the restaurant."

Judith waved her hand dismissively. "I've got more than enough gigs right here at home, David was staying anyway, and, well, Elias may not be able to apprentice with those Vulcans in Dubai this year, but you know what? He'll get over it. They already told him they'll take him next year." She got up and walked over to my bookshelf. The exhaustion in her voice shifted to anger. "But hey, you're prepared to fall on your sword, or put a phaser to your head, or do whatever they teach you about self-sacrifice in Starfleet, so I'm sure you'll do it." She went over to Mister Bayou and pulled out a small package in gift wrapping that I hadn't noticed behind him, and held it out to me. "The day before Mama…died, she gave me this and told me to give it to you."

If Judith knew what was in the package, her eyes didn't reveal it. She gave me a kiss on the cheek and left the room, closing the door behind her as she left. I stared at the small package in my hands: my last gift and message from my mother. It was no bigger than my own palm, which made it even more difficult to guess what was inside. I sat at my desk and placed the package in front of me. The wrapping paper was midnight blue with silver stars and gold crescent moons. This was my favorite wrapping paper: over the years, whenever I would get presents from Mama, she would wrap the best ones in this paper. It was her way of telling me to save this one for last. As usual, every fold was neat, efficient, meticulous. My mother always seemed to put in almost as much care in the wrapping of her gifts as she did selecting them.

Slowly, cautiously, I began to unwrap it, taking care not to tear the wrapping paper as I did so. As I peeled away the paper, more of what was inside began to reveal itself to me, I realized I recognized what was inside.

"Maya Angel," I whispered.

Life Doesn't Frighten Me And Other Poems by Maya Angelou. The small book from my childhood was now old and weathered from time and use. I'd forgotten all about it, left it as a fond memory on a shelf somewhere in my past. But now, Mama had made sure it had found me again. I opened the small book to reread my favorite poem, and right above the title on the first page was Mama's handwriting, a final message placed where she made sure I'd understand.

Do big things, Ben.

I read those words and realized I was returning to Starfleet Academy.

✦

"Report!" I screamed.

The starship bridge we were on looked real, but everyone knew it wasn't. The holoprojections had gotten so good, and since I had entered last, the only thing in the room I was sure was real was me. Of course, that didn't change my reactions or the stress I was feeling.

Laporin didn't bother masking the astonishment in his voice. "The prefix code worked! We have control of the *Kobayashi Maru*, Captain. She's heading into transport range! Shields holding at sixty-five percent."

I wanted to smile but knew better. We'd taken out one Klingon Bird of Prey, but had two more to worry about and a long way to go before we were out of hot water. "Prepare to extend shields when they're close enough and we'll beam—"

Laporin interrupted: "Two more Birds of Prey decloaking aft, we're boxed in. They're firing!"

The conn station Laporin was sitting at exploded, blowing off half of his face. I watched different variations of the same theme play out around the bridge. Susanna, Charlie, Solok, and Cal, all dead. On the main viewscreen, the warbirds continued to fire, rocking the ship with each barrage.

I tapped a panel on my command chair, opening shipwide communications. "Activate escape pods. Send out the log buoy. All hands abandon ship. Repeat… all hands abandon ship."

A familiar voice called out over the ship's comm system: "All right, open her up."

As I suspected, everything in the holodeck disappeared except for the command chair. A pair of massive doors slid open in front of me and Admiral Paris walked in. "I've seen a lot of these, son, but no one has ever lasted six, seven, and certainly not eight-and-a-half minutes trying to beat the *Kobayashi Maru*. Congratulations, Mister Sisko."

Damn. I thought about the admiral's words. First off, I was so engaged in the moment I had no real idea how much time was passing. Secondly, every cadet at the academy knew *Kobayashi Maru* wasn't about winning, and yet they all still tried.

Everyone wanted to be Kirk, to be better than Kirk.

I have to admit I'd thought like that too, but after the events of the last few weeks at home and Mama's message, it just seemed like doing the same thing over and over and expecting a different result was either the textbook definition of insanity or an incredible act of hubris.

"Thank you, Admiral, but respectfully, sir, I wasn't trying to beat the *Kobayashi Maru*. I understand and accept some situations are wildly disproportionate. But if you don't give up, if you stay in the fight for as long as you can regardless of the odds, sometimes big things can happen."

CHAPTER FIFTEEN

FIRST SIGHT—2354

GEORGE MCCRAY'S CRATER PARTIES WERE KNOWN throughout the quadrant. The idea was simple: find a moon orbiting a popular planet or a planet everyone had easy access to, preferably without an atmosphere and low gravity, scan the craters on that moon to find one that is geologically sound, set up a forcefield, add a life support system, and you're all set. You can beam in a bar and everything else you need. The coordinates are by invite only, then six hours later George pulls the plug, and the elite party turns back into a crater.

It wasn't an original idea. Tycho City on Luna was created inside the Tycho crater. That engineering masterpiece took six years to create and had a permanent dome. Crater parties were a simpler version akin to the pop-up nightclubs in Earth's distant past.

Now that George ran the hair salon and barbershop at Starfleet Academy, he couldn't hop around the quadrant, so the parties stayed local to the Sol system and a lot of the younger side of Starfleet found its way in. The first party I went to was on Luna. Somehow George actually had gotten Starfleet's approval—they picked a small out-of-the-way crater on the far side of Earth's moon about the size of an old sports arena. I went along with George and offered my engineering skills, designing and building the forcefield for the party. Of course, that meant I had to go in and set it up first, but I didn't mind.

George had become a good friend and now that I had graduated and was awaiting my first assignment, I knew times like this might not come again. After setting up and stabilizing the field, I used atmospheric canisters to pump in an oxygen-rich atmosphere.

After that, George and his crew started beaming in, then we built a stage, dance area and set up the sound system. In no time at all, I was standing on the stage above the dance floor, watching blue transporter beam-ins all across the temporary club. Pretty soon the place was packed. With the music and the low gravity, the party was a huge hit. Some people had grav boots on and were dancing on the lunar surface while others were flipping and somersaulting in rhythm to the beat. George transformed into another person as a DJ, with headphones on and plugged into four turntables. The technique of mixing music back and forth between expected and unexpected rhythms and sounds to create unique dance music hadn't changed much since it was created on Earth in the Bronx four centuries ago, but George utilized music from the entire Federation. Vulcan ballads mixed with Andorian rap, mixed with Tellarite funk, mixed with Klingon opera mixed with human hip hop. Just like the Federation, on the face of it—it all seemed too different to work, but somehow those differences made it all sound great together.

When I made my deal with George to teach him to cook, and in return he would give me access to these parties, I thought it was a good deal, but I didn't consider I would be nurse-maiding a forcefield the entire time while everyone else had fun. Calibrating field harmonics every fifteen minutes, making sure the oxygen and CO_2 levels stayed safe, and maintaining power levels for the forcefield, sound system, lighting and replicator really wasn't how I wanted to spend my time at a party.

And then I saw her.

She leapt above the crowd, letting the low gravity take her in slow motion. Her one-piece off-the-shoulder cobalt blue bodysuit accentuated her caramel complexion. Like an angel in flight, she did a somersault and came down laughing between a group of people dancing.

I couldn't take my eyes off her.

The rest of the night I tried my best to keep track of this amazing woman through the masses of dancing flesh. I kept losing sight of her, but towards the end of the night, I was performing a check on the forcefield when the angel in blue leapt onto the stage. She was beautiful from afar, but breathtaking up close. She smiled at me as she walked over and gave George a kiss on the cheek. "Great party. Thanks for the invite!" she yelled.

With his headset on George just smiled and nodded, keeping to the beat he was mixing. The blue angel turned and leapt off the stage, disappearing back into the crowd. I went over to George. "Who was that?" I yelled.

George looked at me blankly. "What?" he asked.

"Who... was... that?" This time I pointed back down to where she had jumped off the stage.

George laughed and yelled back. "Her name's Jennifer. If you're gonna talk to her, you better hurry up: she's getting ready to leave."

He was right. I'd been looking at her all night, I needed to go down and introduce myself. I searched the crowd for a few minutes for the now familiar cobalt blue bodysuit. I found her and was about to leap down when she disappeared in a transporter beam.

She was gone.

✦

I've never been one to sulk or mope around. As my father always says, there's no room for worry in the kitchen or in life! However, the day after George's party, that's exactly what I was doing. I just couldn't get that blue angel— Jennifer—off my mind. And now that I had graduated, I had nothing but time to kick myself and think about what might have been.

"It's a beautiful day, don't you think, Ben?" Giselle Mariano said as she slipped her arm around mine. The three of us were at Gilgo Beach—Giselle, Calvin Hudson, and me. Cal and Giselle were going to a volleyball game and dragged me along with them. Cal said if I was going to mope around, I might as well do it at the beach. I told him about the night before, and he just laughed at my sour mood.

As the three of us walked along the beach Cal faced me, stepping in front of Giselle. "Yeah, Ben, *beautiful* day!" he said.

I got the message. Giselle wasn't just beautiful; she was stunning. Emerald green eyes, a short crop of red hair, and an electric personality that made her stand out in every room she entered. We had tried to connect a few times at the academy, but Giselle was on the science track, and with me focusing on engineering we didn't move in the same circles academically or personally. Now that we'd graduated and everyone was awaiting orders, I'd been seeing a lot more of Giselle around. Cal said it was because she liked me, and I was starting to think he was right. If this had been just a week ago I probably would've been having a great time with Giselle and Cal. But it wasn't: after the night before, all I could think about was my missed opportunity. "I'm gonna go get us some lemonades," I said. "I'll be right back."

✦

Lemonades in hand, I came back to where I'd left Giselle and Cal, but they weren't there. I stopped, and started to scan the beach. Maybe they'd headed towards the volleyball game, so I cut across the sand—

"Hey!" cried the young woman lying on her stomach, sunbathing in a blue bikini on a blue blanket who I had just kicked sand onto in my haste.

"I'm sorry…" I stopped mid-sentence as I realized the woman sunbathing was my blue angel. "Jennifer?" I asked. I couldn't believe this was happening.

Jennifer turned over, holding her unbuttoned bikini top with one hand and taking her sunglasses off with the other. "I'm sorry, did we meet last night at George's party?"

I couldn't believe it the woman of my dreams. My blue angel from last night was here in front of me. "Do you realize how incredible this is?" I asked.

She got up, and walked off.

I put the drinks down and followed her. As I walked next to her in silence, she took a moment to look me over and I could see in her eyes she realized I wasn't crazy, or dangerous, just captivated. Eventually, she said, "So tell me the truth. Have we really met before?"

I thought about explaining how I first saw her, and the smile she gave me on the stage. "No," I said finally.

Jennifer looked at me, even more puzzled than a few minutes ago. "Then how do you know my name?"

"George told me, at the party." I said.

Jennifer looked at me expectantly. "Are you going to tell me your name?" she asked.

A few minutes ago I didn't think I would ever see her again and now she was asking me my name! "Ben Sisko. I just graduated from Starfleet Academy. I'm waiting for my first posting."

"Ah, of course. A junior officer waiting to go out on one of those fancy starships."

"Yeah," I said, and then it hit me. "You don't sound like you're in Starfleet. What do you do?"

She smiled. "Oh no. I've never wanted to join Starfleet. I'm a Federation oceanographer. Don't get me wrong, I admire what you do, but the ocean is the frontier I explore. We still have so much to learn, and with all the microplastics and hazardous materials from previous centuries, there's a lot of damage to clean up."

I had never felt like this before. I loved that she wasn't in Starfleet but just as passionate about exploration in a way I hadn't really thought of before. The more she spoke, the deeper I fell. "You're amazing," I said.

Jennifer looked me over again, but this time it felt different. "My mother warned me to watch out for junior officers."

"Your mother is going to adore me," I said.

"You're awfully sure of yourself."

"It's not every day you meet the girl you're going to marry," I said.

Jennifer stopped walking and laughed, but I could see something stirring in her eyes. Then she started walking again. "Do you use this routine a lot with women?"

"No. Never before and never again," I said.

Something was happening. I could feel it. She could feel it. A soft and gentle "Sure" was all she revealed as she started walking again.

I quickly stepped in front of her. "How about letting me cook dinner for you tonight? My father was a gourmet chef. I will make for you his famous aubergine stew," I offered.

Jenifer smiled, her face, flush. "I don't know," she said.

Without thinking, I got down on one knee in front of her and said, "You're supposed to say, yes!"

This time there was an intimacy in her voice: "I'll probably be sorry."

"There you are, Benjamin." There was a coldness in Giselle's voice I'd never heard before.

I looked over my shoulder to see Giselle and Cal walking up to us. Cal looked as shocked as Giselle. "Are you proposing?" he said, only half joking.

I stood up. "Jennifer, these are my friends, Giselle Mariano, and Cal Hudson." I could see Giselle wasn't particularly happy with the way I introduced her, or how close I was standing to Jennifer.

Jennifer shook Giselle's and Cal's hands eagerly. "Jennifer Richardson," she said.

"We were about to go join the volleyball game. You should join us," Giselle offered.

Jennifer looked at Giselle for a moment, then smiled and said, "No thanks." Then she turned to me: "But I will take you up on your offer if you agree to go freediving with me tomorrow morning."

"You have a deal," I said.

✦

I was a few minutes into the dive, nine meters down, and I was in trouble.

For over an hour, Jen had gone over the freediving essentials for beginners. How to breathe before taking the last breath, the best way to break the water's surface, body position as you descend, how to kick the fins, and how to take a recovery breath when you resurface. I was holding onto the freediving line as I descended, which, in this case, went thirty meters down. Jen was on the other side of the line, watching my descent as she made her own.

My lungs felt like they were on fire, desperate for the precious air that I was purposefully denying them. As I moved deeper into the blackness of the ocean depths, I couldn't help but think back to that day so very long ago when Grandma Octavia pushed me into the lake to teach me to swim. Teaching me how to deal with the unexpected, providing me with the tools I would need one day to become the man she hoped I would be, and now the officer I wanted to be.

On that day I nearly drowned, kicking desperately to rise and break the surface of the water. Now, I focused on the training I had been given, and kicked in a steady, controlled rhythm to push deeper into the darkness. I checked the readout on my diving watch. I had descended another six meters, diving fifteen meters with fifteen to go. I tightened my focus and went another few meters, but I quickly realized even if I did make it to the bottom, I wouldn't be able to get myself back up to the surface.

It was time to turn around.

I signaled to Jennifer I was going back up, reversed myself, and quickly began my ascent. As I saw the surface, I fought the instinct to rush, and slowed down as my new freediving coach had trained me. When I broke the surface, I immediately started taking my recovery breaths, so I wouldn't pass out. Jen came up and did the same. As we floated together on the surface, closely facing each other, I waited for her to go through her recovery. I realized I had never felt like this before. Even when I was stuck out on the ocean swimming back to Starbase 137, I hadn't felt this alive, pushed myself this far. "That was intense. I'm looking forward to the next one!" I said as I began laughing.

Jen unzipped the small pouch strapped to her arm and took out a hypospray. She put the device to my neck, and I felt a slight tingle as something entered my bloodstream. "Special tri-ox compound for free divers. It will help you breathe better and recover faster," she said. After a moment of us floating together, she added, "On my first dive, I felt a lot like you do now. You're right. It is intense."

Then Jennifer kissed me.

I had just swam up from the deep blue sea, but I could feel myself falling into something deeper and more wonderful than I had ever experienced before in my life.

After the kiss, Jen smiled. "I've got to go home tomorrow. Want to come?" she asked.

✦

Home, I discovered, was Mars.

Jennifer's family line went all the way back to those first colonists that built the early domed cities. When I told her my Lafayette Hood story, she told me people in her family actually knew the man.

Jen's father, Darius Richardson, was a high school teacher. Tall and thin, he wore horn-rimmed glasses that made him look like he stepped out of an era long past. The glasses didn't take anything away from the intensity of his stare— they accentuated it. As he and I sat alone in his study before dinner, I could feel every ounce of his gaze on me. We'd been in the large room for a few hours but it was feeling smaller with every passing moment. We started off easy, talking sports and my wrestling credentials, but that didn't get me nearly as far as I hoped. Nor did my love of engineering. Mister Richardson was a cautious man that loved his daughter. He seemed adequately satisfied with my demeanor and responses. But as our conversation continued, I got the impression he thought I was a nice guy—he just wasn't sure if I was "the" guy for Jennifer.

"You come from a town with a lot of history, a lot of music, and a lot of emotion," he said. "How much of that history, music, and emotion is in you, Ben?"

"A lot, sir," I answered.

Mister Richardson let my answer hang between us for a few moments before he answered. "That's what worries me, son. New Orleans is the birthplace of jazz, and we all know it's a beautiful art form. But jazz, by its very definition, is about improvisation, making things up as you go. That's the environment you grew up in. That's not an environment for an oceanographer."

I understood his point of view, even if I didn't agree with it. The last thing I wanted to do was have a disagreement about where I grew up with Jen's father. "I'm also a Starfleet officer, sir," I said.

"A junior officer," he replied flatly. "There aren't many oceans on starships, young man, and Jen has never brought anyone else home before. So I'll ask plainly—what are your intentions?"

I knew how I felt, and I knew it was real. But I didn't think there were any words that I could say, or perhaps more adequately, words that he wanted to hear that would express my sincerity in a way he would accept.

So I showed him.

✦

Over dinner, we talked about water.

Athena Richardson, Jennifer's mother, was a Federation geologist who studied lake beds in the hopes of creating new lakes on Mars. She had grey eyes with sandy blond hair that was cut in a similar hairstyle as her daughter. "Ever since she finished school, I've been trying to lure my daughter back to Mars so we can work together," she said. "But since she was five, she has been in love with Earth's oceans. Do you think you can compete with that, Ben?" she asked.

"Oh no, ma'am, not at all," I said. "Yesterday, Jennifer showed me how to free dive. I didn't get as far as I wanted, but I loved it, and can't wait to go again. I've never met anyone who talks about Earth's oceans the way most people I know talk about space. Honestly, I love that."

Jennifer's mother laughed. "You're adorable," she said.

I looked at Jen, beaming. She just rolled her eyes as she smiled back at me.

✦

The pitcher for the Phoenix Phasers threw a ninety-mile-an-hour fastball and struck out the New Orleans Cajun Comet. As the inning changed and the players switched, I leaned forward and looked down the row of stadium seats. Jennifer was sandwiched between two Siskos—my father and Judith. "Are you even watching the game?" I teased.

Jennifer was laughing about something with Judith, and then for some reason, broke off half of the hot dog she was holding and gave it to my father. Almost as an afterthought, she leaned forward and looked down the row toward me. "You watch the game your way, and we'll watch the game ours!" she teased back.

Seeing Judith next to Jennifer made me realize just how quickly my little sister was growing up. And beyond that, Judith's musical career was taking flight. Watching my nineteen-year-old "little" sister sing to a sold-out crowd was something I was not used to. But it was clear this was only the beginning for JJ. She was getting requests to sing around the world and even a few offers from Luna and Mars.

Watching Jennifer with everyone was more than I could have dreamed for. My girlfriend fit right in. My family had always been accepting—they'd loved Zoey and Tryla—but with Jennifer, it was like they welcomed her into their hearts because they saw I had already let her completely into mine.

"She's wonderful," David said.

My little brother was sitting next to me, but Elias was a no-show, yet again. It was different talking to him and Judith after Mama passed. Now, both of them truly felt older beyond their years. "Thanks," I said. Down on

THE AUTOBIOGRAPHY OF BENJAMIN SISKO

the field, the first Phoenix Phaser of the inning was at bat, already with a 3–1 count. "Hey, you're the closing pitcher. Shouldn't you be like, you know, down there?" I asked.

David laughed. "Dad asked me the same thing. Relax, big bro. It's baseball, not Starfleet. We're up three to one. The Comets are doing just fine without me. Besides, we're only in the fourth. I've got plenty of time to go down and get my arm loose."

At eighteen, David had as much muscle on him as I did, probably more. Whenever I saw him, he made me aware of just how out of shape I really was. I watched him do things on the baseball field and Parrises Squares court I didn't think possible. His fastball was usually clocked at around ninety-two, ninety-seven on a good day. With all this athleticism, he was so different from Elias. Even though they were twins, physically it was easy to tell them apart, but otherwise, they thought nearly exactly alike, which worried me. "I've been trying to reach out to Elias, but he won't return my calls, and he's never home when I'm around."

The count for the Phoenix Phaser at bat was now 3–2. David chuckled and I knew it wasn't about the game. "Yeah, he's not gonna respond to you, Ben, at least not for a long while," he said.

The Cajun Comet pitcher threw a wild pitch, hitting the Phoenix Phaser player, giving him an automatic walk to first base. David cursed and then turned his attention back to our conversation, sensing my puzzlement. "Yeah, when Mom died, and you decided to go back to Starfleet Academy, he just never let it go. You're the oldest. He still thinks you should've stayed and helped Dad, helped us figure everything out."

David's words brought all the old feelings back, the indecision, the guilt. Only Judith knew about Mama's message. I never told him and Elias. "I just did what I thought Mama would've wanted," I said.

I could see the regret on David's face. "Hey, I get it. I don't feel that way, Ben, and I don't blame you."

"That means everything to me, Dave, and don't get me wrong, but you and Elias are so much alike. He does. Why don't you?" I asked.

The next Phoenix Phaser was up, we stopped and watched to see what he had. Right away, his first two swings were strikes. David laughed, then continued. "I don't know, maybe it's because I play baseball, and I see how much it's like life. Starfleet is your up at bat. What are you gonna do? Step away from the plate? Nah, that wouldn't be right. Mom wouldn't want you to do that."

I looked at my little brother, at this young man sitting next to me, and I was amazed at his words of wisdom. "Damn, David, now I'm gonna have to watch all your games."

David smiled. "We're recording them for holodecks now, I'll—"

There was a crack of the bat on the field, and the baseball went deep into the outfield and over the wall, tying the score.

"Shit," David said.

✦

"What's in the backpack?" Jen asked.

In the afternoon sun, we sat on the edge of our skiff, letting our fins dangle just above the surface of the clearest waters I'd ever seen. We were just outside the town of Dahab on the coast of the Red Sea in South Sinai, Egypt.

I reached into the hard-shell backpack and pulled out a hypospray and a small automatic buoy—a triangular orange device about the size of a small melon. "Emergency tri-ox and our buoy," I said as I dropped the hypospray back in the pack, closed it up, and slipped my arms into the straps and on my back. I activated the automatic buoy, placing it on the surface of the water next to our skiff. The buoy shot a cable down to the ocean floor, and once it was secured, the faces of the pyramid read the depth of the line—ninety-two meters. Finally, I zipped up my wetsuit. "Ready?" I asked.

Jennifer looked at the buoy. "Are you sure, Benjamin? You've never dived that deep before." Her concern was thick in her voice.

I smiled. "I just did seventy-five a few days ago, plus we have the emergency tri-ox." In just the three weeks we'd been together, Jennifer had changed me. Because of her, I saw the world and myself differently. For most of my life, my dream had been to join Starfleet, but in a lot of ways, that had been the dream of a child. Now that it had been accomplished and I was with Jennifer, I wanted more, and she showed me I could have it.

"Yes, sir!" Jen giggled as she saluted me and dropped into the water.

I followed her in and tapped the buoy, which activated the cable illumination, lighting our path to the ocean floor. We took some breaths to open up our lungs and then our last breath before we dove into the unknown.

Together.

Like space, the ocean is a silent frontier with beauty and wonders unmatched in the galaxy. The water was so clear and with our cable illuminated we could see nearly to the bottom. Unexpectedly, it seemed the light attracted some attention. A pair of dolphins wanted to play with us, circling several times, but when we continued to dive and didn't pay them any attention, they moved on. At about twenty meters, we moved through a school of fish which felt like we were trying to navigate through a tornado of beautiful slivers of orange, blue and green swirling all around us.

When we got to fifty meters I heard them, and to my surprise, felt them, before I saw them. What no one tells you, is how the vibrations pass through you when they sing.

Whale song.

Jen and I stopped and shared the moment with a pod of six majestic humpback whales. The whales were in a vertical position, spaced out around the cable as if it were a campfire, providing the only illumination in their dark forest. One after the other, the whales sang, and while the meaning of their song eluded me, its vibrations and emotion touched me deeply.

We continued our descent, and as we approached the ocean floor my lungs were telling me I had little time left, certainly not enough time to return to the surface, but I already knew this. Jen motioned that we needed to start our ascent, but I held my hand up in the universal symbol, asking to give me a second. As quick as I could, I slipped the backpack off and pulled out the small forcefield generator I'd spent the last three weeks constructing. I quickly looked around and made sure no marine life was around us, and then activated the field. The generator quickly created a bubble with a one-foot radius in the water. Then, slowly, the forcefield began to expand until it was a six-foot sphere, holding the water outside of its perimeter. I reached into the backpack and pulled out a mini O_2 canister, releasing its contents and filling the space with breathable oxygen.

I exhaled and then breathed in the precious oxygen my lungs were craving. Jennifer did the same, clearly thoroughly confused. "Ben, what is this? What are you doing?" she asked.

I got down on one knee and took out the ring box that I'd showed her father a little under three weeks ago, when I asked for his blessing to marry his daughter. I faced it toward Jen and opened it. "Both of our worlds are about exploration into the unknown, so I wanted to do this in your world. Jennifer Williams Richardson, will you marry me and explore the unknown with me, forever?" I asked.

Jennifer was in tears as she looked at the ring.

"Also, I should add that we only have five minutes of power and air."

"Yes!" she screamed with excitement, as she put her hand out, and I placed the ring on her finger.

I stood up to give her a kiss. But I could hear someone screaming, just outside the forcefield.

Wait.

That's not right, Jake, that's not how it happened. I never heard screaming. Wait, the screaming, is it here with me now, or was it then?

Is it both?

It doesn't really matter does it? Someone is, or was, screaming in pain and I'm a Starfleet officer, so I took a deep breath and stepped through the forcefield.

Benjamin Sisko stepped into an ocean of memories.

Images, vistas, and people flowed and flashed around the Starfleet captain faster than the eye could follow. The steady and persistent rhythm of a heartbeat began to grow louder, and with it screaming.

Sisko cried out. "Hello? Where are you? I'm here to help. Hello?"

The screaming persisted, but the sea of memories that swirled all around the captain began to divide and part, creating a path. Ben could hear the screams coming from the end of the corridor. He began to run down the long passageway. As he ran, fluid memories ebbed and flowed along both sides of the path, like waves of a life lived and yet to live.

Sisko looking up at his much taller son. "Look at you. You're older than I am."

Now a young man, Jake Sisko talking to his father inside the Bajoran lightship Benjamin Sisko constructed. "What I mean is, yesterday I got a communication from the Pennington School in New Zealand, and they offered me a writing fellowship."

Jake Sisko, still a boy, sitting on a couch in their quarters. "Starfleet is too much like you. I need to find what's me. Does that make any sense?"

The sound of the heartbeat was all around him now, permeating through him. Sisko reached the end of the hall, and stepped into the memory that was screaming out to him.

Benjamin Sisko watched himself as he held the hand of his wife, Jennifer Sisko, in the hospital room. He stood in the back of the delivery room, and out of the way. Like being on a holodeck, Sisko was able to watch himself like never before.

Jennifer screamed. Her husband held her hand as she squeezed it. "You're doing great, Jen, he's almost here. One last push!"

Sarah appeared next to Benjamin in the back of the room as he watched. Ben turned to his mother. "Sarah, why did you bring me here?" he asked.

Sisko's mother turned to her son, confused. "Emissary, we do not bring you here. You bring us here. You exist here."

After a moment of thought, Sisko smiled. "I didn't know I could, but it makes sense. I think about this moment a lot. One minute I was a husband very much in love, and the next I was a father, with a family. Starfleet, my career, none of it was as important as them and yet they gave me a strength and focus that made everything else in my life better, all because of this moment," he said.

Sarah looked at Benjamin with eyes of uncertainty. "Focus, what is this?"

Ben's face softened at his mother's question. "It can be both an emotion and an expression of mental concentration. A way for humans to prioritize what is important from what isn't."

At that instant, the room filled with the sound of a baby crying. Jennifer Sisko cradled her newborn son in her arms as the Sisko-memory stood over his wife and child. Watching the moment, Sisko whispered to his mother, Sarah, feeling as if he were actually in the delivery room instead of his own memory. He said, "You may not understand this, but in a way, Jake is your grandson. Just like he's a part of me, you're a part of him too, and a part of our family."

Sarah turned to her son and smiled. "Linear procreation, the continuation of our family. You value your ignorance of what is to come. The Sisko will have many tasks."

CHAPTER SIXTEEN

DAX—2355-2362

WHEN THE ORDERS FINALLY CAME IN, I learned I was being stationed on New Berlin on Luna. Jennifer was excited because it meant that she could still work as an oceanographer on Earth. We knew that the posting would be at least twenty-four months so we secured a house. Not long after, I was surprised to learn that Cal was stationed on New Berlin as well.

In those early days my primary responsibility was to provide my engineering skills on the maintenance team at the Luna power station, and when that wasn't needed I was often assigned as an attaché to escort dignitaries. As much as I knew these roles weren't challenging me to my fullest potential, I didn't mind. I was grateful that I was an officer in Starfleet. I knew I had time to build a career, and I was also a newlywed building a life. I saw this as an opportunity to spend time with my family and learn how to become a good husband and father.

Jake, I'm sure you don't remember this. But after you were born, your mom and I took six months of paternal leave. My favorite thing during that time was carrying you around. Of course we had a stroller, but every excuse I could find I put you in a baby harness and carried you around. I told your mom that she carried you for nine months, and I was going to carry you for at least six. I took you everywhere. We went on morning walks, your first warp flight—a short trip to Vulcan to watch your uncle play Parrises Squares.

And when you were about five months old I started to teach you to swim, slowly, in a pool. I wanted to pass on to you the gift that my Grandma Octavia gave to me, but not in the traumatic way she delivered it.

Your mother was exhausted after giving birth, so I took on your hectic nights while she slept, and as much of the days as I could too. I learned to change you, feed you, and bathe you, but I won't lie and say I learned on my own. More than a few times, I was on the phone with your grandfather, picking his brain and finding out what he did for me when I was your age.

Most importantly, New Berlin gave us the one thing we needed most—time. Time for Jen and I to grow into our marriage and bond with you. Time to create the nursery with the starscape you loved so much, time to have fun and go waterskiing together.

Time to be a family.

We only expected my orders to keep me on New Berlin for two years, but we were blessed that it lasted for five. One of the hardest things I've ever done was leave you and your mom, but I was a Starfleet officer, and we knew that meant going wherever I was sent. We decided to keep the house until we had a better idea of what my next post would be like. This would also allow Jennifer to maintain her position as a lead oceanographer for the Earth Oceans Organization and give you, Jake, the stability your mother and I wanted to provide you.

My new orders were to go to Pelios Station, pick up Ambassador Curzon Dax, and escort him to the *U.S.S. Livingston*, where we were both to be stationed. In some ways escorting an ambassador is one of the hardest jobs to do, which is why, according to Starfleet logic, it's given to young new ensigns. As an attaché you're supposed to keep your VIP on time and always moving forward, but you have no real power or influence over them.

When I arrived at Pelios I knew our shuttle to the *Livingston* left the next morning, so there was little time to get Ambassador Dax's affairs in order. I went straight to his office, and was looking forward to seeing him again.

The Trill.

On New Berlin, I had taken documents to Ambassador Dax, and on a few occasions, to save time, he had come by the house to pick up sensitive material I was holding for him. The man never just came in or stood still. He always walked through the place commenting on this or that. We once got into a conversation for two hours about the starscape I created in your bedroom, Jake. He was fascinated that I would take the time and effort to do that. "Not a lot of fathers would do that. I know, I've been one," he said.

Jennifer said he might be a renowned ambassador, but he was also a dirty old man and she didn't like the way he looked at her sometimes.

Now, when I came into his office he waved me in. He was on a call so I sat in one of the chairs assigned for visitors and waited. I was always fascinated how the spots on either side of Curzon's—and all Trill's—temples looked so much like tattoos. They said the strips ran down the length of a Trill's body on both sides. For Curzon, the spots framed his face nicely and accentuated whatever mood he was in. While I waited, I tried to make the best use of time, so I pulled out my PADD and began to create a list of all the items in Dax's office. As I walked around itemizing everything, Curzon watched me while he talked. Before he got off one call, another would come in for him. He spent the entire morning and afternoon that way, leapfrogging from one call to the next. Finally, a personal call came in and he asked me if I could step outside. As I did, his voice softened as he began to speak to someone named Revella.

After two hours Curzon came out of his office, he looked at me perplexed. "My apologies, Ensign, I forgot you were here. Let's set something up for next week, we'll talk then," he said.

Next week?

"Ambassador, the shuttle leaves tomorrow morning at 0700. We have to be on it, sir," I said.

Curzon laughed, and pointed his index finger at me indicating he wanted me to follow him as he walked out of his office. "Ahh, ahhh…" he said, searching for my name.

"Sisko. Ben Sisko, Ambassador," I said.

"Right! Starscape!" he shouted.

We turned down the hall towards the Pelios Municipal building transporter station. I didn't like where this was going. As we got outside the control room, he stopped. "Listen, son, at my age orders are more like suggestions. The *Livingston* can wait for me a couple of weeks." He walked into the transporter room, and winked at the young female transporter chief as he stepped onto the pad. He reached into his pocket and tossed me a card. "My apartment key. I'll be in late tonight. Right now I have a pressing appointment with a young lady named Revella, and I don't intend to be late. Energize."

And just like that, he was gone.

✦

Eighteen hours later Curzon Dax walked into his apartment.

"What the hell is this?" Curzon said.

"This is your apartment, Ambassador," I replied.

"I know that, but where the hell are all my things?" he asked. The ambassador's voice reverberated off the walls, punctuating the emptiness of the room.

I was sitting in the only piece of furniture in the entire apartment, a very comfortable Klingon rocking chair. I'd been rocking for hours and saw no reason to stop because the ambassador had finally come in, but I did feel an obligation to answer his question. "By now, Ambassador, I'd say all of your possessions from here and your office are well on their way to the *Livingston*, as we should be."

Dax was angry. "I'm shocked, Starscape. Is this how you treat an old man?"

I laughed. "Ambassador, you're a lot of things, but you are not an old man."

Curzon's anger instantly disappeared. "This is true. Hey, did you know that Kang gave me that rocking chair? Nice, isn't it? You better get up out of it. We don't have much time," he said.

"Time for what?" I asked cautiously.

"We've got to charter a fast private ship, take my one remaining worldly possession with us, and see if we can get to the *Livingston* rendezvous in time. But you're carrying the chair," he said.

✦

On the *Livingston* I was less an engineer than Curzon Dax's personal assistant. Anytime Dax had a mission or needed to go anywhere, he requested Ensign Sisko accompany him. It got so bad that the skipper of the *Livingston* stopped giving me ship-bound duties and assigned me to the ambassador.

I stood next to Curzon when he was one of the first individuals to make Federation contact with the Tzenkethi. They towered above us, a species that exhibited reptilian features, almost like prehistoric dinosaurs in appearance, but with advanced armor for clothes. Afterward, over drinks, he asked me if I found them intimidating. "Are you serious, Old Man?" I asked. Ever since Pelios, the nickname stuck.

Curzon waved his hand, "Klingons, the Cardassians, and now the Tzenkethi. A lot of species are intimidating because most set out to be. But once you look past the posturing, strip away the layers, you start to see what's really behind the masks these species wear. Intimidation is just a tool they use: the real question is *why*," he said.

On another occasion, we went to Pressnes II to negotiate a contract for their dilithium sculptures. The Pressnians are the only people in the quadrant that use dilithium crystal for rare art and not as a power source. After a ten-minute conversation with the planet's foremost sculptor, Dax realized the woman was a fraud. In actuality, the children of the planet had an innate ability to sculpt anything. So he exposed their worldwide child labor ring.

Pressnes II was on the fast track to becoming a member of the Federation. When Curzon took his findings to an admiral, he was told the matter would be addressed once Pressnes became a Federation world. Somehow, the next day the information was leaked to the Federation News Network. The Pressnian government didn't want their membership petition dismissed. In the span of four days, changes were made. Heads rolled, people were indicted, and an independent UFP group was brought in to oversee the cleanup. That was when I started to understand that Starfleet and the Federation weren't the only paths that led to justice.

Being assigned to Curzon meant that I was around the ambassador nearly all the time. And that meant I've seen and heard many things I wish I hadn't. Curzon Dax had certain appetites that would put other men to shame. He would always party too much, drink too much, *Curzon* too much. It seemed like burning the candle at both ends at night was the only way the Trill could be an effective ambassador during the day.

During a visit to Qualor II to assist in repairs of their weather regulator systems, Curzon wanted to sample the nightlife. There were two things everyone knew about the planet. One: that it had a Federation ship depot in orbit. And two: that it was a place anyone could have a good time. With its neon lights, shops, restaurants, and entertainment centers, the planet had become a service industry catering to the needs of others, regardless of what those needs were.

While we were out and about, Curzon met a young Caitian woman. Caitians, for all intents and purposes, are feline humanoids. Physically, they're covered in fur, and they have short faces with whiskers, fangs, large eyes, slitted pupils, and long furry tails. Their personality was this interesting combination between what I was used to from both humanoids and felines.

This young Caitian woman had grey fur with black stripes running down her arms and legs. She also had a white patch of fur that ran from her chin to her belly, and she would purr every so often, which delighted Curzon no end. He said he wanted to take her back to his hotel to "learn more about her species." Whenever on assignment, Curzon always stayed planetside, instead of on the ship. He always said if you can't eat and sleep where the people you're visiting live, then why are you even there?

When I was a kid in New Orleans, you could always tell the tourists because they'd be walking around with a PADD reading *Ward's Guide to New Orleans*; it was cute. Now here I was at two in the morning with a PADD reading *Ward's Guide to Qualor II*, with a blinking red alert telling me we were in an area known to have a high crime rate. Normally we'd just beam up to the *Livingston* and then beam back down to the hotel, easy. But there was no way we could beam up with Curzon's "guest" without a multitude of explanations. So there I was, looking for the closest public transporter. I was walking slightly ahead of Curzon and his date when a Caitian man with orange fur and a vicious sneer stepped out about five feet in front of me. At the same time as two more Caitians appeared behind us, they had gray fur with black stripes. All of the men had their claws out—something which, until that moment, I didn't realize Caitians had. The male in front of me hissed, "Give us the PADD, your combadges, and tricorder, and no one will be hurt." The items he was asking for were more than worth their weight in latinum and they knew it.

I backed up until I was standing next to Curzon and his companion. Dax shot a quick glance in my direction. He was clearly shocked. He'd been so concerned about getting back to the hotel he realized he had been caught totally off guard, and that perhaps his companion wasn't whom she appeared to be.

I slowly took my combadge off.

Curzon whispered. "What the hell, kid?"

"I know what I'm doing, Old Man." I said as I tapped the combadge.

"*Livingston*, emergency transport, two to beam up!" I quickly turned and slapped my combadge on the Caitian woman. Curzon's face was a mixture of both surprise and horror as he disappeared into the familiar blue stream. I didn't know if the young woman I just beamed up was a participant or victim, but I knew ensuring her safety was the right thing to do.

"You didn't do anything," one of the men behind me said. "You're carrying all the stuff we want anyway."

I raised the PADD as if in surrender and closed the distance between myself and the Caitian in front of me. I held out the PADD for him to take and grinned. "No problem, I was just getting them out of the way. Here you go," I said.

The Caitian reached for the PADD, taking a step forward, and his weight shifted slightly to his back leg. Without any hesitation, I took his extended hand and pulled him forward and off balance. At the same time, I swept out the leg he was stepping forward with. The pull and push caught him totally off guard, and as he fell backward uncontrollably, his knee made an ugly popping sound.

I screamed as I felt claws tear through my uniform and rake across my back. I wondered how one of the two humanoids had closed the distance so quickly, and then it hit me.

Speed, agility: there was no mistaking they were felines, and they meant business.

Working on pure instinct, I spun around and quickly hooked my right hand behind the Caitian's left shoulder, pulling him towards me as I leaned back and pushed my left hand into the same shoulder. He wasn't ready for the shift in momentum, and as we started falling together, I slipped out from under him and was on top of him by the time he hit the ground. The feline was protesting with a hiss when I knocked him unconscious. I looked up just in time to see the third Caitian in midair, claws and fangs eager to sink deep into my flesh.

And then the world took on a familiar hue of blue.

✦

I was promoted to a full lieutenant for my actions that night, protecting the ambassador and the civilian that was with us. The Caitian woman was cleared of any association with our attackers. At the same time, Curzon received a reprimand for recklessness, and I noticed after that night he stopped calling me "kid" and "Starscape."

I was now, in his eyes, simply Benjamin.

Curzon was definitely an acquired taste, and most people didn't like what they were getting. But over the years, I accepted him for who he was, faults and all. I came to see that he had forgotten more about art, diplomacy, and science than most people ever learned. Having him as a mentor in my formative Starfleet years gave me a universal perspective, understanding, and friendship that few ever have the privilege of being a part of.

✦

Jake, in a lot of ways, I always felt Jadzia was the child Curzon never had. Children are supposed to take the best parts of the parents and surpass them, and while she wasn't Curzon's kid it did feel to me like everything good and healthy and nurturing about my friendship with Curzon made it into my friendship with Jadzia. And a lot of the bitterness and cat-and-mouse poking and prodding that Curzon was famous for ended with him. Until that point, I had only known Dax as Curzon, but in a lot of ways, when he became Jadzia, I felt like inside this twenty-something lieutenant, the Dax I'd known was able to grow up.

I was always close to Curzon, and our friendship ran deep, but there was a depth to my friendship with Jadzia Dax that started at the deepest level of my friendship with Curzon and then went further. It was a friendship beyond what friends have, the love beyond what lovers share.

When that was taken away—no not taken, ripped, stolen from me and from all of us that knew Jadzia—for the first time in a long, long time I felt lost. There's a stability that the people you love bring with them, that says *I'm here in your life and I'm not going anywhere.* It says we'll be able to laugh and cry together, learn and fail together, we'll be able to lean on each other. When that's no longer there, when it's just gone, it can feel incredibly disorientating. The first time that happened for me, with Grandma Octavia, I was just lost. And then with Grandpa James, losing him almost literally killed me. Mama understood that, and it's why the message she left me was so important.

Loss and grief, if not processed properly, son, can be worse than the loss itself.

When Jadzia was murdered, I felt that same disorientation, but this time I at least knew enough to know I needed perspective. I knew that I needed to be around what felt familiar and safe. And while Deep Space 9 had become our home, it wasn't the home we'd come from. Seeing Dad again, seeing the sights and smelling the aromas that can and will forever only be New Orleans, even cleaning clams until one in the morning, brought with it an inner peace that only home can bring.

Do you understand what I'm saying, son?

Now, where Jadzia Dax was the best friend I ever had or ever will have, Ezri Dax is the gift I didn't know I needed. Ezri sees everything differently than Curzon and Jadzia. Ezri doesn't have the same kind of nostalgic love of the past that they did, and that perspective gives her a candid power that few have. Ezri also has a sense of hope and wonder that is becoming rare in Starfleet but she's in many ways a realist. I know a lot of people, when they first met her, just saw her trying to sort through eight different lifetimes when she had only planned to live her own. But even then I could see the Ezri in Dax. Dax has had a profound influence on the hosts, even altering their personalities. Now I feel like it's gone the other way, and Ezri is most assuredly in the driver's seat influencing Dax.

I want you to do something for me, Jake. I'd love to see you and Ezri have a friendship. And no, I'm not expecting anything romantic, especially because she's about two hundred years older than you. But where Curzon and Jadzia and I were good friends, there's an opportunity for you to have a real friendship with Ezri. The Old Man will be straight with you and give you a perspective unlike anyone else on the station; you can give her a sense of family and stability she's going to want, even if she doesn't know it yet. Think about it. I have, and I think it will be good for the both of you.

CHAPTER SEVENTEEN

OKINAWA—2362

I WAS ON TWO WEEKS' LEAVE FROM THE *U.S.S. LIVINGSTON*. Jennifer and I had started to talk about her and Jake coming back with me when my leave was over. We missed each other terribly, but I think Jennifer also worried about me being around that "dirty old man."

While we were filling out the paperwork, war broke out with the Tzenkethi. I knew something was wrong when reports started to come in redacted, and Federation Network News reporters were being pulled from some starships and being sent to others. Then there was news that really got my attention—the *U.S.S. Renegade*, the ship I knew Tryla Scott was on, had been in a major skirmish on the Tzenkethi boarder. Some were saying the *Renegade* had been ambushed. A few days later, I learned that Tryla had somehow gotten a field promotion and been made the captain of the *Renegade*. The rumor was that when the Tzenkethi were about to take the bridge, her skipper promoted her to first officer and ordered her not to reveal her rank. Tzenkethi were known for kidnapping, interrogating, and killing Starfleet captains, but ignoring junior staff. Her orders were to get the *Renegade* out of harm's way once he was killed. But instead, Tryla led an assault against the Tzenkethi, retrieved the captain's body and saved the ship.

The day after that, I received new orders. I was to report to the *U.S.S. Okinawa* in two days. It was headed to the Tzenkethi border, and I was being reassigned to it because of my experience with Curzon on the *Livingston*.

Jennifer didn't say much, but it was clear she was worried. I could see her thinking about all the worst-case scenarios that could befall a Federation starship in a warzone. That night, Jake, we took you out to the amusement park for ice cream, bumper cars, and the roller coaster. You had a great time, and because we were with you, so did we.

We decided not to think about tomorrow because it hadn't arrived yet.

✦

Two days later, when I shipped out, you and your mother went with me to the Starfleet transport hub on New Berlin. From there Starfleet personnel would either take a shuttle or transport to wherever they needed to go. I was beaming up directly to the *Okinawa*. The starship had just finished receiving updates at the Utopia Planitia Fleet Yards and picking up new personnel was one of the last things it needed to do before heading to the Tzenkethi border. The three of us walked to the transporter pad together. "I'm coming back," I said.

Your mom kissed me, and I could feel everything she wanted to say but couldn't in that kiss. "You better," she said, finally.

Then you began to cry, Jake. I think at that moment all you understood was that I was going away again for a long time. I wiped away your tears and kissed you on the forehead. "I love you, son," I said, and then I did the hardest thing I'd ever done up to that point in my life.

I turned away from you and your mom and went to war.

✦

As I materialized with other new personnel on the *U.S.S. Okinawa* transporter pad, I realized this was the first time in my Starfleet career, and in my life, that I was truly alone. I had shared my first posting with Cal Hudson for five years. After that I was fortunate enough to have met, became friends, and served with Curzon Dax for nearly three years. This was my first time working without such a safety net.

"Welcome aboard the *Okinawa*. I'm Commander Thatcher." The middle aged, red-haired woman was a direct descendant from her historical namesake, Margaret Thatcher, and was rumored to be just as tough as that

Iron Lady. The commander was reading out assignments and finally got to me. "Mister Sisko, report to Chief Engineer Isaac in main engineering."

As I made my way through the corridors of this *Excelsior*-class vessel, I realized the *Okinawa* was the largest starship I'd ever been on. The *Excelsior* class was designed and created back in the late twenty-third century to be a bridge between Starfleet's past and its future. The original transwarp drive for the ship was far ahead of its time and was never fully realized. But the ship achieved its design goals in many other ways, proving itself to be viable and reliable even now in the twenty-fourth century during war time.

Main engineering felt as if I'd entered another world. The warp core sat at the heart of the room, just as engineering did for the ship. It was three stories high, with the main engineering deck on the second story so that it lined up with the center of the warp core and its dilithium crystal chamber assembly. A low, steady hum of power coming from the core could be both heard and subtly felt throughout the room. As I stood there admiring the technological marvel, Chief Isaac stepped up beside me. His presence snapped me out of my moment of reverence. "My apologies, Chief, I—"

Chief Engineer John Isaac gave me a relaxed smile and held up a hand cutting me off. His long, thick graying dreadlocks were pulled back and tied together into a neat regulation formation behind his broad shoulders. The eyes said more than the man's face, but neither revealed his age except for thin lines in the bronze skin around his eyes. "No need to apologize, Mister Sisko, you're an engineer, not a tourist. Trust me, I get it," he said. He went back to looking at the warp core and I joined him. "You'll find the *Okinawa* is something special. I've been reading your file and about your time at Starbase 137, I like the intensive cross training they did. I spoke to Commander Thatcher, and we're going to adopt the same policy here in engineering, so let's get you started."

✦

Three months into the war the first major engagement happened. Seventeen Tzenkethi ships conducted a surprise attack as Federation ships were mobilizing in the Temecklia system. All the Federation vessels were lost. Six hours after the battle, the *Okinawa*, the *Yasuke*, and the *Kasai* were dispatched to look for survivors.

It was the first time I'd ever seen anything like it. Ships from both sides were still on fire. Atmosphere was venting from pieces of demolished vessels. Specks were flailing around through space in a manner that only bodies can. Deflector power was reduced to a minimum because we didn't want to repel an escape pod that could be mistaken for wreckage.

After seven hours of searching, we located two escape pods, the *Kasai* had found three, and the *Yasuke* two. On our final pass of the debris field we found another escape pod and, as with the others, we beamed the injured directly to sickbay and tractored the escape pod into the shuttle bay. A few minutes later I noticed something strange on my engineering console. "Chief, my board is saying sickbay is losing oxygen, that can't be right—right?" I questioned.

Chief Isaac looked over at me, and then glanced up as he spoke "Sickbay, this is engineering, everything okay up there?" he asked.

There was no response.

The chief looked back at me then up again. "Bridge, Engineering. Captain, we may have a problem in sickbay," he said.

Nothing.

The chief's hands played quickly across his station. When he spoke, it was more to himself than any of us. "Looks like comms are down shipwide, but I can't find any reason." Isaac pulled open a drawer marked *EMERGENCY*. Inside were two of the latest phasers, and tricorders, and two ancient yet pristine communicators, with a retro-styled flip-open front. The chief handed me one of each. "These communicators aren't linked to the comm system or our badges. Go to sickbay, find out what's going on, report back," he said. Isaac then pointed to two other engineers: Daneeka, a Tiburonian with light green skin, ears that resembled fish fins, and tiny ridges that started just above his eyebrows and ran across his bald head, and Moodus, a Saurian female, whose grey reptilian skin and large round black eyes gave the impression she was always watching, even when she wasn't. "You two go with him."

As we headed for the door, the chief kept talking, I could hear him trying to cover the growing stress in his voice with confidence and calm. "I'm sending another team to the bridge. It's probably nothing," he said.

Daneeka and Moodus walked out of engineering, and I was right behind them when the *Okinawa* rocked violently, and we heard thunder from somewhere far off within the ship. I put my hand in front of the door slot to prevent it from closing. "Computer, what the hell was that?" I demanded.

The computer answered the question in a calm even tone. "An explosion has occurred in the main shuttle bay."

The chief and I locked eyes, our faces filled with questions, and then Engineering began to fill with transport signatures. I smiled as I thought the bridge was sending assistance, but as the transport cycle finished, I could see there were four Tzenkethi standing throughout Engineering.

"Computer lockdown engineering. Authorization Isaac, three, omega!" the chief snapped.

As the Tzenkethi fully materialized, the door nearly took my hand off as it slammed shut.

I could hear weapons fire and screams from the other side.

Moodus put her hand on my shoulder, "Ben, do we still try to get to sickbay?"

There were a million questions swirling around in my head. How did the Tzenkethi get aboard undetected? What was happening in sickbay, on the bridge, the shuttle bay, and now Engineering? Were the captain, the chief, all the people I'd worked with for the last six months alive or dead?

Would I ever see you and your mom again?

It took less than a second for me to snap back into focus and take action. "No, we've got to get to auxiliary control. The Tzenkethi are trying to take the ship, and we've got to take it back!"

I was watching Daneeka. He was standing in the middle of the hallway, blankly staring at the floor, and I realized he was listening for something. Then suddenly, his head snapped up, and he screamed, "Run!"

Daneeka started off in a sprint towards the turbolift and we were right behind him. I looked over my shoulder; the corridor was clear. We entered the lift, I gave our destination, and just as the door closed a Tzenkethi came around the corner. The Tiburonian slumped down to the floor, shaking. "I could hear them, they're so heavy. I can hear them stomping around like a Takaran wildebeest," he panted.

I held out my hand to help him up. "You did good, you saved us," I said.

Daneeka looked at my hand for a moment then took a breath before taking it and standing up. "Thanks," was all he said.

"How much time do you think we have?" Moodus asked.

I understood the question. Chief Isaac had locked down Engineering, denying the Tzenkethi—and everyone else—access to everything in the engine room. Which was both good and bad. "Well, there's only two ways to undo that lockdown. The captain can do it, or..."

Daneeka knew where I was going and finished my thought: "Or the Tzenkethi get the chief to rescind it."

Daneeka and I looked at Moodus as she slumped back against the wall. "Or they point a phaser at the warp core and blow us all up. Great. I hope patience is a Tzenkethi trait," she muttered.

✦

The turbolift opened into hell.

A few feet in front of us was a makeshift barrier haphazardly made from two doors that had been quickly removed from an adjacent office. Three members of the crew that I didn't recognize were behind the barricade: two ensigns and a lieutenant. The lieutenant, a Vulcan male, was bleeding badly and looked as if he'd been mauled by a targ.

The ensigns were a young human woman firing down the hall wildly with a phaser rifle, and a Betazoid male helping the lieutenant. Both were wearing blue uniforms. The Vulcan lieutenant was wearing gold, and was unconscious.

At the far end of the hall, a pair of Tzenkethi were returning fire. And in-between, in the center of this makeshift no man's land, was auxiliary control and a slew of bodies, both Federation and Tzenkethi.

We stepped off the turbolift and the ensign with the phaser rifle turned and almost fired at us. As she turned to fire back down the hallway, I could see she was doing her best to keep it together. "They tore apart the security protecting auxiliary control, we dragged the only one alive back here. We need help!" she screamed to no one.

I knelt down next to the bleeding Vulcan lieutenant and the Betazoid ensign working on him. His hands and uniform were soaked in the Vulcan's green blood. "How is he, Ensign?" I asked.

The Betazoid looked shaken, he was definitely feeling our fear and anxiety, maybe even from everyone on the ship. "I-I'm not certain, I'm a dental hygienist, not a doctor," he said.

I leaned in close to the barricade, pulled out my phaser, and fired a few shots down the hallway. If I couldn't get into auxiliary control at least I could keep the Tzenkethi from getting in there too. "Do whatever you can," I said to the ensign.

My communicator beeped.

Stunned, I looked at the old communicator for a second before flipping it open. "Sisko here," I said.

Over the phaser fire, I could make out the chief's voice utter a single word. "Report," he whispered.

"We're outside of auxiliary control, but we're pinned down. We can't get in!" I said.

"Good man. Listen, Ben. They're killing people in here. You've got a minute, maybe two, before I'm going to have to come out of hiding and give them access. Get in there!" Isaac whispered.

The connection ended.

There wasn't much time left and I realized if I didn't do something bold, we may all be out of time. "Daneeka, help the ensigns get the lieutenant into the turbolift. Moodus, take the phaser rifle and cover me," I ordered.

Daneeka and the ensigns began dragging the lieutenant into the turbolift. Moodus looked at me messing with my phaser. "What are you doing?" she asked

I moved the phaser setting from heavy stun, past kill and into overload. I knew it takes about ten seconds for a phaser to overload and about two seconds to throw my makeshift grenade the distance it needed to go. I held onto the device as its whine and the warm surface became a white-hot scream. "Something crazy," I said and I threw the phaser.

✦

The world came back to me in slivers. I could see, but I couldn't hear. I remembered I was on the *Okinawa*, but not where.

I could taste blood in my mouth.

There was a shard of metal in Moodus's leg, but she was pointing to something but I didn't understand. I looked to where she was pointing and saw a rod-sized shard lodged in my shoulder. Moodus was still pointing, and I realized it wasn't at me but past me. "Ben! Get to auxiliary control!"

I knew she was screaming, but everything was muffled, distant. I stumbled off in the direction she pointed, but I could feel myself starting to fade out while on my feet. I focused back in and realized I was now standing in auxiliary control, and I hadn't remembered walking into the room. The world was starting to return to me but in a jigsaw of moments.

"Get in there!"

"The *Okinawa* is something special."

"We need help!"

Instead of going over to the panel that overrode control from engineering, I found myself standing in front of transporter control. I used the transporters to scan for Tzenkethi life signs and found eleven.

I beamed them far away into deep space.

✦

"Lieutenant Commander Sisko." I opened my eyes, groggy and dazed, either from my makeshift bomb or whatever medication I was on. The rank wasn't right, I knew that, but I would recognize Captain Leyton's voice anywhere. I turned my head to see my captain standing next to my biobed, his arm in a sling. My entire body hurt. "Sir?" I said.

"Congratulations on your promotion, Commander. Your incredibly quick thinking and bravery saved the *Okinawa*. I've transferred you out of engineering and into command. You should also know I've promoted you to first officer," he said.

There was so much to take in about what Captain Leyton was saying, I couldn't process it all. But one thing didn't make sense. "Sir, you already have a first officer," I said.

Captain Leyton's face shifted from sadness to surprise and back again. "I'm sorry, Ben, we did tell you yesterday, but I guess you were so out of it. Commander Thatcher died saving the bridge from the Tzenkethi. If it weren't for you and her working independently yet in tandem, we'd all be dead right now, son."

I tried to think of something to say about how I felt about the *Okinawa*, about Commander Thatcher and never being able to replace her, but wanting to honor her. About the captain's decision, and even though it wasn't something I ever sought, I would do my best to see in myself what he and others have always seen in me. But in truth I was so exhausted, physically, mentally, and emotionally, that I just said, "Thank you, Captain. I'll do my best, sir."

After Leyton left sickbay, I couldn't stop thinking about his words and the promotion. My entire time at the academy people had told me I was better suited for command than engineering. Tryla told me, West told me, but I didn't listen. As I lay in sickbay, Jake, I began to understand that the only person I wasn't listening to was myself. When people suggested command to me I thought they were crazy. For me that was an unattainable challenge to consider. Don't get me wrong, I loved engineering, I still have a love for it. Engineering is what got me into Starfleet. But lying in that biobed I realized I never considered command because somewhere deep down I was afraid they might be right. Sometimes success is much more frightening than failure. If I did transfer to command, and if I was good at it, then at some point I might be responsible for people's lives.

And I didn't want to be.

But when the *Okinawa* was in trouble I didn't think about any of that. I just did what I thought was right and tried my best to keep people alive. If it had been up to me, I would've happily gone right back to engineering and I probably wouldn't have realized any of this until I was retiring, if ever. Luckily Captain Leyton did something for me that, even though I didn't realize it, I was too scared to do for myself.

Take a true leap into the unknown.

Engineering has always been challenging, but it was safe, much safer than Command. In Command there are no excuses to hide behind, you have to be honest with yourself and with your crew.

All of which brings me to you, son.

When you told me that you didn't want to join Starfleet, I was disappointed. But as you explained your reasons, I could see even then you were on your way to becoming your own man. It took a lot of guts to stand up for yourself in the way you did. I've seen people twice your age have difficulty doing what you did when you were just fourteen, Jake.

I was so proud of you that day.

I remember that after you made your declaration and left the room, I realized I had come full circle. I had been a son on one end of that conversation, and now I was a father on the other end. I was in my father's shoes when I told him I didn't want to be a chef and that I wanted to join Starfleet. Because of you, son, that day you helped me to understand my father a little better.

I've never had the opportunity to say this to you before now, Jake, but I've seen kids of Starfleet officers that feel the deeds of their parents were something they had to live up to. When the Bajorans started calling me 'The Emissary' it worried me on a whole different level, in ways I never mentioned, and only a parent would understand. What kind of weight was that putting on you? A father that's both a Starfleet captain and able to talk to the Bajoran gods? That's a hell of a burden to put on a kid that's trying to find his way in life. But you never let anything I did, or any narrative people tried to give me, affect you. You've never fallen into that trap, you've always understood your life is just that.

Yours.

You've walked the unbeaten path to find yourself, you've always spoken truth to power and you've confessed to the universe your fears and your humanity. It's clear to me, Jake, you were well on your way to becoming your own man long before you became one.

CHAPTER EIGHTEEN

SARATOGA—2362-2367

FOR WEEKS ON THE *OKINAWA* I COULDN'T SLEEP. I'd lay awake looking up at the ceiling trying to figure out what it was that was keeping me up, and then after a while I had to finally admit that I already knew what it was. I had a great position on a fantastic ship. My job was challenging, and people liked me—in short, I had a great career. But I hadn't seen my wife or son in nearly a year. I was miserable and I didn't know what to do about it.

So I made a call.

Just seeing Dax over subspace improved my mood. It was the middle of the night for me, but Dax was on Risa where it was a few hours after sunrise. I motioned to the drink he was holding. "Starting a little early, Curzon?" I asked.

My mentor snorted. "Starting?" he said. "I haven't gone to sleep from last night's party. So the sooner you tell me what's going on," Curzon took a sip from his drink, "the sooner I can get back to it, Ben."

I laid it all out to my friend, and in typical Curzon Dax manner he smiled and said, "I told you not to get married."

The look on my face must've told Curzon he had crossed a line. He put his hands up in surrender. "My bad Ben, I know, sometimes I play too much. My apologies, my friend."

I loved Curzon, but loving him meant understanding sometimes he was like a phaser with a hair trigger that would fire indiscriminately. "Accepted," I said.

The Trill took another sip of his drink. "Do you love her?" he asked. I opened my mouth to really lay into him, but he held up a hand and I could see he was deadly serious. "It's just you and me, and no shame, here, Ben. If you had to choose between them and Starfleet, which would you choose?"

I had wanted to be in Starfleet since I was ten years old, it was a dream that had become real and helped me understand who I am, but it was nothing in comparison to the two people that were now a part of me. "They're everything to me, Dax, everything," I whispered.

My friend was about to say something when a young lady I'm sure was younger than me came into view only wearing a sheet. "Daxy, when are you coming back to bed?" she said.

Dax smirked and downed the last of his drink, but when he looked back at me it was like he'd left something in the bottom of that glass. "Look, Ben, there are a lot of people in Starfleet and the Federation that have made their work their life. I should know, I'm one of them. But life is too big and too short not to be lived fully. You already know what to do, kid." He held my gaze for another few seconds and then reverted back to the old familiar Curzon. "Now if you'll excuse me, I've got a party to get back to!"

The subspace line disconnected. I set up a link with Starfleet Command and queried how many ships were immediately looking for a first officer that also allowed families aboard. There was only one.

The *Saratoga*.

✦

I materialized onto the *Saratoga*'s transporter pad, expecting to have an ensign escort me to the captain's ready room. Instead, I was greeted by the ship's second officer. I thought I knew every species in the Federation that had a member in Starfleet, but this individual escaped me. He was humanoid, and from a distance I could see how someone might mistake him for human, but up close it was clear that he wasn't. His skin was a pale yellowish white with matching yellow eyes. From the moment I materialized, his hand was already strangely outstretched, waiting for me to shake it.

"Welcome aboard, Lieutenant Commander Sisko," he said. "I am Lieutenant Commander Data. I know you have had a long trip, I hope it was pleasant."

The name rang a bell, I remembered reading about Data years ago on the Federation News Service when he joined Starfleet. As a kid I'd read a lot about androids, how Captain Kirk had met more of them and other forms of artificial intelligence than any other Starfleet captain. Reading his adventures, I admired how he always managed to outwit something that was designed to be smarter than any of us. Now as I stood in front of this artificial lifeform wearing a Starfleet uniform, I couldn't help but feel he was trying his hardest, in this moment, to put his best foot forward.

I stepped off the transporter pad, and he shook my hand in much the same way I had as a kid, shaking the hand of an adult. It was firm and thorough, but there was no ease or comfort in it. It felt rehearsed, staged. I looked at the second officer, who was clearly doing the best he could with the human gesture, so I let it go. "Thanks, Commander. I wasn't expecting anyone to roll out the red carpet for me."

The lieutenant commander jerked his head back in surprise, immediately looked down at the floor, and then back up at me tilting his head slightly before he spoke again. "I do not understand, sir. Why would a red carpet be installed for your transport to the *Saratoga*? Is there some significance to the color red in your personal history of which I am unaware?" he asked.

I chuckled and saw the transporter chief doing her best to hide an unprofessional grin. "No, forgive me, Mister Data, it's an old Earth idiom. It means to—"

Data interrupted me, unable to contain his excitement. "Ah yes, roll out the red carpet—to formally greet or welcome an important guest who has just arrived. I see, thank you for the clarification. Captain Storil is in holodeck one awaiting your arrival, sir. If you will follow me, please."

I fell in step next to the second officer and asked the obvious question. "Why the holodeck? I thought you'd be escorting me to the captain's ready room."

In a very human way, Data looked down and then to the side before turning his head to look at me directly. It was clear that while he still had to work on his greetings, along the way he had picked up human subtleties when we withheld information. "The captain believed the holodeck would be a more appropriate setting for your interview."

"I see," I said as I entered the turbolift. "Have all the candidates had their interviews on the holodeck?"

The second officer looked down again, determining what he could, and could not say. "Yes sir, I believe the captain is finishing up with Commander Studivent as we speak."

Studivent was easily one of the best in Starfleet. He was known to be hotheaded at times, but thus far it had served him and Starfleet well. I didn't realize he wanted this position, but I shouldn't have been surprised. Captain Storil was an exceptional captain. He and the crew of the *Saratoga* did things with the *Miranda* class ship that people said weren't possible. A few years back the *Saratoga* came to the aid of a dilithium mining facility on the edge of Federation space under attack by eight Orion raiders. The *Saratoga* and its crew held off the assault until reinforcements arrived, destroying four raiders in the process. People started calling the *Saratoga* the little ship that could.

The more I thought about it, meeting on the holodeck made me nervous. Being a Vulcan, I figured Storil would put me through a series of questions perfectly designed to delve into my psyche and allow him to see whatever it was he was looking for in a first officer. An interview that was so intense and demanding it was the second-best thing to a mind meld. That's what I'd prepared for, but the reality was totally unexpected. Maybe that was Storil's point, I thought. Maybe he was going to pit me against a Gorn on Cestus III, or he and I would attempt to steal a Romulan cloaking device together.

Whatever it was going to be, I'd find out in a few minutes and worrying about it wasn't going to do me any good. I needed to think about something else. "How long have you been on the *Saratoga*, Mister Data? I hope it's been a rewarding experience?" I asked.

It was subtle but Data performed another human action as he spoke to me by keeping his gaze on the turbolift doors. "I have been… filling in as the second officer for two months, three weeks, four days, seventeen hours and thirty-six seconds, sir. My time here has been… well spent."

In his own way, by being precise, Data avoided my real question. I was fishing to find out if the android had any personal interest in staying on as my Operations officer if I got the job. But Data wasn't giving me any information that I could use or would influence my interview. I already knew that he'd been assigned as an interim officer aboard the *Saratoga* after the first officer, operations officer, and security chief were all lost on an away mission. While surveying a moon in the Orelious system, the away team happened upon an ancient munitions depot and accidentally triggered an explosive device. The subsequent chain reaction resulted in the annihilation of the away team, the destruction of the moon and severe damage to the Saratoga. No doubt assigning Data as the interim officer brought his particular skills to the repairs of the *Saratoga*, and allowed the crew the time they needed to grieve their friends and coworkers before assigning new people to those posts.

As we exited the turbolift, Data said, "Sir, may I ask you a question?"

"Shoot," I responded. Data stopped, looked at me, surprised and horrified by my response. He opened his mouth to say something, but already knowing where it was going, I cut him off. "Sure," I said this time. "What do you want to know?"

Data closed his mouth, and began walking again, then continued. "Usually, sir, when someone meets me for the first time, they comment on the fact I am an android and how unusual the experience is for them. You did not." We stopped in front of the entrance to Holodeck One, where I could see a sincere and perhaps refreshing curiosity on Data's face. "May I inquire as to why?"

Smiling, I realized I really liked the lieutenant commander. "Well, Data, I know you're an android, you know you're an android. I really didn't see a need to bring up what we both know."

Data smiled. "Ah, I see, sir." The android stopped and tilted his head slightly again. "Thank you, sir."

I was about to reply when the holodeck doors opened and Commander Studivent stormed out. I was so shocked, by the time I thought to take a peek inside to see what environment was being projected, the doors were already closing. Studivent was physically agitated, and looked a little older than I'd expected from his Starfleet photo. There was a time when his smooth caramel complexion and blue eyes would have belied his true age. But now, the salt-and-pepper beard masked a square jaw and brought a seasoned, tempered appearance that matched the three pips on his collar. He turned and looked back at the closed holodeck door for a moment, then turned back to us. "That man is the most illogical, irrational Vulcan I've ever met." I could see he was doing what I had just done, comparing my face with what he'd no doubt seen in the Starfleet database. After a half second to make the adjustment, he let go of whatever he was feeling and smiled as he shook my hand. "Ben Sisko, right? Good luck, you're going to need it!"

I noticed that Data was eyeing how Studivent and I shook hands, no doubt storing the interaction for future reference. I was about to say something when the commander headed off toward the turbolift. Lieutenant Commander Data watched Studivent walk away and then quickly turned to me before he followed. "Please, sir, enter when ready, Captain Storil is expecting you." With that Data walked briskly down the corridor, catching up with Studivent just before he entered the turbolift.

Anxious to get this over with, I turned and entered the holodeck.

I had half expected to walk into the middle of some battle or even a warp core breach in progress. What I didn't expect was that I would be back in New Orleans. The holodeck doors opened to a small space that was almost as familiar to me as my own living room back home.

Preservation Hall.

The hole-in-the-wall jazz club really wasn't much larger than a spacious living room. The holodeck doors opened behind rows of fold-out chairs that only seated about fifty—in this case, holographic—people. About another forty holograms hugged the walls of the hall, packing the place much like it would be on a Friday night. Beyond the seats, there was no stage, just a small area separating the audience from where the band played. As I eyed the band, I couldn't believe what I was seeing.

They were wearing Starfleet uniforms. It was the bridge crew.

I'd taken the time to memorize the faces and history of the bridge crew I was interviewing to become a part of, and nearly all of them were here. Lieutenant Hranok Zor, the *Saratoga's* new bald Bolian tactical officer, was on the drums, which seemed somehow appropriate for his tall thin blue frame as he sat behind the old, run-down drum set. Ensign Kemeko Tamamota, the operations officer, was calmly holding her saxophone. She was a little older than the other officers and carried herself with confidence as she shared a laugh with Ensign Rachel Delaney, the helm officer, who surprisingly, was holding a trombone. The brass instrument seemed larger than the small young woman, but she held it with an ease and authority that I'd seen all the time back home. Captain Storil wasn't there, but I noticed in the corner, there was a piano that no one was sitting at.

That couldn't have been a coincidence.

I started making my way along the wall around to the front of the club, and the band. There were so many holograms crowding the small space, I started to command the computer to delete them so I could get to the front of the room quicker and to see if the bridge crew disappeared as well, but then I thought better of it. This was Captain's Storil program, which meant it was a test.

I was surprised a Vulcan knew about this place. Preservation Hall wasn't like some juke joint in the early days of jazz and blues. The small venue had been a mecca for jazz since the early 1960s when the art form was only known on Earth. As kids, it was the only jazz club our parents would let us go to by ourselves. No bar, no food, no photos, and no bathrooms. Preservation Hall has always been about music and only the music.

I finally made it around to the front and approached my fellow officers. The question I was thinking must've been on my face. Ensign Delaney smiled as I approached. "Welcome to the Bridge Crew Band, sir. And no, we're not holograms."

Delaney was an incredibly soft-spoken human woman with a mass of curls that made her seem even younger than she was. But what was most striking about her, and this Bridge Crew Band, was how relaxed the four of them seemed together, especially since Zor and Delaney had only joined the *Saratoga* a week ago. If this was any indication of how Captain Storil ran the ship, I was impressed. "Good to know, Ensign. So why are we all here?" I asked.

A voice from behind me answered the question. "I thought by now that would be obvious, Commander. This is your interview."

I turned to see Captain Storil sitting in the front row. His chiseled face and pointed ears accentuated his glare. In every way, Storil appeared to be your standard Vulcan, down to the same damn mushroom bowl haircut that hasn't changed since humans first met Vulcans in the twenty-first century. But it was quickly becoming clear to me that this wasn't a typical Vulcan. Here we were in a holodeck simulation of one of the most prominent Earth jazz clubs in history, and beyond all logic, sitting on the captain's lap was a trumpet.

Storil got up, walked over to me, and held my shocked gaze for a moment before speaking. "Station, please, Commander," he said.

I walked over to the old broken-down piano that was in the corner; its keys were chipped and no longer a bright ivory but a faded far-off beige that only comes through time and use. As I sat down, I realized there was no sheet music for me to read, and with my back to the Bridge Crew Band, the only way for me to know my place was to listen and feel for it. For the first time in a long time, I could feel myself start to sweat under my uniform.

Great.

I looked over my shoulder to say something to the captain, but he was already turning to face the audience, the holograms began to clap and whistle. Storil waited patiently for them to die down, and when they did he put the trumpet to his lips, and began to play one of the most emotional instruments in human history. He began with a brief solo, holding the longest, purest, cleanest note I'd ever heard. As he broke into his piece, the rest of the band picked up on it and slipped in under his tempo immediately. Thankfully, I recognized the opening to the Cuban classic 'El manisero'—a beautiful song about a man of the people, a peanut vendor, of all things—so listening to the rhythm, I turned back to the piano and started playing.

I could hear Storil hand off the piece to Ensign Tamamota and her sax. Zor, Delaney, and I played under her as she stepped into a solo. I shot a quick glance over my shoulder; the captain was waiting, keeping time by tapping his foot. As Tamamota finished, Lieutenant Zor, who had been doing a soft shoe on the drums, let loose into his solo. I closed my eyes, and I began to feel the rhythms of my fellow players.

We were jamming. This was jazz.

Beyond the absurd contradiction of seeing a Vulcan playing the trumpet in a jazz club, I began to understand Captain Storil's brilliance. It was only logical to expect individuals that play well together and understand each other's cues and rhythms in music to do the same within the command structure.

As Zor finished his solo I played a little riff to bring in Delaney's trombone. The young ensign picked up on this and leaned in, letting loose on the instrument. I looked over my shoulder and could see the young woman having fun. There wasn't any place now for a trumpet, so the captain had tucked the instrument under his arm and was clapping on the beat. Sensing that Delaney was closing her solo, I turned back around and it was my turn to let loose. My whole body was moving now as my hands played across the keys. It had been years since I'd felt like this while sitting in front of a piano. I had forgotten the freedom of not thinking and just letting the moment take me, letting the jazz inside me out.

But now it wasn't just about me, I was being held and supported by the rest of the band. I closed off my solo, now completely in step with the rest of the Bridge Crew Band. Captain Storil eased into the end of 'El manisero' with another solo, bookending how we started. As the music stopped, the holographic audience went wild with applause and then abruptly disappeared. Captain Storil walked over to me and placed his hand on my shoulder.

"Welcome aboard, Mister Sisko," he said.

✦

"We need more time, Commander," Professor Sisko said.

I could hear the underlying stress in my wife's voice. "I'm sorry, Professor, but I have the same answer for you the operations officer had. Your request is denied," I said.

This wasn't the response Jennifer wanted or was expecting. "Commander Sisko, as the administrator of Cetacean Operations, it's my job to care for the wellbeing of everyone in this department, Starfleet or not, humanoid or not. These mammals have been in the same tank since they were first installed here. They need a break, Commander," she said.

I had to admit that I agreed with Jennifer. "You have an excellent point, Professor. However, your solution is that while the *Saratoga* is in dry dock for repairs, we install a holodeck here in Cetacean Operations?"

"That's right."

"That's just not feasible, Professor. For one, the holodeck draws a significant amount of power. For another, we don't have the time to make that type of upgrade," I explained.

Jennifer's voice tightened. "Which is why we need more time. Quite frankly, Commander, no other life forms can assist Federation starships with navigation the way these dolphins can. And if we want to keep exploring all these strange new worlds, then we need to pay more attention to the well-being of those that help us get there."

Jennifer was a scientist and administrator of this department but not in Starfleet, and here I was a senior Starfleet officer on the ship. With influence over her department. We'd talked about working together on a ship or starbase and the conflicts it could invite. And now here we were. "Professor, I appreciate your position, and I'll be frank with you as well: a holodeck down here just isn't going to happen. However, while we're in drydock I will speak to the captain about retrofitting one of the holodecks so that our friends here can be beamed in and make use of it."

Professor Sisko's gaze softened. "Thank you, Commander. I appreciate that," she said.

I smiled and turned to leave. Jennifer caught my arm, leaned in, and whispered. "Remind me, why did I fall in love with someone in Starfleet again?"

"You didn't have a choice," I whispered back.

✦

My father has always said bad news has a habit of coming in threes. Starfleet secure subspace communications reported that a shipwreck was found in a sector near Dytallix B. The debris was identified as Captain Walker Keel's ship, the *U.S.S. Horatio*.

The next day, Captain Storil called me into his ready room. After sitting quietly for nearly ten minutes reading the same report he'd just read, I handed it back to him and asked the obvious question: "How do we know this alien conspiracy to take over Starfleet is really at an end?"

The captain raised an eyebrow. "We have to trust the findings of Captain Picard and the *Enterprise* crew. In the interim, we can only stay vigilant, Commander." Storil tapped a few commands on his PADD and then handed it back to me again. "I thought you would appreciate this additional information," he said.

I never mentioned to Captain Storil that I knew Tryla, now Captain Scott, but he'd obviously done his homework. The PADD reported that Tryla and Admirals Savar and Quinn had made a full recovery. But the next line was unusual—it said Scott had resigned her commission as captain, stating, "*At the end of the day, it's our actions and not our beliefs that define who we are.*"

I read the words and tried to find the Tryla Scott I knew in them, but couldn't. Looking back, I now realize Tryla may have been speaking about different aspects of herself, obscure sections of her character I was completely unaware of back then. I could only hope that wherever she was, she was happy.

I tapped the PADD, turning it off and handed it back to the captain, with a change of subject. "Do you know Captain Picard, sir? I'd love to meet him.

As I understand it, our old second officer is now his."

The captain took the PADD along with the change of subject. "Lieutenant Commander Data would have been a useful asset to the *Saratoga*, but it is illogical to think about what might have been." Storil leaned back in his chair. "The Starfleet captaincy command structure is not as vast as one might think. I'm sure we'll both meet Picard sooner than later."

✦

"Sir, we're being hailed by a ship of unknown origin. They're identifying themselves as the VinShari. They say we're in their space and demand we stop for an inspection," Lieutenant Zor said.

The *Saratoga* was ferrying personnel and equipment to a new starbase that Starfleet was constructing near the Shackleton Expanse—Narendra Station. I turned to Captain Storil in the center seat. "That's bold, asking a Federation starship to pull over for an inspection. Can you scan the vessel, Lieutenant?" I said.

After a pause Zor replied, his voice filled with concern. "Captain, I'm reading the ship has warp sails, and some organic and energy-based projectile weapons. They appear to be configured in what I can only describe as... cannons and harpoons, sir."

Storil raised his eyebrow. "On screen, maximum magnification."

The main viewscreen switched to an aft view, and behind us at some distance was a ship that looked a lot like a nineteenth-century clipper ship from Earth. "Warp sails, cannons, harpoons. Who are these people?" I said.

Captain Storil got up and took a step towards the image on the viewscreen. "Lieutenant, please send the following message. 'VinShari, this is Captain Storil of the Federation starship *Saratoga*. The area we are in is recognized as open space by the United Federation of Planets. We're en route to our Starbase 364 and wish to open diplomatic relations with you.'"

After a few moments of silence, the security station alarm sounded. "They're firing cannons!" Zor announced.

"Shields up, red alert!" I commanded.

I was expecting to feel a shudder against the shields, which is what I was used to in other, energy-based conflict situations. But, this time, the cannon shells tore through the shields like they weren't even there, and everyone was knocked off balance. As we all got back to our feet, everyone looked a little shaken. An attack like this was in uncharted territory. And yet, there was no stress or anxiety on our captain's face. Seeing how placid he appeared, I was immediately reminded of our conversations on the holodeck…

✦

I walked into the holodeck and was surprised that it was a recreation of Sisko's. The place was packed, every table filled with customers as if it were a Friday night. A fair approximation of Nathan was working hard in the kitchen, there was a young woman at our old piano playing away, and an older man with a trombone playing next to her. I didn't see my father or anyone else I knew. After searching the sea of people for a few moments, I spotted Captain Storil sitting alone at a table outside. I walked up to the table, smiling. "Captain, when you said you wanted to have lunch I presumed the mess, or your quarters. You really won't be getting the full Sisko's experience here in the holodeck," I added.

Captain Storil waited for me to sit then he began to speak. "I will get right to the point, Commander. You have a very structured and disciplined mind. If you are willing, I believe there are skills I can impart to you that will allow you to bring calm to chaotic situations."

I sat back in my chair. "I'm sorry, Captain, I hope you don't mean a mind meld, because the answer would be no," I said.

"Not at all," Storil said, emotionless. "Nor am I speaking about meditation, exactly. These are concentration techniques taught to Vulcan children."

I smiled. "Sure."

The Vulcan folded his hands together on the table. "Tell me, Mister Sisko, how many distinctly different sounds do you hear?

I thought about the question, and it was difficult to come up with an accurate answer. There were so many different people talking. But above the human hologram noise, I could hear the piano, and the trombone. Every few moments I thought I heard Holo-Nathan say something I couldn't make out in the kitchen and then of course there was the sounds of metal forks and knives clanking against porcelain. "I'm not sure sir. There's a lot I can't make out… Perhaps six or seven different sounds?" I said.

Storil sighed. "I can hear thirty-nine distinctly different sounds. As a human, you should be able to make out at least twenty-seven. When you can identify the different parts of chaotic structure you can begin to control that structure. I see we have work to do, Commander. We will start with these lunches twice a week."

I had spent enough time around Vulcans to know that they're very emotional people, they've just become really good at hiding the different ways they show that emotion. The captain and I worked well together, dare I say even liked each other. And while I have no doubt his offer to train me in the ways of Vulcan children was legitimate, I also think he just wanted to get to know me better. "I look forward to it, sir, but let's not meet here again. My father would go crazy if he learned we were eating at a holographic Sisko's," I said.

✦

The captain always, always kept his cool in the face of danger. I wasn't Vulcan, but his tutelage, being under his command, did give me those tools he talked about and allowed me to remain composed in chaotic situations. "Damage report," I said calmly.

"Structural damage to decks four and five, emergency force-fields are in place." Ensign Delaney said.

"Captain!" Lieutenant Zor said with some stress in his voice. "Looks like their harpoon weapon is powering up."

The captain sat back down in the center seat and crossed his legs. "Suggestions?" he asked.

"We need to take the wind out of their sails—literally," Delany said.

"Captain, with their weapons able to cut through our shields we can't go toe to toe. Torpedoes might do the job, but we'd have to hit them from all sides, simultaneously. Overwhelm them," I said.

The captain tilted his head slightly, and I knew from experience he was calculating, options. "Lieutenant Zor, launch a full spread of photon torpedoes, but set them to detonate in staggered intervals around the VinShari ship. Fire," he instructed calmly.

We watched six torpedoes launch from the *Saratoga* like depth charges adrift in a sea of stars. They caught up to the VinShari ship and began to detonate all around the vessel, explosions buffeting it from all sides.

Zor confirmed what we all could see on the viewscreen: "Vessel is dropping out of warp, major damage to their warp sails, sir," he said.

Ensign Tamamota looked at the viewscreen. "Did those guys just try to mug us?" she asked.

Everyone on the bridge laughed, except for the captain, who instead, simply raised an eyebrow. I looked at the viewscreen, where the alien style clipper ship was becoming a speck as we pulled away at warp speed. "Nice neighbors," I added.

When I think back to all of the harrowing and exciting moments like that one on the *Saratoga*, that encounter was the first time I can recall feeling truly connected to people. I think that was because I had you and Jennifer, the most important parts of my life, with me. Seeing the both of you at the end of every shift meant that I was home, and as an extension of being home these people became family. We worked together, lived, and played together.

That's why it was so devastating when I lost them all.

CHAPTER NINETEEN

WOLF 359—2367

"CAPTAIN, YOU'VE SEEN RIKER'S REPORT," ADMIRAL HANSON SAID. "Picard has been altered, changed somehow. The Borg are using him to attack us. We're mobilizing everything we've got. Intercept of the Borg Cube will take place at Wolf 359. That's where we'll make our stand."

Captain Storil got up out of the *Saratoga*'s command chair and stood in front of the main viewscreen. "We will be there, Admiral," Storil said.

The admiral forced a smile, "Excellent, *Saratoga*. You don't want to be late to this party. Hanson, out," he said.

Admiral Hanson disappeared from the main viewscreen to be replaced by a sea of stars. I said, "Helm, set course for Wolf 359, maximum warp. Engage!"

As the stars began to streak by at warp speed I joined the captain in front of the viewscreen, hoping to prompt him to say something in this moment to the crew. But Captain Storil turned and sat back down in the center seat calmly as if he had just been told a shipment of self-sealing stem bolts had been delivered. Not that Starfleet was about to engage in a battle to save humanity, the Federation, and perhaps all humanoid life and culture in the Alpha Quadrant. Storil was a great captain, and a hell of a jazz musician, but he could also be very Vulcan. I could tell he wanted to say something, but I knew that was exactly why he wouldn't.

When the *Enterprise* returned from system J-25, seven thousand light years from Federation space, and alerted Starfleet about the Borg, we'd believed we had the amount of time it would take a vessel traveling at maximum warp to reach us from J-25 by what we considered normal and standard conditions—about three years. There were briefings and meetings about what people were calling the "possible Borg threat," but nothing really changed. Meeting after meeting took place and after nearly a year, none of the projected designs had received a green light. And then the unimaginable happened—we learned the Borg weren't playing by our rules. They had traveled seven thousand light years in less than one year, and they hadn't sent an armada, just one Borg cube.

Because that was all that was needed.

Earth had declared a state of emergency for the first time since the incident with the whales nearly a century earlier. The reason the Borg wanted to start with the assimilation of Earth wasn't just because it was the birthplace for humanity. They also knew Earth was where the Federation was founded, and in many ways, where hope throughout the Alpha Quadrant started. And for the Borg, what they admired or envied, they assimilated, but what they didn't understand, or felt was irrelevant—like hope—they destroyed. En route to Wolf 359, we spent the time recalibrating our shield harmonics and phaser bandwidths, but there was a silence on the *Saratoga*'s bridge that was full of dread.

✦

"Resistance is futile. You will disarm your weapons and escort us to sector zero zero one. If you attempt to intervene, we will destroy you," Locutus said.

I looked at the thing that was once Jean-Luc Picard. The Borg were using him as a harbinger of what was to come if we failed. The creature was devoid of all reason, all humanity.

Forty ships, with ten ships in each wave. The *Saratoga* was sent in as part of the first wave, the idea being each successive wave would learn from the success and failures of each preceding attack.

Adapting on the fly.

That was the plan, at least in theory. What happened was very different. Twenty seconds into the battle, the *Melbourne* was destroyed. Forty seconds after that we were hit, the bridge exploded, and only Lieutenant Zor and myself survived. Captain Storil, Ensigns Tamamota and Delaney, my friends, the Bridge Crew Band, lay dead all around me.

One minute there had been a mighty task force of forty starships; the next there was a graveyard.

When I looked at all of those dead faces around me, it took everything I had to hold myself together. All I could think of was finding you and your mom, Jake. As I tried to make it to our quarters I saw people in the halls that I'd known for years, but I didn't recognize them—the panic and fear had changed them so quickly.

So completely.

Our home was obliterated. I called out for Jennifer, and when she didn't answer, I suddenly remembered what it felt like when I called out for my grandpa all those years ago, and he didn't answer. Then I saw you, and I could tell you were all right, and a part of me was too, because you were.

When I saw your mother, I knew something was wrong, but it didn't matter. Whatever it was, I told myself, we could fix it. I told myself there was time to fix it. You were the same age I was when I'd lost so much, when death started to change me, and I didn't want that for you, son.

I tried to lift the beams and girders your mom was pinned under. Even though the heated debris burned my hands, I pulled with all my strength, with everything I had, but it wasn't enough to free her.

So I stayed.

Somehow, Zor knew. He had known enough to follow me, having seen on my face what I'd seen on the faces of the others in the hallway. Starships were exploding around us, being destroyed by a demon that had once been a Starfleet captain, the best of us. The *Saratoga*'s computer was warning that there were three minutes until a warp core breach. But I didn't care about any of that. All I could think of was saving my family. I had to get Jennifer free. If Zor hadn't grabbed you and sent you to the escape shuttle and then dragged me out of there, away from Jennifer's body, I don't think I would have ever left.

Lieutenant Zor saved us, he saved our family, and I will always be grateful to him for that. But even though he physically pulled me out of there, the truth is it wasn't until years later I was able to mentally and emotionally leave the *Saratoga*.

Jake, we both know the pain of losing a family member unnaturally. There are times when death comes upon us in our lives when it shouldn't, through murder, or war or something unjustified. In those times, especially when it happens to someone we hold dear, it can change us, darken us. And for a time, that's what happened to me. If you ever find yourself in that place, son, don't let go of the light in your life that anchors you. For me, ultimately, it was my love for you and desire to be the father I knew you deserved that led me back to myself. I found I couldn't hold onto both what was darkening my soul and the love I had for you and your mom.

I had to make a choice, and in the end, it wasn't a choice at all.

CHAPTER TWENTY
DEFIANT—2367-2369

AFTER WOLF 359, STARFLEET AND THE FEDERATION were in a state of both shock and paranoia. There was talk that Starfleet should, for the first time in its history, move from a charter of exploration to defense first. While all this was happening, everyone wanted to make sure the "359 survivors" were being taken care of, while simultaneously wanting to know from us what it was like being at Wolf 359.

In the immediate aftermath, I was numb. The only thing I was able to do was be a father to you. My dad and Jennifer's father, Mister Richardson, took care of the funeral arrangements—a memorial at Gilgo Beach, where we were married. Everyone came, even Elias. People were coming up to me saying the same things that we always say when we don't know what to say. And then Elias was just suddenly in front of me. It had been over ten years since I'd seen my younger brother. He opened his mouth to try and say something comforting, but then just hugged me instead. Any other time, there'd be so much I'd want to say to my brother and ask him, and be mad at him for and laugh with him about.

Instead, I just hugged Elias and wept.

I was struck by how much my own childhood had prepared me to help you through yours. If for nothing else, I was thankful that I'd gone through that to make things easier for you. After a month of spending time with your old man, I was able to get you back into school and restart some normal rhythms in your life. I watched you go off on your first day in a new school, introduce yourself and never look back. I couldn't have been prouder.

Starfleet issued mandatory counseling for all of us and three months of leave. There were a wave of early retirements and even some suicides. A vacuum started to appear at the command level, and Starfleet needed experienced officers to replenish its ranks. As a 359 survivor, and with my command-level experience, I was promoted to full commander. And instead of being told where to go, I was asked what command I would like—a rarity in Starfleet.

"Why Utopia Planitia?" asked Admiral Whatley

I'd met Charlie Whatley a few times while on Starbase 137. He was good friends with Master Chief West. I liked him, and now that I was in his office, I felt he might be receptive to what I had to say. "Admiral, I've been keeping up on plans for a Borg response, and honestly, sir, we're getting nowhere. We can't respond without a ship, and a ship means Utopia Planitia." I handed the admiral a PADD I'd been working on all week. "Here's the personnel I'd like to put together to build our prototype," I said.

He looked over my proposal in silence for several long minutes. Afterward, he put it down and smiled. "Well, Ben, it seems like you've been putting some serious thought into this. You've selected some heavy hitters, and I like your rationale that a smaller team can get more done than a large think tank has been attempting to do. All right, I'll approve the project, and I love the name. *Defiant* has a nice ring to it."

✦

"I have to admit, Commander, this isn't the transmission I was expecting," Leah Brahms said.

From what I could make out behind the doctor, I could see I'd caught her in engineer La Forge's office on the *U.S.S. Enterprise*. Leah Brahms was critical in the design of the *Galaxy* class starship warp engine propulsion design. With dark brown eyes and hair, she was a brilliant woman with a cool exterior and penchant for saying exactly what she thought. "Understood. I won't take a lot of your time, Doctor Brahms. I'd just like to know if you've had an opportunity to review the classified material I sent you?" I asked.

"Yes, I have, it's intriguing. But I don't think I'm what you're looking for, Commander."

"I understand your concerns, I do. That's why you'd be involved in the design and initial construction, that's all. But more than that, I'm asking you to be part of a team of just four individuals that will build something to protect us all. You're not really going to say no to that, are you?" I asked.

Doctor Brahms looked at me for a long time, then finally spoke. "Damn. Alright, Commander, I'll be in your office on Utopia Planitia in a few days. Brahms out."

✦

I watched Lieutenant Commander Zor manipulate the large holo-model of the *Defiant* that was hovering over the design table we all sat at. "With the smaller profile we've given the ship, we could add phaser arrays port and starboard as well," he said.

Commander Elizabeth Shelby was shaking her head. "Phasers don't work against the Borg. We need another option."

This was the usual rhythm of the room. Shelby and I would discuss our creation's weaknesses, Zor would adjust the holo-model as we spoke, and Brahms would only speak up when she had something to say. As usual, Doctor Brahms was quiet, at the opposite end of the design table, working on a separate PADD.

Commander Shelby had been on the *Enterprise* when Picard was abducted by the Borg. Before Wolf 359, the lieutenant commander was really the only specialist on the Borg Starfleet had. She was in charge of Starfleet tactical analysis for the Borg, and she knew her stuff. After the massacre she had been assigned to lead the task force to rebuild the fleet, but quickly found herself weighed down in a mire of politics and red tape. I'd argued with her that her proposed *Ares* project was too bloated. She agreed with me and folded the best parts of her project—herself and her engineering crew—into the *Defiant* project. In the last month, we'd gotten farther than her design team had in six. "We need pulse cannons, along the lines of what the Klingons have," I said.

Shelby smiled. "Each pulse could automatically be attuned to a different frequency nutation," she mused. "I don't see how the Borg would be able to adapt to that."

For years Starfleet always believed bigger or sleeker meant better, but we changed that edict. Going with a smaller profile, something that would be more difficult to lock onto with a tractor beam, something that could easily slip around salvoes while effortlessly returning fire. A smaller ship but with the power of its larger counterparts. Our tough little group was putting together a beast of a ship. Working with these three geniuses around the design table, I was reminded of working on an earlier *Defiant* at Starbase 137. I was even more sure of the ship's name now.

Doctor Brahms slid the PADD she was working on down to me. "What's this?" I asked.

Leah leaned back in her chair. "Pulse phaser cannons, routed through the warp core," she said, as she gave a genuine smile.

✦

"Borg have increased to warp seven. They're firing their cutting beam!" Lieutenant Zor said.

"Evasive maneuvers, stay with them!" I ordered from the center seat.

The stars streaked by as the *Defiant* slipped around the cutting beam and opened up with its pulse phasers, tearing off huge swaths from the face of the cube.

"They're increasing to warp nine-point-four. They'll reach Earth in two minutes," Shelby said.

The *Defiant* began to shudder.

"Match velocity," I ordered.

Our tough little ship began to rock violently, as the engines began to whine. Doctor Brahms was screaming over the engines, "I can't hold it. It's too much power. She's tearing herself apart!"

The lights came on in the bridge, and I could see the disappointment on everyone's face. The cradle was the last phase a starship had to pass before an actual trial run. Once inside the cradle, the prototype starship would behave exactly as if it were under the same conditions in space. The *Defiant* was certainly living up to her namesake.

Leah Brahms didn't try to mask the frustration in her voice. "Commander, the four of us have been at this for two years. After ninety-four tests in the cradle, we have a ship that can fight the Borg but not fly, and that's not a ship. It's time to move on," she said.

The bridge was silent.

"Anyone else?" I asked.

Shelby looked apologetic before she spoke. "We should take what we've learned with the *Defiant* and integrate it into other, larger starships that are built to handle the power. Then, when we develop new systems, we can come back to the *Defiant*, maybe salvage her," she said.

I looked at Zor. At first he didn't make eye contact with me and I know it was because of our history on the *Saratoga*. Finally, he looked up. "They're right, Commander," he said simply.

I heard what they were all saying, and in any other situation, at any other time, it would have made sense. But back then every night when I closed my eyes I could see Jennifer's face in the debris and nothing was going to stop me. "You're all welcome to leave, but I don't have that option. Dismissed."

✦

After the failed tests in the cradle everything started to move quickly. The resources and personnel I had access to were reduced and then reduced again. Doctor Brahms and Commander Shelby both left the project. Zor tried to stay, but after a while it felt like pity, so I told him to go with my blessing. I tried to go to Admiral Whatley's office to discuss the issue with him, but he never seemed to be in. It had taken only two years for the Borg to fall out of the public consciousness. Of course, there was still an annual memoriam for those lost at Wolf 359, but that had become a separate case. During these two years at Utopia Planitia I would like to say I was a great father to you, Jake, but the truth is I know I wasn't. There were times when I let the *Defiant* project take over my day, my week, and my month. Spending more time at the shipyards than with you and your grandfather. I still had authority over the project, so I was still putting the *Defiant* through its paces using automation in the cradle, rather than being with my family.

Somewhere along the way, my work had become my life, and I hadn't even realized it.

One morning when I walked into my office, Captain—now Admiral— Leyton was waiting for me. I was excited to see him until I realized he wasn't smiling. "People that know you are telling me you've changed, that the *Defiant* has taken over your life. Can you tell me this isn't true, Ben?" he asked.

I was silent.

Admiral Leyton sighed. "The *Defiant* is being mothballed. Starfleet has put four of its best and brightest on this for three years and we don't have anything to show for it. It's time to move on, Ben," he said.

There was no mistaking that Leyton sounded a lot like Doctor Brahms. I had no doubt the admiral had spoken to her first to get an expert opinion on the mechanics and science of the situation before coming to me to hear my side. "One day, Admiral, the *Defiant* is going to save the Federation."

Leyton scoffed. "That may be, Benjamin, but it won't be today—or tomorrow, for that matter." The admiral took a breath and seemed as if he were trying to reset the mood. "Look, Ben, it's over. You're going to have to let this one go. I spoke to Shelby, and as a courtesy to you, we're not going to scrap the *Defiant*. The ship will stay here at Utopia in storage. Shelby is going to take some of the lessons learned and integrate them into the new line of *Akira*, *Steamrunner*, *Saber*, and *Norway* classes, so it won't have all been for nothing."

Leyton's words set me off and I didn't stop to think. I just reacted. "Frankly, Admiral, I don't think anyone that wasn't at Wolf 359 can understand what we're up against. They're *machines*, and they can afford to be a hell of a lot more patient than us. Three years from now, thirty years, or three thousand, it doesn't matter to the Borg. If the *Defiant* isn't finished, and if we don't protect ourselves now, we will regret it. And those eleven thousand souls that died, including my wife, would have all been for nothing!"

I knew my words crossed a line, but I just didn't care. I fully expected to see anger on Admiral Leyton's face, but instead, I saw the very last thing I wanted to see.

Pity.

I could see I hadn't ended our friendship, but I had certainly placed a strain on it. When he spoke to me next it was clear it was with all the weight and authority of an admiral. "You're being reassigned, Commander, period. End of story. The Federation is taking over a Cardassian station in orbit of Bajor, and I've recommended you run the place. They call it Terok Nor, but we're designating it Deep Space 9."

CHAPTER TWENTY-ONE

TEROK NOR—2369-2371

I WASN'T HAPPY ABOUT THE DECISION TO ABANDON the *Defiant* project, and uprooting you from school, Jake, and leaving Earth certainly wasn't ideal, but it is part of the life being in Starfleet. At the same time I started to think that maybe my time in Starfleet had run its course. As much as I loved it, I will always love being your father more. I started looking into becoming a project director for the construction of orbital habitats on Earth.

But, as I waited for a response on that, I did my job and followed orders.

For fifty years the Cardassian Union had occupied Bajor, pillaging the planet of all of its resources while torturing and enslaving the Bajoran people. During this period, they resisted the Cardassians every minute, every hour, every day. They became terrorists, spies, and anything else that was necessary to free their world. In the end their perseverance prevailed, and when the Cardassians finally left, one of the reasons was that the Bajorans made it too dangerous and too bloody for them to stay.

After the Cardassians pulled out, Bajor had no infrastructure, no economy, no food. They asked the Federation for assistance, not as another occupying force but as what the Federation has been for over two hundred years. An organization that helps without stipulation or condition.

The Bajorans needed help and they were going to need it quickly.

On the trip from Earth to Deep Space 9 I selected my senior staff. I wanted as many of them in place before or by the time I arrived. My first choice was the easiest. I had recently learned sadly that Curzon had passed away, but that the Dax symbiote had been passed to a new host, Jadzia, now Jadzia Dax. Reading her file, it was clear this young woman was an exceptionally gifted science officer and that she would be an incredible asset to DS9. I was eager to meet her for the first time and rekindle my friendship with Dax.

Once we started working together, I realized things felt familiar, but was nothing like working with Curzon. My old mentor was often playful to the point of being distracting. Regardless if he was on duty or off, he was usually more interested in what enjoyment he could extract from any particular moment than his responsibilities. In less than four hours on Deep Space 9 for the first time, Jadzia Dax had managed to do what hadn't been done by the Bajorans or the Cardassians—explain where the Orbs of the Prophets had originated from. And, in doing so, the Trill science officer helped make one of the most profound discoveries of the twenty-fourth century.

A stable wormhole in the Alpha Quadrant.

Maybe it was because she was a Starfleet officer, maybe it was because she was immersed in the sciences, or maybe it was just her age, but Jadzia always took the job very seriously. However, when she was off duty, that was when I got to see more of Curzon in Jadzia. There were times when Jadzia felt like a young, unsure lieutenant. There were times I could see Jadzia becoming the seasoned lieutenant commander on duty. And there were times it was clear she was also a three-hundred-year old soul. It may have taken seven lifetimes, but I always felt that Dax was most comfortable in the Jadzia Dax combination. Even though I spent more years with Curzon, I've fought side by side with Jadzia, and I've been her confidant. She will always be my best friend.

I've been in Starfleet long enough to know every ship or base has a baby. Some kid that's so young, so green that whether they know it or not, whether they look it or not, they're the baby. On the *Livingston* it was Lieutenant Kustanovich, who ate whenever he was nervous, which was a lot. I knew the moment I selected him it was going to be Doctor Bashir. The young man truly loved medicine but had a romanticized, perhaps somewhat juvenile, idea of what it meant to be in Starfleet, but, didn't we all when we first started? When I think of Julian now, and how far he's come, in so many ways, adhering as best he could to his ethics and principles. We've all done things we're not proud of, we all have secrets that we don't want brought out into the light of day. But Julian Bashir is one of those few, rare individuals that has had his worst secret exposed for all the world to see and we can still look at him and say he's a good and decent man. And he is certainly no longer the baby.

I've watched Bashir go from someone everyone thought they needed to look out for to him holding his own when we defended the station against The Circle. I think early on we all prejudged the doctor based on initial assumptions. But I've never known anyone to be a better example of character revealed.

Even while being held prisoner by the Jem'Hadar, Bashir tried to help them break their addiction to ketracel-white. He refused to leave a world the Dominion poisoned with the Quickening, bringing hope to a planet that had none. It's also true that you can work years with someone and not truly know them until you spend a weekend with them. When the doctor and I were trapped in the past, back in 2024 during the Bell Riots, I got to learn a lot about Julian Bashir. I've seen people fold for a lot less than being accidentally transported into the twenty-first century during one of the bloodiest riots of the period. Bashir had my back the entire time. We fought together, slept in alleyways together, and nearly died together. That time I spent with Julian was the only reason I let you go with him to a medical conference anywhere remotely close to where the Federation had been fighting with Klingons during our conflict with them. As a parent, even though I never thought you would get anywhere close to the enemy, I needed to know my child was in good hands. And yes, Jake, I know at the time you were seventeen and tall as me, but you were still very much a child.

My child.

As a father, it's not the experience I wanted you to have. But I'm glad Julian was there to have your back in the way I knew he would, in the way he had mine. I was also impressed with you, son. That experience didn't scare you off from writing, or cause you to become a different or even softer writer. Instead, it informed your craft and helped to reveal your character.

With everything Julian has seen and experienced, he's still managed to maintain a youthfulness that I admire. Whether it is playing darts with Chief O'Brien, or his many holodeck adventures, like masquerading as a secret agent, or introducing us all to Vic Fontaine. I'll admit there have been times I've seen it all as a little pointless, but now looking back I see more clearly that Julian has found unique ways to relieve stress in his life and, in doing so, like a good doctor, he has provided us with a prescription to do the same.

✦

I wanted to be an engineer in Starfleet for a long time, but I've been in command so long now I can't imagine doing anything else. But I don't regret a second of my trajectory. That first love, Starbase 137 and Master Chief West taught me a lot of things, but I think more than anything, those experiences gave me a profound respect for engineers and what they can do.

When I needed to find an engineer to run DS9 I realized I needed to find my own master chief. Miles Edward O'Brien came up in every search I ran for Starfleet engineers that had experience in the Cardassian theatre. As my parameters narrowed, his name remained. He had combat experience in the Cardassian War. He was resourceful, innovative, and well-liked by those around him. He was a non-commissioned officer and even built models as a kid, like me. I was surprised to learn that this gem was being wasted in the *Enterprise*'s transporter room.

I liked Chief O'Brien as soon as I met him. In another era he would've been what people called a "blue collar" hard-working man. But I think my like for him shifted over to respect when there was an accident while the chief was escorting our first visitor from the other side of the wormhole, an entity known as Tosk, back to his people. The chief took responsibility for the accident in his report, even though it was clearly a malfunction of the docking ring's security system. You can always tell the character of someone, Jake, by how they treat the most vulnerable. This Tosk was considered a slave to be hunted in a game, and while I'm not passing judgment on that species, I will say the chief treated Tosk as a friend, with respect and honor, which told me everything I needed to know about him.

In those early days when the station was a shambles, it seemed like something was breaking down every other week. A lot of that time reminded me of when I was at Starbase 137. Then, as now, there were a million things that needed to be done, each one with as much priority as the next. Back then, West wanted updates, but we took care of what needed to be done. As long as we got it done and it met Starfleet specifications, the master chief didn't say anything. I found myself taking on that same attitude with O'Brien. Micromanaging the man wasn't going to help him work. However, just like West, I'd learned that from time to time, it's always good to remind those that have free rein that there is a chain of command. But the truth is, with Miles it really wasn't necessary. He was one of the hardest-working people I'd ever met, and also one of the kindest.

O'Brien arrived on Deep Space 9 two days before I did. The Bajoran Provisional Government wanted Bajorans to work with members of Starfleet in the Operations Center, but none of the Bajorans knew our protocols. So the chief held classes before the morning shift for the Bajoran staff without telling anyone. When I found out about it, I didn't say anything, but it was unfortunate that we had to shut down the classes after the assassination attempt on Vedek Bareil.

Despite him being the most qualified person, I almost didn't select O'Brien as my chief of operations. After what happened with Jennifer on the *Saratoga* I knew Starfleet officers would do their duty, but I found myself hesitant to purposefully put families potentially in harm's way. This is the reason none of the other members of my senior staff have families of any kind. The only reason I went through with my decision with Miles was because, as I read about the couple's experiences on the *Enterprise*, it was clear Keiko had been in dangerous situations several times and dealt with them very well every time.

There are people that believe the captain of a starship or commander of a starbase is the most important person in that command structure and should be protected at all costs. It's a longstanding military tradition, and while I understand it, as captain, every life under my command is precious. That being said, I've seen Miles, a father, willing to put his life on the line for me. I've seen him do it when he and I were being held against our will, and I've seen him do it when we were fighting side by side on more occasions than I care to count. When Jadzia was murdered and the war was going badly, I felt I had to take a step back, get a new perspective, think things through. As hard as that was for me to do, knowing I was leaving DS9 in the chief's care made it a little easier. O'Brien always did more than I asked him, always stayed longer than he had to, and worked harder than anyone else. Much of the success of Deep Space 9 can be attributed to this one man.

When we talk about people that played a pivotal role in the success of Deep Space 9 and the war, people that will probably go down in the annals of history as an unsung hero and is one hell of an engineer, I have to talk about Rom.

The truth is, Jake, that I noticed and thought of Nog long before I thought of Rom. He was the peripheral character you see in a story. He was Quark's brother, Nog's father, but I hate to admit I never really gave much thought to who Rom was. It wasn't until Nog made a bold step for his life and told me he wanted to join Starfleet that I took notice. Nog said some things about his father that I'll keep just between him and me, but one of the things he said that stood out to me was that he felt his father could've been chief engineer of a starship, if he'd had the opportunity.

Honestly, at that moment, I didn't see it.

But I did see a tenacity in Nog that I hadn't expected, and I knew that had to come from somewhere. Three years later, the entire Alpha Quadrant saw Rom's ability. We are all very lucky Rom got the opportunity to show what he had to offer and he became much more than a chief engineer of a starship. He's the genius that came up with self-replicating cloaked mines. That one tactical engineering idea managed to hold back Dominion reinforcements from the Gamma Quadrant and give the Alpha Quadrant the one thing it desperately needed: time. Now that he's been named the new Grand Nagus, I think the Alpha Quadrant is going to learn all over again what Rom can do when given the opportunity.

✦

When I arrived, I was surprised the station was even in orbit. The Cardassians had stripped their facility of every viable piece of technology. In some areas, they'd even removed the lighting so we'd literally be in the dark when we took over. I'm sure you remember what it was like in those early days, Jake. With the station in that state, I was worried about you even if I did my best not to show it. I asked Odo to keep an extra eye on you, but, when I did that, he thought I was making a racist remark. After assuring the Constable that it was just a figure of speech, I think my words actually broke the ice between us.

Very early on, it was clear to me that Odo was used to people treating him differently because he's a shapeshifter. But in a galaxy of wonderous unknowns, I constantly remind myself there is no true normal. In a federation of planets and four quadrants of the galaxy, we are all different. If anything, I found more of myself in Odo's desire for justice and search for his people—his family. If people hadn't been so afraid of his ability to shapeshift, they too would have seen themselves in him.

Quark was the first Ferengi I ever met with a sense of family. Not to say that other Ferengi didn't also have a sense of family, but when I caught Nog involved in nefarious affairs and suggested that if Quark became DS9's community leader, the charges could be expunged, he agreed. That was when Quark showed me that, for all his schemes and backroom deals, he valued family over profit. I'd never seen that before. The truth is if he had left Nog to rot in the security cell I would have let him go and kicked Quark off the station myself. I came to see fairly quickly that Quark is both more and less very much like Ferengi everyone is used to dealing with. Quark worships profit: he lives for it. I wouldn't be surprised if he slept with the Rules of Acquisition under his pillow every night. That's just the kind of Ferengi Quark is.

But he's also no fool.

You can't have profits if you're enslaved, or worse if you're dead. Some Ferengi, some people, wouldn't let the threat of these things stop them, and would just push forward regardless. But Quark is the type of Ferengi and businessman that prefers the thirty-fifth Rule of Acquisition over the thirty-fourth. He understands peace is always much better for business than war.

That being said, Quark will always find an opportunity within a crisis. During our first encounter with the Jem'Hadar, we were captured by them. If not for Quark's greed, we would have never learned that our cellmate Eris's collar was a ruse, and that she was actually a Dominion plant sent to gather information on Starfleet and the Federation.

Jadzia really liked Quark and his bar. It was the only place on the station with holosuites, and just about the only place you could catch Morn and have a deep conversation with him at almost any time, twenty-six hours a day. I'll admit these three things together made Quark's Bar appealing even to me on occasion.

So while I'm appreciative for some of the things he's done, even thankful, I've never taken my eye off of our resident community leader.

Jake, as a reporter you're astute enough to know when something's missing from the story. And even though I've been talking about the aftermath of Wolf 359, there's one name that really hasn't come up.

Jean-Luc Picard.

After his rescue by the *Enterprise* and the reversal of his Borg assimilation reversed, to my astonishment, Starfleet deemed him fit to resume his captaincy. There were a lot of us that felt that decision was wrong, and desecrated the memories of everyone we lost that day. After what had happened, Picard got to go back to his life, to his ship, his crew, and those he loved.

Well, the survivors of 359 didn't. I didn't.

When we arrived at Deep Space 9, the *Enterprise* had already been there for two days, and I was told Picard wanted to meet with me. I have to tell you, seeing that man was something I held off on for as long as possible. When I finally walked into the *Enterprise* lounge, I was struck by how much the space reminded me of our living room on the *Saratoga*. When I looked at Picard I wasn't just angry, I was seething with a rage and hatred that had been living inside of me for nearly three years. A rage that had replaced my love, and was now living in the part of me that Jennifer had once treasured and nurtured, but was slowly rotting.

I didn't care that Picard was a superior officer, and I sure as hell didn't care that he was trying to be cordial. I couldn't strike a fellow officer, but I wanted to hurt him. I hated Picard for everything he took away from me, from our family, and even from the Federation at Wolf 359.

When the wormhole aliens, the Prophets here in this place showed me my pain, they showed me that I was very much like them, living a nonlinear existence within my grief, still stuck in that final moment on the *Saratoga* with Jennifer. When I saw that, and I admitted it, dealt with it, I was finally able to look at Picard differently as well.

The sad truth is that poor man was the Borg's first victim that day, and hating him only made my own pain worse. When I stopped feeding that emotional but irrational anger for him, I found something unexpected within myself—room for empathy and compassion for others, and for myself.

When you let go of hate, the first person you free is yourself.

✦

After my meeting with Picard, two things became very clear to me. First, it was obvious to me that he and nearly everyone in Starfleet had an opinion on Cardassians, Bajorans, and the occupation. I had read everything Starfleet had on Cardassians. I read mission reports and even a Cardassian evaluation profile constructed by Captain Jellico. But all of this felt like it was the wrong perspective: it was all from the outside looking in.

I wanted to find someone that had a deeper, personal perspective on the situation and the Cardassians. I had spoken to Kira when I first arrived and even though she started to fill in some of the blanks for me, the major had just come out of an unimaginable trauma, and we were just starting to get to know each other; she was confrontational and distrustful of me back then. I needed to speak to someone that could see the big picture. I needed a Bajoran who was also in Starfleet.

Luckily, as chance would have it, one was on the *Enterprise*.

"Cardassians have an overblown sense of entitlement and privilege that they use as justification for their atrocities," Ensign Ro Laren said.

Laren wore a Starfleet uniform but even in her quarters on the *Enterprise* I could see, like Kira, Bajor lived inside her. And even though she'd gone through a court martial, it was clear to me this woman was a genuine Starfleet officer. She was beautiful but had the face of someone that had seen far too much in too short a time. "So when you're told you deserve something just because you're Cardassian, you believe it, and it automatically elevates you and lowers everyone else," I said.

Ro nodded. "That's right, but that's not the real problem with Cardassians, Commander," she said.

This really piqued my interest. Of everything I'd read, this was new. "Go on, Ensign," I said.

"Bajor was occupied by Cardassia for fifty years, Commander. They tortured and enslaved us for every day in more ways than you can imagine, and we got to know them pretty well. Their smug superiority is a mask that covers a deeply rooted fear of not being good enough and of others being better, and that makes them very, very dangerous," she said.

I understood Ro Laren's message. "Because," I said slowly, "they'll do anything not to feel that way."

CHAPTER TWENTY-TWO
BAJOR—2371-2373

BAJOR IS THE FORTY-SECOND WORLD I'VE VISITED and even then, immediately after fifty years of occupation by the Cardassians, its beauty was undeniable. Yes, there were places of mindless and savage destruction, and brutal strip mining. But then I would see a few untouched acres of green fields on a rolling hill, or a lake as blue as the sky that the Cardassians used to swim in, or the beautiful remnants of Bajoran architecture that would let me know what once was.

Kai Opaka was one of those beautiful remnants of Bajor that had made it through the occupation.

I have never really understood the maxim "to walk by faith and not by sight" until I met Opaka.

Her faith in the Prophets sustained her through half a century of unimaginable cruelties. She reminded me of Grandma Octavia in so many ways. A strength that came from a place deep inside herself. Always looking for solutions within, her sense of spirituality, her kindness, and desire to put others before herself. I imagine if Opaka had met my grandmother, she would have been pleased with her *pagh*. Opaka wasn't interested in politics, power, or persuasion. Only the spiritual wellbeing of Bajor and the will of the Prophets. When she told me I was to be the Emissary, I honestly thought it was a lot of what we used to call mumbo jumbo, but now I see how far ahead, and patient,

Opaka was with me. She was not a nonlinear entity, but her faith gave her the ability to see far beyond all of us.

When we lost Kai Opaka it felt like the end of an era for Bajor. When a major sea change like that occurs on a world, it can be a time that ushers in new prosperity or unbridled chaos for its people.

Kai Winn was everything Opaka wasn't. Winn used blind faith and the station of Kai to elevate herself and not the Bajoran people. For Kai Winn, the will of the Prophets was always somehow beneficial to her. Power was not just sought, but coveted. However, in the end when Bajor needed her, when I needed her, Kai Winn became the true spiritual leader of Bajor it always deserved, and for that I am grateful.

And then there was Kira Nerys. When I met Nerys, she was combative, opinionated, blunt, honest, and took charge. She was like nothing I expected, and everything I knew I needed. In the Federation, part of a first officer's job is to be a buffer between the captain and their crew. They have to make sure everything runs smoothly and that everyone's needs are met. In many ways Kira's job wasn't only to be a buffer between myself and the station crew, but between the Federation and Bajor.

Although, at first, I had to remind the major that meant not speaking to Starfleet admirals without my authorization.

Being in Starfleet I've gotten close to people before, fought beside them, been injured with them, gotten in and out of life and death situations with them. But Nerys was different from the start. She never went to an academy or had a dream of joining anything like Starfleet or the Federation. She simply wanted to free her people. And this woman, this freedom fighter terrorist that started as a child, acquired skills and tactics that would be the envy of some Starfleet captains. Yet instead of simply becoming a killing machine, she didn't allow the Cardassians to rob her of her morality and of her ability to love, or of aspects of her innocence.

One of the best times I've ever had was taking Nerys to a baseball game. The game didn't matter, I got to see Nerys allow herself to be vulnerable with me for one of the first times, and have fun in an unexpected way. With her past it wasn't lost on me how much courage that took, and it said everything about our friendship.

But if I'm honest, that friendship took time to develop on both our parts. Even though we butted heads a few times, right from the start it was clear to me we worked well together and both of us wanted what was truly best for Bajor. Captain Storil taught me the benefit of having a friendship with a first officer. So I didn't force it, and because Nerys had never learned as a kid how to hide the truth, she often spoke her mind without any filter.

I liked that, a lot. Even when—especially when—I was on the receiving end of her comments.

But even as I warmed up to my first officer, I could tell she was reluctant to do the same. How do you have a friendship with someone that is the Emissary to the Prophets? I've never just been Nerys's commanding officer. Almost since the first moment she met me, I've also been the Emissary. Honestly, I think there were times it was a little uncomfortable for both of us, and it was certainly a learning curve for me. But it's funny how sickness and injury can change the nature of a relationship, Jake, or make you even more appreciative of one that has always been there.

During a battle on the *Defiant* with Jem'Hadar warships, I was injured. I knew it was bad because it was hard to concentrate, difficult to hold onto thoughts, and I kept slipping in and out of consciousness. But through it all I kept feeling this hand gripping mine. Like a tether the hand wouldn't let go, wouldn't let me slip away into the darkness that kept trying to claim me. And then there was this voice hovering over me. Ever present, familiar, determined.

I almost died that day, Jake. But it wasn't the Prophets that saved me, or one of Doctor Bashir's devices. I didn't die because Kira wasn't going to let that happen. She wasn't talking to me as the major to her captain, or a Bajoran to her Emissary, but just Nerys talking to Ben, trying to keep her friend alive.

I've been to so many worlds and met so many people, but the truth is that meeting someone like Kira is rare, and being able to work beside them and to call them your friend is rarer still. I would walk into fire for Nerys and I know she would do the same for me.

✦

Jake, I've been thinking a lot about friendship.

When I was growing up, I didn't have a friendship like you do with Nog. Everyone was so close. My sister and brothers were my friends. I really didn't meet anyone that I connected with until I got to the academy where I met Cal Hudson. We grew up in two very different places—New Orleans and Austin, Texas—but we still saw the world and people in many of the same ways. The truth is there were times that I felt closer to Cal than I did David or Elias. I think part of that is because I'm the only one in our family that's in Starfleet, and it was the same with Cal and his family, so he and I shared a common bond.

Cal threw my bachelor party and, of course, was my best man, although I barely saw him at the wedding. How do you lose a best man at a beach wedding? He was too busy talking to Gretchen, Jennifer's maid of honor. It turns out the two of them had walked nearly a mile away to some rocks and were talking for almost three hours! A few months after that, we were doing it all again, but now I was his best man, and throwing his bachelor party.

If you're lucky, Jake, you get to have two families in life: the one you're born with and the one you acquire along the way. For some, the family you choose is more loving than the one you start with. That was Cal's story and why I think he was so alone, maybe even a little isolated, when he lost Gretchen. I couldn't be there for him when he lost her, and he couldn't console me when I lost your mother. It's the nature of working in Starfleet, and it's life. That's why it's important to make those connections and friendships with people that you feel are special when you can, Jake. Sometimes you may not see them again for years, but if the connection was real to begin with, it won't matter. You will always be able to pick up right where you left off.

You're about to become an older brother, and with that will eventually, hopefully, come a friendship with your little brother or sister. I can tell you it won't always be easy, but there's nothing like having that kind of connection.

Now that Nog is a lieutenant in Starfleet, you'll probably see even less of him than you did during the war. Your friendship with him challenged my own preconceived notions about Ferengi. It made me aware of prejudiced thoughts and opinions I didn't even realize I had. I'm very thankful to the two of you for that. When Nog came to me and told me he wanted to attend Starfleet Academy, I was reminded of just how easy it is to label and stereotype someone based on the actions of others or a false narrative. Nog has proven to be one of the best officers I've ever served with. I'm thankful for his friendship with you, grateful for his service, and proud to have been his sponsor.

Unfortunately, the other side of the coin of friendship can often be betrayal. I hope you never know what that feels like, but one day you might, so let's talk about it.

During my time on Deep Space 9, disappointment and betrayal by those I trusted seemed to go hand in hand more times than I care to admit. In a lot of ways, Cal and I were mirrors of each other. We were in the academy together and served together for a long time, long enough to become good friends, long enough to trust each other, long enough to make the pain of what he did run deep.

Cal didn't betray me, didn't betray our friendship, but he did lie to my face. I can make that distinction because Cal betrayed himself, Starfleet, and the Federation long before he made the decision to lie to me. By the time he got to that bridge, he had crossed so many others that he probably felt lying to me was just a necessary step to help the Maquis. I believe he thought I would cross that bridge with him because of our friendship. He was right to think there wasn't much I wouldn't do for him, but betraying myself and my principles was a bridge too far, and one I wouldn't cross for him.

I'd be lying though, if I said I didn't understand Cal. Perhaps not the cause, but where he was in his life when he joined the Maquis. He'd gone through the pain of losing Gretchen to a rare temporal neurological degeneration. After that, all he had was the uniform, and he lost perspective, just as I did with the *Defiant* project. He didn't like the Federation–Cardassian Treaty, and I think it provided him with a fight he needed. I often wonder about the choices he and I would have made in the midst of our pain if our roles were reversed. The truth is I was becoming just as lost as Cal, he was just further along, and sometimes when you get so far along a wrong path, it's difficult to see the road back. Cal couldn't see his road back, and it got him killed. I wish I'd seen something in time to help him, but he was always better at holding up heavy weights than I was.

I never saw Eddington coming. He used my open hand of friendship to pull me in, and betray me. Jake, if it had just been me, that pill would have been a hell of a lot easier to swallow, but it wasn't. Eddington used me to betray Starfleet and the Bajoran people. I couldn't let that stand. What Cal had done was bad enough, but Cal at least focused his energy on the Cardassians that were attacking former Federation citizens. Eddington attacked Federation and

Cardassian alike and lied to himself that it was because his cause was just and he was fighting the good fight. That's not a freedom fighter. That's a glory hound.

Starfleet officers are known throughout the galaxy for being paragons of integrity and character. But people don't realize the dark pitfalls that lay waiting within the desire to do good deeds. Eddington and Cal weren't the first I've known to stray off the path and tell themselves they were doing it for a righteous cause. Admiral Leyton did the same damn thing as Eddington. Leyton tried to take over Starfleet because he was sure he knew what was best for all of us.

Cal allowed himself to get sucked into the Maquis, but Eddington was different. The more I listened to him talk, once he revealed his true self, the more I came to see he never felt he strayed from the path. Michael Eddington felt it was Starfleet and the Federation—everyone else—that had betrayed him and those in the Maquis. He was so caught up in his own integrity and character, so caught up in doing what he felt was the right thing, that he never even saw just how far away from the path he truly was.

That's a minefield I've had to walk through myself, son.

The road paved with integrity and character isn't a wide one. There are many twists and turns that take you off the straight and narrow path, and they will all be for reasons and causes you tell yourself are just and true. I've felt it myself. My desire to bring Eddington to justice started to become an obsession. At one point, I came to see Eddington as a cautionary tale, and I realized I needed to take extreme measures to defeat him, but not so extreme that I would lose myself.

And when it was all over I realized it wasn't over at all, Jake. There are always tests, trials of character and judgment just waiting to tempt you, to break you. Some are obvious and can be clearly seen in the light of day, but there will be others that won't come to you straight on, but in the night, in the guise of a deed to help that is so great it would be worth your own discomfort for the sake of others. But even then, especially then, it can be difficult to live with the choices you make. Because if you start hiding behind the excuses and rationales of those choices, perhaps that's pointing towards a larger truth? And if I do that, then in my own way, how different am I from Cal, Leyton, or Eddington?

CHAPTER TWENTY-THREE
EMISSARY—2369-2372

JAKE. I'M NOT SURE THIS NEXT PART IS GOING TO MAKE SENSE. The longer I'm in here, the more I come to understand. However, linear time has no meaning here. So doesn't that mean the moment I set foot in here, I've always understood what I now understand?

Are you starting to see my point, son?

I've come to understand I have powers, no, let's call them… the abilities of the Emissary. One was sending you this message. There are others, but it's taking… time for me to sort it all out.

Don't laugh.

All of this has me thinking a lot about not just what's happening to me, but also about faith, and the responsibility of power.

Before I came to Deep Space 9 the extent of the faith I had in my life was for Starfleet, and the system it created that had endured for so long. I had faith in the officers, and the people I worked with every day. Faith in their skills, faith in their ability to work together, faith in the technology and ships those people created and relied on. That was it. And then, I met Nerys, Kai Opaka, and the Bajoran people. Their faith sustained them through unimaginable horrors during some of Bajor's darkest moments. I had never met people like that, I'd never stayed anywhere long enough with people like that to understand them, long enough to learn from them. Their faith and spirituality inform everything in their lives, everything. Nerys' faith makes her a better warrior. Kai Opaka's faith led her to a dead moon to spend the rest of her life helping a group of people she didn't even know. Nerys, Opaka, the Bajorans, I watched them, worked with them and it was impossible to not be somewhat influenced and inspired by them. Through these people I found myself exploring new—or maybe some old—possibilities of faith.

You know that at home, we've never been very religious, yet when I was growing up, the Bible always had a place in our home. I think it was more a source of comfort than a guide. In my line of work, I tend to see things that could be misconstrued as higher powers all the time. There have been times Starfleet personnel and technology have been mistaken for gods. Some say the Bajorans do this when they call me their Emissary. Personally I've never sought power, especially power like this, but now, being among what people would consider gods has given me the faith that there is more out there beyond what any of us can comprehend.

When Kai Opaka first squeezed my ear lobe to read my *pagh*, she called me the Emissary. That word, that role, that responsibility has brought with it a weight that, at times, has felt almost impossible to bear.

It started in little ways. At first, on Bajor, I would be called Emissary instead of Commander. Out of respect I would let it slide and just smile. Then it started to happen on the station. First on the promenade, then on a turbolift, or in hallways. Over time there wasn't a public place where a Bajoran wasn't at some point referring to me as the Emissary.

In those early days, I was uncomfortable with the title. I never wanted to disrespect the Bajoran people or mock their faith in any way, so, as usual, I smiled and stayed silent. When I met Federation President Jaresh-Inyo, I found myself sympathizing with, and perhaps understanding, the man in ways few could. There were times I would look into the faces of Bajorans I'd never met before and often see expressions of hope, and even the expectation of salvation.

When Akorem Laan came through time and claimed to be the first true Emissary, I thought I'd found my out and was eager to relinquish the role. But after seeing Bajorans assaulting each other in an effort to return to the D'jarra caste system, I realized I was wrong to give it up. Thankfully when Akorem and I asked the Prophets, they, too, agreed with me.

Even later, when I became comfortable as the Emissary and the responsibility it carried, I still never wanted or sought the power or the influence. Regardless of my lineage, I am not a messiah, or some magical being. I am just what I have always been.

A man.

Which is the whole point now, isn't it, Jake? The Bajorans call the entities that live here in the wormhole Prophets. They treat them like gods, and I've certainly seen them do things that could be defined by some as god-like.

But having incredible power doesn't make you a god, it just makes you powerful, and sometimes abusive. Q has nearly incomprehensible power, but the more he wanted to be worshiped as a god, the clearer it was to me that he was no better than an incredibly insecure, and perhaps even short-sighted, human. Q didn't seek validation from other super-beings on his level, like the Organians or the Metrons. No, he always wanted to be propped up by those that didn't know any better, that he desperately hoped would see him as a deity.

Across the universe, on countless worlds, the mythologies of so many diverse species have taught us the same thing over and over. Gods are never judged by the power they wield, but by how responsible they are with that power, and with how they treat those in their care.

I don't know what the Prophets are. I don't know if they've always lived here in the wormhole, or if long ago they were once like us. Living and dying with hopes and dreams and families. I do know, Jake, that sometimes, they can be detached, even cavalier when it comes to their power. Then, other times, in their own way, they appear to have a deep understanding and even love for Bajor.

I don't ever want to become like that.

I've been thinking a lot about this since I've been in here. A part of who and what they are is inside me, but I'm a part of them, too. Does this mean I'll start to become more like them, or will my spending time in here influence them and help them to learn from me? I can only hope—

"Ironic. One who does not wish to be among us is to be the Emissary."

This time there was no transition from the infinite white of the Celestial Temple, no burst of blinding white light, no ocean of memories. There was simply before and now. This time the transition, in many ways, was like what it was to be in a transporter, only faster, instantaneous.

It was as if he'd relocated from one place to another at the speed of thought. One moment Captain Sisko was inside the Celestial Temple, and the next he was on a beach at night. It was obvious this was Bajor. Her five moons hung suspended high above in the night like pearls adorning the planet. A group of barrowbugs were leaving their mound in wet sand for drier land. Emerald green waves pushed onto the beach and then slipped back into the ocean, obeying the tidal rhythms. Benjamin Sisko looked at the woman that stood across from him on the otherwise empty beach. A moment ago, he'd recognized her voice, and now she stood in front of him. Covered in the traditional lavender and orange robes of Bajor's spiritual leader, only her face and hands were exposed, so that she might always speak the truth and provide a helping hand.

Kai Opaka.

"Opaka? What are you doing here?" Sisko questioned.

The Kai walked over to the Starfleet captain, pressed her thumb and forefinger to his earlobe, and read his *pagh*. "Who are you?" she asked, finally removing her hand.

Sisko looked confused. "What? Don't you know me?"

Opaka scowled. "Know you? How can I know someone who doesn't know himself?"

Sisko shook his head in confusion as he turned both of his hands inward, pointing at himself. "We've been over this before, I don't understand. I'm the Sisko, the Emissary. Is this Bajor's future or its past?"

Opaka laughed. "What comes before now is no different than what is now, or what is to come. It is one's existence."

Sisko took the Kai's hands in his. "What? I don't—that was seven years ago. Opaka, what are you trying to tell me?" He asked.

The Kai smiled. "We are of Bajor. You are of Bajor."

Opaka pulled her hands away from Sisko, and as she did her body coalesced into a translucent wisp of blue energy. Sisko watched from the shore as the energy life-form ascended high into the Bajoran sky. When the energy wisp was a small point on the horizon, barely visible, it happened. An explosion of light erupted in the Bajoran sky. Coiling into rings of energy around an open doorway of power.

The wormhole opened over Bajor and the speck of blue entered.

CHAPTER TWENTY-FOUR
SONS OF CARDASSIA 2369–2375

I WASN'T GOING TO TALK ABOUT HIM, BUT I REALIZE IT'S NECESSARY.

Dukat.

Whenever I meet someone, I make an effort not to have any preconceptions about them. It's not always easy—as I said earlier, I judged Nog and Rom by other Ferengi. Usually, I like for people to tell me who they are through their words and, more importantly, their deeds. It's how I was raised, and it has served me well throughout my life.

When I first met Dukat he was menacing and brutally honest. He walked into my office on Deep Space 9, which two weeks prior had been his on Terok Nor. He told me he missed the office, but what he really meant was that he missed the power that came with it.

As he walked around attempting to mark his territory, Ro Laren's words came to mind: "They have an overblown sense of entitlement and privilege." I could see the truth in her words. Dukat was offended that I was sitting at his desk. I could feel he wanted to remove me physically from the chair—and perhaps more.

But that was just the first day. Over time I came to see Dukat clearly as a narcissist, but I also saw him as an exile that loved his world even though it didn't love him, and as a father that loved his daughter. The truth is that none of us are completely good or bad—we all have our secrets and our shames. I watched

Dukat wrestle with demons and try to reconcile those parts of himself, and become better. My fundamental mistake with Dukat was that I didn't realize he was never going to try to become a better person. He was simply always attempting to attain higher levels of power. From that first day in my office (and it was *my* office!) Dukat always defined himself by the power he wielded. The power he believed the universe owed him. The power he used to make others suffer. The more power he acquired, the more he needed because it told him who and what he was.

Powerful.

I've wrestled with the burden of command my entire adult life. First as a commander, then as the Emissary and now as a captain. The most important part of being in command and having power is in making decisions that will forever affect people's lives, decisions about who lives, and who dies. The lives that have been lost in battle from my decisions haunt me every day.

Dukat could only do the same two things over and over: make people suffer, and gain more power.

On and on it went, first the Bajorans with the occupation, then the Alpha Quadrant with the Dominion War, and yes, I believe if I hadn't stopped him, eventually, the galaxy.

I've called Dukat evil before, and I do think that fits him, but I also think Ro was right all those years ago. I believe Dukat needed to define himself with power because he didn't know who he was without it, which really scared him.

Fear.

Sadly, it's clear now that was the real reason for his breakdown, not Ziyal's death. Fear. When Dukat was at the height of his power, supreme ruler over all of Cardassia, had retaken Deep Space 9, and had Starfleet and the Klingon Empire on the ropes, he lost one battle that didn't cost him the war, but set him and the Dominion back. The Changelings retreated, accepting from their perspective that sometimes you must take one step back to take two steps forward. In their strategic retreat they preserved power in what they considered a temporary setback.

But not Dukat.

For all intents and purposes he was shown to be powerless, impotent, and he lost it, his insecure psyche cracked. I think that was when Dukat became truly dangerous, truly evil. That was also when he decided to add a third ambition to his other two.

Destroying what I cared about.

That's why he left me alive when he could have killed me; that's why he killed Jadzia, when he could have left her alive. It's why he worked so hard to lead the Cult of the Pah Wraiths and become the antithesis of what I represented to the Bajoran people as their Emissary. It's why he aligned himself with the Pah Wraiths and Kai Winn. Power, suffering, pain, fear. On and on, over and over. When I pushed Dukat over the edge in the fire caves, in many ways, he was being consumed and imprisoned in the flames of his own creation.

Since I'm talking about one Cardassian I know, this has me thinking about the other.

Elim Garak.

I can't say I ever liked Garak, but I did find him necessary, and honest. I know it may sound strange, Jake, to hear me call Garak, a well-rehearsed liar, and known spy, an honest man. But over time, I started to understand that the more lies Garak told, the more of his own truth he revealed. Of course, this never meant that I could spot his tell, which was invisible. But there were certain things you could rely on Garak to do. First, from the day we all met him he lied constantly about his varied professions, his skills, whether or not he was a spy and if he'd killed people.

But he never lied about the fact that he was a liar.

This is something that he made sure everyone was aware of. I would never turn my back on him, but over time I think we all began to understand that we could trust Garak to be Garak. His friendship with Doctor Bashir didn't make sense on paper. But then I realized sometimes our friendships and the relationships we seek out are not always who we're compatible with, but who we'd like to be. Sometimes it's not even the individual we're friends with but the quality that friend imbues. There may be other reasons behind Garak and Bashir's friendship, but I think a large part of it is because Garak admires our good doctor, and sees a person he could have been.

Secondly, Garak never lied to himself.

Dukat lied to himself all the time. He made excuses for the atrocities he committed and by doing so prevented himself from truly understanding who he was, and who Cardassia was. I never saw Garak lie to himself about who he was, and in doing so he saw himself and Cardassia honestly. Regardless of anything Garak may have said I believe this is why he aided us, especially during the Dominion War. His own self-interests aside, he saw the changes in his homeworld, and I think those changes impacted him. The direction Dukat and the Founders were taking Cardassia under the rhetoric of improving life for all Cardassians. In reality, Cardassia and its people were just resources being used by Dukat to amass power, and by the Dominion to gain a foothold in the Alpha Quadrant. Garak saw this and allowed his skills to be used as an instrument for change.

Garak fought with us against Cardassia to save Cardassia.

At this point, son, you may be asking yourself why am I giving you my impression about Garak? To my recollection, other than a passing acquaintance, you've never truly interacted with our resident tailor. But should for any reason your paths cross, I wanted you to know what my thoughts, feelings, and impressions of the man are. One day you may have to decide for yourself if he can be trusted.

And when it comes to certain circumstances, I believe he can be.

CHAPTER TWENTY-FIVE

DOMINION—2370-2375

I KNEW THE ALPHA QUADRANT WAS IN TROUBLE when we encountered the Jem'Hadar. It wasn't their appearance. Thanks to Curzon, appearances had stopped intimidating me long ago. It wasn't even that they had the personal ability to cloak. What made me see just how serious a threat the Jem'Hadar and Dominion were was when they went up against the *U.S.S. Odyssey*, a *Galaxy*-class starship. Without any hesitation whatsoever, they went on a kamikaze run to destroy the ship. The Jem'Hadar were the enforcers for the Dominion, who would kill their own soldiers to prove a point. This was the first time I encountered a major political power that had created a species of disposable people just to be used as its military. The Klingons, Romulans, and Federation forces were all made up of individuals from those groups—not a separate species entirely. I also found myself thinking about when the Tzenkethi tried to take the *Okinawa*. The Tzenkethi were ruthless, and they could have just pointed a phaser at the warp core and blown up the ship and themselves to prove a point, but they didn't.

The Dominion just had.

When I saw the *Odyssey* explode, it was clear to me I had to do everything in my power to prevent that kind of insanity from reaching the Alpha Quadrant.

✦

"You've seen the footage of the *Odyssey*. I need her, Admiral," I said.

Admiral Whatley leaned back in his chair at Utopia Planitia. "What makes you think that overgunned, overpowered little ship that can't fly past warp nine is going to help you against this Dominion, Ben?" he said.

I leaned in, and grinned. "I built her, Admiral, and she's defiant."

✦

Thank the stars for Miles Edward O'Brien. We would never have gotten the kinks worked out of the *Defiant* without him. Part of the reason that I had asked the *Defiant* be attached to DS9 was because I had seen the miracles the chief had performed, and I was confident he could do what none of us could, and fix my girl.

When we made first contact with the real power inside the Dominion—the Founders—it became clear the situation was worse than I could have ever imagined. The Changelings weren't warmongering zealots or a species just looking for territory. The Founders' sense of purpose and order had created the Dominion. It allowed them to take over the Gamma Quadrant for over a thousand years, through fear.

Long ago, Changelings were hunted, tortured, and destroyed, simply because they weren't solids, because they were different. The Changelings vowed never again to be hunted and tortured. They used their abilities to destabilize power structures and overthrow governments. After that, the Changelings created the Dominion to keep an entire quadrant on its knees and under their control. In his mission report, Odo stated that the female Changeling told him, "What you control can't hurt you."

Jake, fear can be a powerful motivator. For some, it can make them want to protect themselves and those they care about. For others, they may want to wield it as a tool to obtain power and control. Admiral Leyton used the Changeling threat to try to take over Starfleet. The Cardassians are so afraid of being weak that they have killed millions and committed unspeakable atrocities in the pursuit of strength. Kai Winn and the Cult of the Pah Wraith use fear to elicit obedience and worship. And the Dominion wanted to enslave the entire Alpha Quadrant in order to protect themselves.

Son, I've always understood how terrible slavery is. As a kid, I've already told you how your grandfather took me to one of the Remembrance Centers, how it educated me and had a powerful impact in a way I'll never forget. But, back then, I had never physically experienced anything to do with slavery, it was just words in a book, and a painful part of history. That changed when the chief and I found ourselves stranded in a compound belonging to a woman named Alixus. She tried to get me to convert to her way of thinking. To give up my uniform, wear what they wore, and to give up trying to find a way off the planet. When I refused, I was locked in a sweat box, a cramped metal box that sat out in the sun. I was denied any food or water. I understood that Alixus was trying to break me. She was hoping after being let out of the box I'd see the error of my ways, beg forgiveness, beg for water. Agree to anything she wanted.

What Alixus didn't understand was that I didn't go into that box alone. I went into that box with the strength given to me by my father, my grandfather, and my ancestors that had overcome much, much worse. I went into that box wearing a uniform that represented over two hundred years of courage and justice. As I sat in the darkness and heat, feeling the slow effects of dehydration, suffocation, and exhaustion rack my body, I didn't know if I would come out of the box alive—but I knew I would come out free.

I thought a lot about that box after meeting the Changelings and seeing what they wanted for the Alpha Quadrant. The Federation had been introduced to the Founders and the Dominion on my watch, and it was up to me to prevent the Founders from bringing their perfect form of slavery to the Alpha Quadrant.

Less than a year after our first contact with the Founders, the Tal Shiar and the Obsidian Order launched a joint preemptive strike against the Founders' homeworld. When the joint task force was destroyed by the Dominion, I could feel then what was starting to happen. Some said that the Founders' greatest power is their ability to change shape, but I think what's even greater is their ability to seek out, twist, and shape their adversary's paranoia and fear for the Dominion's purposes.

The Federation was founded on the simple yet elegant belief that there is more that connects us than separates us. Everyone matters, and we are all stronger together. The Founders understood that the strength of the Federation, and most of the powers in the Alpha Quadrant, are constructed to withstand confrontation from without, and not violent, structured dissent from within. So they took on our faces, and trusted positions of power, in places of authority, to lead us to our own destruction.

Romulans, Cardassians, Klingons, and the Federation. The Founders were holding up a mirror to the Alpha Quadrant, showing us the worst parts of ourselves. It was ugly, and they were using our own fears, prejudices, and paranoia to help us destroy ourselves without them firing a single shot.

Divide and conquer.

The Tal Shiar and Obsidian Order were dismantled in the Dominion's opening play against the Alpha Quadrant. Trust and communication were eroding between the quadrant's major power structures. When I thought about what was happening, I was reminded of a quote from Sun Tzu: "The supreme art of war is to subdue the enemy without fighting." I started to feel more and more like we were being isolated, corralled into a position so that when the time came, we'd be easy to slaughter.

I never spoke about this to anyone or put these feelings in my reports, Jake. As a leader there are some things you have to keep to yourself, burdens you have to bear so that the people in your command won't have to feel the weight. And even if they do feel the same way, then they shouldn't see their fears on the face of their leader, that's not my job.

As their captain, it's my job to stand shoulder to shoulder with them in the darkness and then lead them into the light.

CHAPTER TWENTY-SIX

FREIGHTER CAPTAIN—2371-2375

JAKE, I HAVE TO ADMIT I NEVER EXPECTED TO FALL IN LOVE WITH KASIDY.

When you told me she was a freighter captain, I'm not sure I knew what to expect. Besides, after your mom, I never expected to fall in love ever again. Meeting Fenna and the emotions we shared was an extraordinary situation. There was emotion, there was mystery, and there was chemistry, but Fenna wasn't real. She was a subconscious projection of a woman that looked just like her but had her own trauma she needed to work through. At first, that experience hurt, but then over time, I realized it taught me that there was still a place in my heart for love.

And even though I realized that, it didn't mean I was going to ever look to fill that place. The truth is, son, if you hadn't nudged me in Kasidy's direction, it would never have happened. If anyone else had tried to fix me up with her, even Dax, I would have said no.

Thank you.

I realized as soon as I saw her there was something there. Love is different every time, but if you're lucky it does get deeper as you move forward. I also think love should be kept private, even when expressed publicly.

I was surprised how quickly and how easy it was for Kasidy and I to become friends. I'm always in meetings or taking care of something or putting out some fire somewhere, and yet, before I knew it, she and I had seen half a dozen baseball games together. Grandpa James always told me we find the time for the things and people that are important to us, and he was right. Somewhere during those baseball games, I'd fallen in love with Kasidy Yates. Our love had grown not out of what we said to each other, but in the silences we spent together. From the first moment I met her, we started communicating with, and to, each other in those moments of silence in a conversation. I had never had anything like that before, not like this. So much was being said, and heard, and felt by both of us in those moments. With this woman, I was learning something new about myself. I was finding a place within myself that I had never been to before. I was learning to communicate and love in a way I didn't know I could.

Which made her betrayal so difficult.

I lost Cal to the Maquis. Eddington betrayed me and his uniform because of the Maquis. And now the woman I was in love with was delivering shipments to the Maquis. They were all different, but it felt the same. I was losing people I trusted to this, and all three lied to me about their involvement. When we finally caught Kasidy red-handed, Odo was upset we didn't take her into custody, but I knew I had to give her the opportunity to come back on her own. If she didn't, I was prepared to hunt her down.

But she did return of her own volition, and that said everything to me.

And because she did, I knew then that we had the possibility of a future together. As I looked at her in that docking bay as she turned herself in, I had a moment very much like I did back on Gilgo Beach. I knew I was looking at the woman that I wanted to marry. But a lot of years had passed since I was that young, eager junior officer and a lot of life had been lived since then. So I didn't say anything. I knew that no matter how I felt, a lot of things had to happen first. Kasidy had to stand trial and pay for her crimes, I had to sit with my feelings, and then she had to return and see if we both still felt the same about each other.

When Kasidy came back we picked up right from where we left off. If anything, the time apart made me see how much I missed her and wanted to spend my life with her. I asked her to marry me when it felt right. The Prophets said if we married I'd know nothing but sorrow, but even now, even here in this place, Jake, this bond of marriage doesn't weaken me. It strengthens me and gives me the most powerful motivator to return.

Family.

Sometimes the universe brings you an unexpected gift.

I never thought I would be a father again. Jake, one day you're going to see that there's nothing more important and powerful that two people can do together than have a child. That's why love is such a necessary ingredient. It strengthens the bond between the parents and the new life they've created.

Soon, just like me, you won't be an only child anymore. You will be where I was all those years ago. You're going to be an older brother. Just follow your instincts, and I know you'll be a great brother.

CHAPTER TWENTY-SEVEN

WAR—2372-2375

THE CHANGELINGS HAD MADE IT TO EARTH.

The Founders had infiltrated the Romulan Tal Shiar and the Klingon High Command. The more I tried to hold everything together, the faster it was slipping through my fingers. Every victory I achieved against the Dominion brought about a deeper loss.

We thought we stopped a Changeling threat on Earth only to realize it was just a corrupt admiral. And we never learned what the Changelings were actually doing on Earth.

✦

When the Klingons accused the Cardassian government of being controlled by Changelings and demanded we stand with them in an attack against Cardassia, the Federation did the right thing and refused. But the eroded trust with the Klingons became the linchpin for a new Federation-Klingon war. Unlike Curzon, I hadn't had a lot of experience with Klingons, so I requested that Starfleet send me the only one we had.

Lieutenant Commander Worf.

As much as Nerys aided me with Bajor, Worf did the same with the Klingons. I can say without him, the outcome of the Federation-Klingon war would not have been the same. He not only became an incredible asset to me, but I could see elements of myself in him. He admitted to me that after the destruction of the *Enterprise* -D he had lost his perspective, and was struggling to find his way. I saw other parallels: the woman he loved had also been murdered, and now his son was also without his mother. Here on Deep Space 9 he was in unfamiliar territory, and uncertain if he wanted to stay in Starfleet. I understood what that felt like, and offered Worf the position of strategic operations officer on DS9. I watched Worf not only shift from security to command, much like I did, but over the years, I saw him slowly adjust in ways he didn't think he could, while always remaining Klingon.

When he first arrived he was a great officer, but standoffish, even rigid when off duty. Although he'd never admit it, his relationship with Jadzia did begrudgingly soften some of his edges.

I didn't see the connection between him and Jadzia at first, but once they were together, it became obvious and just made so much sense on so many levels. I think their relationship made them both happy and gave them both a sense of fulfillment in a way that neither really wanted to admit.

When Worf returned from the Dominion internment camp, I noticed another change. I thought my strategic operations officer might double down on his Klingon heritage. After all, it was the warrior inside him that kept him alive and allowed him to defeat so many Jem'Hadar in hand-to-hand combat while he was kept in captivity. But I started to see Worf more in Quark's when he was off duty. Usually, it was with Jadzia, but sometimes with O'Brien as well. And now that he was friends with General Martok—the real Martok (whom we all decided we liked, and who had much more personality than his Changeling counterpart) Worf was just friendlier. I know Klingons always seek a warrior's death, but I think Worf's experience had taught the Klingon to enjoy life.

When he and Jadzia got married, their wedding was one of the brightest periods for all of us during the war. It was a reminder that life goes on, that no matter what is happening around you in the galaxy, there is never a bad time to be in love. And when Jadzia lay in the infirmary, mortally wounded by Dukat, I stood in the background and watched as my best friend said goodbye to her husband. Worf screamed in what I know was a Klingon ritual to warn Sto'Vo'Kor that a Klingon warrior was about to be among them, Klingon or not.

I understood and felt his rage.

We both grieved Jadzia Dax and dealt with her loss in our own ways. Worf lost his par'Mach'kai, and I lost my best friend. Thankfully, we both got a part of what we lost back when Ezri Dax came into our lives.

When my strategic operations officer told me he had just slain Gowron, Chancellor of the Klingon High Council, in ritual combat, and that in his first and only act as the leader of the Klingon Empire, he abdicated the position and gave it to General Martok, I realized there really wasn't anything to say, except that I was glad the most honorable man won. Through the years, Worf has never been everything that the Klingon Empire or Starfleet wanted him to be, but I'm fine with that because he's always tried to do the right thing.

✦

When the war with the Dominion finally did break out, after three years of trying to hold back a dam of inevitability, it was worse than anything I'd imagined. Federation and Klingon forces had been severely weakened from infighting instigated by the Changelings. We'd squandered people and ships, precious resources that left everyone vulnerable. But perhaps even more critical was the mental toll this had been taking on the individual factions and on the Alpha Quadrant itself. Conflict after conflict with each other was slowly wearing us all down. For the most part Starfleet had stopped exploring, and recalled ships that were sorely needed in the fight.

We were just trying to hold on.

Thankfully, now that we were allies once again with the Klingons, our union was the only thing keeping us alive and holding back the relentless onslaught of the Dominion.

The Alpha Quadrant had been destabilized by the Changelings just like they had destabilized and dismantled the opposing powers in the Gamma Quadrant when they created their Dominion. It felt like now that we had been severely weakened and demoralized, the slaughtering had begun.

Something had to be done.

We made first contact with the Dominion on my watch, Jake. The war started on my watch, it was my responsibility. These people, these Federation families struggling, and fighting for their very survival, was all on me. The starships burning in space, the destroyed families, the broken worlds finding themselves enslaved, all the deaths.

All because of me.

Son, I think a lot about all those names, so many names. So many I don't know and will never know, but some I'll never forget. I think a lot about T'Lor, Rooney, Bertram, Hoya, and Muniz. I think about that unit on AR-558.

Something had to be done.

██

██

████████████████████████████████

█████████████████████████*

Jake, there's an old saying: if you have to dance with the devil in the pale moonlight, leave before the music ends. I've talked to you about a lot of things here, son. But none of them are as important as morality and character. Who you are, who you become in the face of adversity, and what you do, is everything. Your actions will follow you in the dark of night and the light of day. There may be times in your life, Jake, when you're tempted to do the wrong things for the right reasons. Times like that can lead you into very dark places, son. If it does, and you ever find yourself lost in that dark place, please, listen to yourself, and what you know is right. Please let your morality and character guide you through the darkness and back into the light.

✦

When the Romulans came into the war, we were able to hold the line. But even with the combined military of the three most powerful forces in the Alpha Quadrant, it wasn't easy. The Dominion had built shipyards and Jem'Hadar breeding facilities that were working around the clock while we were still dealing with manpower and ship losses from battles with each other the year

---

* It wasn't an easy decision to share the transmission my father sent me, but I believe it was a necessary one. That being said, I've redacted this section because some words between a father and son should remain private.

before. The war hadn't stopped being any less of a bloody business, but at least now, together, we had a chance of victory.

In our struggle with the Dominion, we'd lost so many lives, so many battles, but I could finally see a path to winning the war.

And it started with our first real offensive, the retaking of Deep Space 9.

When I first arrived at DS9, I would walk the station at night and often think about the resiliency of the Bajorans. During the days of Terok Nor, every window and viewscreen was an architectural representation of the Cardassian iris, overseeing and ever-present. The brown and gold color schemes of the walls were a reminder of the Cardassian soil, and bounty of its land. Bajorans lived in shanty towns on the promenade under the oppressive rule of the Cardassians. Day and night literally being worked to death in the ore processing plant.

When the occupation ended, all of that changed in a little over a week. Bajorans were being asked to return to the place of their trauma now that the Federation had renamed it Deep Space 9. The truth is DS9 didn't work solely because of the Federation, it worked because the Bajoran people came back and infused the station with their perseverance, their hope, and their faith. The shanty towns became real shops on the promenade. A Bajoran temple brought with it fellowship and families. Children went to school, and people felt comfortable enough to laugh and to love. I would often find myself on the upper pylon, gazing out of a Cardassian iris, not seeing some vigilant totalitarian eye, but an invitation into the unknown with a view of the wormhole that made you feel you could reach out and touch it. Somehow all of us that worked and lived on the station had made DS9 their home. When we took back the station, we were fighting for all this just as much as its strategic value. Deep Space 9 had become a symbol for a way of life free of oppression and tyranny.

After a year of being on the defense, Starfleet finally decided it was time to push back. Command put me in charge of the invasion of Cardassia and the chief noticed the weakest link in the Cardassian defense was the Chin'toka system.

I honestly don't recall much about the mission. During the operation, the Prophets were attacked by Dukat and a Pah Wraith. They reached out to me for help in their despair, but I couldn't focus. Since the Prophets exist outside of linear time, I realize now they were reaching out to a version of me that didn't exist yet. They were reaching out to who I am now and confusing it with who I

THE AUTOBIOGRAPHY OF BENJAMIN SISKO

was then. I was experiencing a type of temporal feedback, and I didn't have the ability to understand that, or help them.

Thankfully, it's like I've always said, a starship is much more than its captain, and the *Defiant*'s crew got the job done without me. After Chin'toka it felt like we'd finally taken one step forward, but it had cost us five steps back. Everything was upside down. Jadzia was gone, I'd returned to Earth, and Starfleet found it difficult to gain new ground. We were bottled up in the Chin'toka system for months in a stalemate of sorts. And then the Dominion convinced the Breen to join their side in the war. To demonstrate their commitment to the Dominion and intent to the Alpha Quadrant, the Breen attacked Earth. This new alliance threatened to wash away the small gains we'd made and put the Founders back on track to victory.

I returned to Chin'toka with the *Defiant* and another three hundred ships to tip the balance of power back in our favor. But it didn't matter. As soon as we engaged the Dominion fleet, we learned of the Breen's energy-dampening weapon. A single shot rendered the *Defiant* inoperable immediately. We were dead in the water, and the fleet was defeated in minutes. I could feel the blasts from the Dominion fleet tearing into the *Defiant*'s hull, ripping her apart, and shattering a dream I'd brought to life with three geniuses so long ago.

With the *Defiant*'s bridge in flames, I gave the order to abandon ship.

In the escape pod with Chief O'Brien, we looked out the viewport, and I could see the *Defiant* and the rest of the fleet in flames. Mighty starships that soared through space only moments ago were now little more than twisted girders and burning wrecks. The Dominion was making an example of my ship, hitting the *Defiant* again and again with torpedoes. They cracked open her primary hull like an eggshell, making a sport of it. I watched from the escape pod viewport as the *Defiant* exploded, and in an instant I was taken back to the *Saratoga* and Wolf 359. But unlike the Borg, our enemy's patience had run out. They were now hellbent on our destruction.

The Founders and the Dominion forces had turned our fleet into a scrapyard, and I wondered if this was a harbinger of what was to come. The Starfleet and Romulan fleets had been rendered powerless by a single weapon.

The only things protecting the Alpha Quadrant was a fool that had found the strength to become a leader, and a leader that didn't have the strength to stop being a fool.

Legate Damar had started a rebellion on Cardassia and Gowron began his own private little war against the Dominion. Squandering Klingon ships to make himself look better.

In their own way, both gave us the time we needed to come up with a defense against the Breen weapon and make one final push against Dominion forces that had retreated from Klingon, Federation and Romulan-occupied worlds and back into the Cardassian system.

My crew and I went to the last battle of the war in a new ship with an old name.

Defiant.

On the way to the war, before I stepped out onto the new *Defiant*'s bridge, I took a moment in my ready room just off the bridge. I reached into the inside pocket in my uniform. I'd been keeping it there with me for the last few years. I opened the small thin book, badly weathered now, much worse than before, even water-stained from when we crashed on that uncharted planet in the nebula. I'd seen the title on the first page thousands of times—*Life Doesn't Frighten Me* by Maya Angelou. But in the last several years, the title had become invisible to me. It was the handwritten words above them that I came to this small book for, time and time again.

Do big things, Ben.

I traced my fingers along Mama's words one last time. Then I put the small book back into my tunic, and stepped onto the bridge.

CHAPTER TWENTY-EIGHT

DEEP SPACE 9—2371-2375

IT WAS SUPPOSED TO BE JUST A TEMPORARY ASSIGNMENT, but a Cardassian monstrosity became a liberated dwelling for the Bajoran people, a symbol for freedom, and along the way it became my home.

The station is where I got to be a sailor again and build a Bajoran lightship with my own hands. DS9 is where I became the Emissary to the Prophets, a captain, and a Klingon! Because of this post, I got to meet James T. Kirk and set a young man on his path in Starfleet Academy.

I came to this station when I didn't care about it, and I had to abandon it during a war when I didn't want to be anywhere else.

Deep Space 9 helped me find myself when I was lost. The station gave me a cause to fight for, a people to believe in, and a planet to protect. The station was where I fell in love again when I never thought I would. Most importantly, Jake, DS9 is where I got to see you grow up into the man and writer that you are today.

I am so very proud of you, son.

When you were born, your mother was in labor with you for seven hours. When you finally arrived, and Jennifer was holding you for the first time, she looked up at me and said, "Now our lives together can start."

It's hard to explain, but I feel a little like that now. This place, where I am now, outside of time, is a womb of sorts, a place I will be reborn from.

Time has no meaning here. The eons of eternity are just pages in a book. I'm beginning to understand.

Jake, even with everything I'm going through here, everything I'm learning about myself, I need you to understand that being the Emissary to the Prophets and a Starfleet captain is nothing in comparison to being your father. This isn't a secret, son, just a truth that every parent knows. My true role was always to be your emissary, and now an emissary to both my children.

I want, no, I *need* you to learn this for yourself, Jake, and you won't be able to do that on the station, waiting for me. It's time for you to go, son, find your place in the galaxy and, more importantly, find someone to share your life with.

Nothing is permanent, Jake. The universe's only true constant is change. Whether in the form of incredible rewards or unimaginable disappointments, change will always happen. Who we are and how we choose to react in the face of change is what will last, what will endure, and what will be remembered of us.

And what we will remember about ourselves.

When I get back, and I will come back, Deep Space 9 will be there for our family. But right now it's time for you to begin your journey. Make it a good life, Jake-O.

Because I'll be watching.

CONCLUSION

STARDATE: TODAY

I'm sure you were expecting this closing to be written by Jake Sisko.

Truthfully, so was I.

After the introduction and everything that has transpired within these pages, Jake's words here would be, to coin a phrase, only logical.

But as my fingers paused over the typewriter, for the first time in a very long time, the words wouldn't come to the surface. To be more accurate, the words I thought would end this journey didn't feel right to me. So I hope you'll allow an old writer this one indulgence.

I held onto the dream of Benjamin Sisko, and the future he lives in, when the world around me was filled with despair. I was brutally beaten

for daring to hope for better. It took me ten
long years to get my first *Deep Space Nine*
story, "Emissary," published. Now, on the 30th
anniversary of that first publication, this
autobiography is a testament that the dream
continues because it belongs to all of us.

Deep Space Nine isn't just science fiction. It is a
challenge to expand our ways of thinking and reach
towards a future that includes everyone through
infinite diversity in infinite combinations.

After everything I've lived through, and continue
to endure, I know there's only one way to turn
that future into reality.

We can only do it together.

Thank you for believing in the dreamer and the
dream.

BENNY RUSSELL

January 03, 1993

ACKNOWLEDGMENTS

This book has been 30 years in the making.

We would never have gotten here without the imagination of the Great Bird of the Galaxy, **Gene Roddenberry**, and the incredibly hard work of the writers, crew, and cast of *Deep Space Nine*. Especially **Rick Berman** and **Michael Piller** for creating the show, **Ira Steven Behr** for his vision, and the performances of **Mr. Avery Brooks**.

Titan Publishing has always understood the impact DS9 and Benjamin Sisko have held within the Star Trek universe and pop culture. My thanks to everyone at Titan for their tireless effort on this project. Especially **George Sandison** for all your hard work, encouraging notes and putting your faith and patience in me and my direction. From our first conversation, it was clear we shared a similar love and respect for this unique *Star Trek* series.

Russell Walks, you made this collaboration not just easy but fun and breathed a phenomenal visual life into this autobiography. I am very grateful for all the hard work you put into this project.

My thanks to the team at **CBS** for your incredible passion, attention to detail, and insightful suggestions.

Dayton Ward, the love, vigilance, and hard work you commit to *Star Trek* inspires me every day.

Una McCormack, I really appreciated our conversations at the very beginning of this journey. Your words came at the right time.

To those that helped set me on this path.

Alonzo Speight, you'll always be my first writing mentor, and good friend. Thank you for giving a passionate kid Syd Field's Foundations of Screenwriting.

Dennis O'Neil, I took your class on writing for comics, but my conversations with you showed me what was needed to become a writer. And I'll always be grateful you let me audit the class that second year.

To my inner circle.

Mike Hood, thanks for taking my calls at insane hours and being a sounding board. You are and always shall be my friend.

Rai, you're the center of my circle and everything good in my world. I love you very much.

And finally, to my first best friends and my foundation. To my **Mom** and **Grandma**, you always made sure to keep my head in the stars and my feet firmly on the ground. I owe you both everything.

ABOUT THE AUTHOR

Derek Tyler Attico was born in Harlem, New York. He began his writing career in 2005 when his short story "Alpha and Omega" won first place in the *Star Trek* Strange New Worlds short story contest. He is also the author of the *Deep Space Nine* story "The Dreamer and the Dream" and is a contributing writer to the *Star Trek Adventures* role-playing game. He lives in New York City with his family.

For more fantastic fiction, author events,
exclusive excerpts, competitions, limited editions and more

VISIT OUR WEBSITE
titanbooks.com

LIKE US ON FACEBOOK
facebook.com/titanbooks

FOLLOW US ON TWITTER AND INSTAGRAM
@TitanBooks

EMAIL US
readerfeedback@titanemail.com